BRUTE HEART

A Novel

To Susan,
Life is precious
in every form it
takes. Ginger Dehlinger
05-14-2011

GINGER DEHLINGER

Brute Heart

©2009 by Ginger Dehlinger, Copyright Registration Number TXu 1-655-577

This is a work of fiction. All of the characters, both human and animal, are either the product of the author's imagination or used fictitiously. Any resemblance to actual persons, pets, or farm animals, living or dead, is entirely coincidental. All of the human characters in *Brute Heart* are named after communities, counties or geographical features found in the state of Oregon. The names of the animals are imaginary.

Bucks Tavern, the V-Bar-J ranch, Pretty Pet, The Kitty Korner, Keeney's Dairy, the Davidson Park Veterinary Clinic, and the Prineville rendering plant are fictitious entities. Any resemblance to actual business establishments is entirely coincidental. The rest of the business establishments, streets, highways and geographical features named in *Brute Heart* are authentic, although some no longer exist.

Address all inquiries to:
Ginger Dehlinger
gdehlinger@live.com
http://bruteheart.blogspot.com

ISBN: 978-0-692-00982-6

Cover Design & Photo: Neal Colburn
Back Cover Photo: Famer
Interior Layout: Fusion Creative Works, www.fusioncw.com

Printed in the United States of America by Maverick Publications

For additional copies, visit: http://bruteheart.blogspot.com

DEDICATION

to my mother, Elsie Vasicek Leaming Lee

ACKNOWLEDGEMENTS

Brute Heart is an amalgam of personal experiences, historical happenings, news articles that have been fictionalized, and pure imagination. I've always enjoyed writing and have been an animal lover all my life, so about fifteen years ago, I began putting into words some of my childhood memories and stories heard at family gatherings. I also wrote little snippets about family pets or animals in general, adding to them or making changes from time to time.

My experience with alcoholism is first hand. My father was an alcoholic, although he was *not* Cooper Miller. My father was strict, uncommunicative and often unreasonable, but he wasn't a tyrant. In *Brute Heart* I share some of the emotional aspects of living with alcoholism, its effect on family members and the tendency for the condition to be passed from generation to generation. The physical abuse described in the novel is pure fiction.

Jordan Miller, the main character in *Brute Heart*, is purposefully flawed, patterned after other women raised by critical, controlling, and often alcoholic fathers. The experience usually shatters their self confidence and makes them vulnerable to abusive relationships with boyfriends, husbands, or authority figures, creating a dependency not unlike alcoholism and almost as difficult to shake.

Assisted suicide (Oregon's Death with Dignity Act) was a hot topic during the nineties. The more I read about it, the more I wanted to explore the ramifications of humans determining the circumstances of their own deaths. Over time, I wove the family and animal stories, what I learned about assisted suicide, living with alcoholism, and dealing with emotional abuse into what might be called a "patchwork" novel with a compelling story.

I would like to acknowledge the help I received from the eight people who read an early draft of my work: Susan Loomis, DVM, Dan Murphy, MD, Karen Lilly, Deanna Berry, Maria Wattier, Jane Williamson, Carla Hoagland

and Karen Andrew for their advice and support. I also want to thank my writing group, The Writing Sojourners, for their valuable input.

I also wish to thank Gary Asher for walking me through the publishing process, Shiloh Schroeder for formatting my book, and Riki Strong for being my proofreader.

My heartfelt thanks goes to Dick Dehlinger for sharing his Henley heritage with me. I'm grateful for the suggestions he made after reading my first draft and for cooking many wonderful dinners while I wrote, rewrote, and edited my manuscript.

Finally, I am fortunate to be a native Oregonian, and I would be remiss if I did not acknowledge my state's natural beauty and geographical diversity for providing inspiration as well as a splendid backdrop for my story.

BRUTE
HEART

CHAPTER ONE

The Holstein cow had been in the second stage of labor for over three hours, yet no muzzle appeared in the vulva when the cow strained, not even the tip of a little hoof could be seen. Too exhausted to stand, the cow lay on a bed of straw, straining, relaxing, and straining again as it struggled to expel the fetus. The veterinarian would have to work quickly, or the unborn calf would begin gasping for air, breathe in uterine fluid, and die.

When she inserted her hand into the birth canal, the veterinarian felt rump and tail, not head and leg, indicating a breech presentation. Being a small woman, she might need another pair of hands if the cow stopped straining and the calf had to be pulled. The farmer hovering nearby was prepared to use ropes, but Jordan Miller, still perfecting her veterinary skills, didn't want to go that route unless it became absolutely necessary.

With one cheek pressed against the cow's buttock, Jordan firmly but carefully began pushing the calf back into the cow's uterus. A few precious inches of reclaimed space would give her enough room to straighten the calf's back legs and pull it out backwards. This effort took strength and a keen sense of timing, because she could only reach inside the cow when it wasn't straining.

As the minutes ticked by, the farmer began pacing outside the stall and she started to sweat. Each time she pushed, she could only get the calf to move a fraction of the distance it needed to go. Meanwhile, the cow was pushing, too, but in the opposite direction.

"Stop straining, I've almost got it," she said to a cow that wanted nothing more than to get that calf the hell out of itself.

Slowly working her hand between the fetus and the uterine wall, the young veterinarian was finally able to grasp one of the calf's hind legs and maneuver it into the birth canal. After turning the first leg around, it was easier to reposition the second one, however with both of its hind legs extended, the calf would soon begin to breathe, if it hadn't already.

She swatted the cow on the rump. "Now push. Push!"

With Jordan pulling the calf's hind legs, and the cow straining, the calf shot out of the birth canal right into the surprised young woman's lap. Steam rose from the black and white calf sprawled across her legs, but the little animal wasn't moving.

Jordan held her breath while she placed the small wet creature on the straw near its mother. Checking its mouth for an obstruction, she saw the calf's tiny rib cage lift once, twice, then begin rising and falling in a steady rhythm. Slowly the calf raised its head, its brown eyes filled with wonder as it looked first at Jordan, then at the farmer, then at its mother. In no time it was standing on its feet snorting fluid out of its nostrils.

• • •

When Jordan and the farmer left the barn, the cow was vigorously licking her baby bull, and the calf was investigating its mother's faucets. These bonding moments always warmed Jordan's heart. They took her mind off her troubles, and helped her justify the years and the money she spent training for afternoons like this.

She would have stayed with the cow and calf a few minutes longer, but she had another emergency to attend to—a human emergency from the sound of her mother's phone call that cold March morning. Her mother, Annie, never called long distance during peak hours and wouldn't think of interrupting her daughter at work, so their rambling, one sided conversation had been on Jordan's mind all day. Although the call lasted less than two minutes, and Annie barely spoke above a whisper, Jordan was sure the emergency had something to do with her father, and she was pissed.

CHAPTER TWO

Snowflakes swarmed in the headlights of her Jeep, as Jordan Miller drove down a wind-drifted side street. It was a dead end street in a tumbledown part of town where the snowplows always came last if they came at all; where cracker box houses and mobile homes going nowhere, peeled and rusted on seedy lots the size of Scrabble pieces.

Although she knew this neighborhood by heart, it would be easy to get lost on a night so white, so she slowed her Jeep to a crawl. She was used to driving in weather like this, but this much snow in March was unusual for eastern Oregon. During the five hours it took her to drive to Klamath Falls, her windshield wipers couldn't keep up with the heavy snowfall, and every ten miles or so she had to roll down her window, stick her hand out, grab the driver's side wiper mid sweep and snap it against the windshield to break off the accumulation. She knew it was risky to drive in such conditions, especially in the dark, but her mother's phone call that morning had frightened her. Snow or no snow, she had to get home.

When the faint glow of a porch light appeared off to her right, Jordan released her death grip on the steering wheel and parked next to a snow bank. A wisp of a woman, she laid her head back, closed her eyes, and scrunched her aching shoulders. One at a time she wiped the palms of her hands on the legs of her jeans, and after the feeling returned to her fingers, she pulled a knit cap over her chin length auburn hair, threw a hastily packed tote bag over her shoulder, and locked the car.

As soon as she stepped outside, snowflakes began landing on the tips of her eyelashes, lingering there for less than a blink before melting. More of the white stuff floated inside the collar of her parka and down the back of her neck, as she half sprinted, half stumbled toward the porch light.

A familiar tension lodged in her chest when she reached the front steps.

She took her time stomping the snow off her boots. She peeked through a gap in the front door curtain, and though her breath fogged the glass, she could see it was dark inside. She removed her cap, shook the snow off of it and slowly turned the door knob.

The front door opened directly into a square living room, lit only by a wedge of light from the adjoining kitchen. Jordan thought it felt odd, even a little lonely, not to be blasted by the TV noise that normally greeted her when she walked into the house.

She was surprised to see a large, metal frame bed where the couch was supposed to be and wondered what in the world it was doing in the living room. Even more remarkable, her father appeared to be sleeping in it; although he did sometimes sleep on the couch.

A familiar snout nudged her in the crotch as the family dog gave her a friendly inspection. Sonny, short for Sonofabitch, was a gray-muzzled golden retriever who still believed he was a watchdog. When Jordan knelt down to give him a hug and tousle his fur, the old dog grunted with pleasure. Satisfied he had been properly acknowledged, he padded over to the strange bed and curled up beside it.

Crackling sounds marked the startup of the oil furnace, giving Jordan her first whiff of the suffocating housebound air that hung around all winter—a stale blend of oil fumes, fried onions, and cigarette smoke. The air was especially heavy and offensive when she hadn't been around it for a while, and she wrinkled her nose at the smell of it.

Arms outstretched, Annie rushed from the kitchen and grabbed her daughter in a wordless embrace. It was a tighter hug than usual, and when the two women parted, Jordan noticed the dark circles under her mother's beautiful eyes, the same gray-green eyes she saw in her own mirror every day.

"What's going on, Mom?" she asked, pointing at the bed that was taking up a third of the space in the living room. "Are you okay?"

Annie raised a shushing finger to her lips. "I'm fine," she whispered, her eyes serious. She nodded toward the bed. "We can't talk here. Let's sit in the kitchen."

Jordan took another quick look at her father before walking from the crowded living room into an even smaller kitchen. She took off her parka, and squeezed her petite body between the kitchen table and the end of the counter so she could sit in her favorite chair. The kitchen was so small it was impossible to open the oven door if someone was sitting in front of the stove, so she always tried to get a chair on the opposite side of the table where she could sit with her back to the window.

"I got here as soon as I could," she said. She pushed up the sleeves of her gray sweatshirt and tucked her hair behind her ears. "Highway 97 was a mess. I practically went cross-eyed staring at the snow in my headlights. Half the time I wasn't even sure I was driving on the right side of the road, and I almost ran into this semi that jackknifed on that section along the lake where it gets so icy. I'd still be there if a snowplow hadn't come along."

Annie patted her daughter on the arm. "I've been worried sick waiting for you. I wouldn't have been able to forgive myself if anything happened to you."

Jordan smiled inwardly as she moved a dirty plate to the other end of the table and brushed some crumbs onto the floor. "I got away later than I planned, Mom. I delivered a calf this afternoon that was born breech."

Annie raised her eyebrows. "Did it live? What about the cow?"

"They're both fine. Before I left, I had the farmer give the calf two liters of colostrum. That plus the cow's milk and the little bull is probably running around the barn by now."

Jordan watched her mother settle into her customary chair at the foot of the table. The light in the kitchen seemed to have softened the dark circles under her mother's eyes while revealing other changes. Usually meticulous about her appearance, Annie's thick, reddish-brown hair was bushy and dull. She wasn't wearing any makeup, not even mascara, and there were stains on the front of her light blue sweater.

"Did you eat dinner?" Annie picked up a partially completed crossword puzzle, folded it into the rest of the newspaper and set it aside. "I didn't feel much like cooking tonight. I could fix you some soup."

"No thanks, Mom. I stopped for a sandwich at the Wheel Café. The place was packed with refugees from the storm. They ran out of pie before I got there, and I was really looking forward to a piece of coconut cream."

Jordan leaned closer to her mother. "It's really good to see you, Mom, but what is that bed doing in the living room?"

Annie inspected the chewed tips of her fingernails. Tiny wrinkles were beginning to crease her forehead, but she was still attractive for a woman in her late forties. She smiled weakly, filling her eyes with the welcome sight of the daughter that made her so proud. Inwardly she struggled with how to put into words what she had to tell her, and making matters worse, what she had to ask of her.

"How about I make us some coffee?" she said. "Then we can talk."

Annie took a can of coffee out of the refrigerator and carefully measured enough for one pot. Small and birdlike, she smiled occasionally and made small talk as she flitted about the small kitchen.

Jordan began to relax as she looked around at what she thought of as the only cheerful room in the house. She was about ten when her family moved from the farm into this rental house in town. She could still remember how hard her mother worked to spruce up the place, how she magically transformed the shabby kitchen with three coats of yellow paint, and then sewed the yellow polka dot curtains that still framed the kitchen's two small windows. Once crisp and colorful, the fabric was limp from repeated washings and the polka dots barely distinguishable. Looking closer, the paint on the walls and cupboards also appeared to have faded to a yellow more bilious than bright.

"It's terrible about those people in Rancho Santa Fe, isn't it?" Jordan said, trying to make conversation. "I've been listening to the news reports on the radio all night. You heard about it, didn't you?"

Annie shook her head.

"It's probably not in the paper yet. Anyway, thirty nine people who belonged to this group called Heaven's Gate committed mass suicide yesterday. It's hard to believe people could die that way, like lemmings jumping off a cliff."

Annie looked confused. "They took their own lives?"

"I know. It's terrible, isn't it, Mom."

"Why would they do such a thing?"

"I know. That's what everybody is ..."

"Please stop." Annie covered her ears. "I don't want to hear about it, Jordan—not tonight."

She poured water into the coffee maker then pushed the button to start it. As soon as she returned to her chair, she lit a cigarette. One of her legs jiggled under the table, and a delicate shudder moved across her shoulders.

A small silence hung between the two women before Jordan said, "Okay, Mom, when are we going to talk?"

Annie gestured for her to lower her voice and pressed her slackened lips together, trying not to cry. Her eyes filled with tears in spite of the effort.

"Mom? Are you and Daddy finally getting a divorce?"

Annie left the table to look for a tissue. She returned with two mugs of coffee and a paper towel, which she used to dab at her tears. She glanced anxiously into the living room, and took a long drag on her cigarette before she answered.

"Your father has bone cancer," she said, clearing her throat. "It's terminal."

Jordan felt as if someone had punched her in the chest. "Why didn't you tell me? I would have come home sooner if I'd known he had cancer." She placed a hand on her mother's forearm, rubbing it lightly while digesting the news. "I don't hate him, you know ... not really."

Annie nodded, holding onto her mug as if it might float away. A brief silence stretched into a minute. "He wants you to end it."

Jordan gave her mother a blank stare. "End what—end the fighting? That would be a switch. Or is he looking for me to end his pain? Surely his doctor has prescribed something for that."

Annie looked up, her face reddening as tears flowed down her cheeks and off the end of her chin. "He wants you to end it for him!" She covered her face with the paper towel. "Do I have to spell it out for you? End his suffering. End it for good!"

Jordan stiffened. *Does she mean...?* Her lips went numb and the color drained from her face. She got up from the table and turned her mother's chair around so they could face each other.

"Mom, will you please look at me?"

Annie lowered the damp paper towel. Her upturned eyes begged for understanding and resolution.

"If I understand you correctly, what Daddy is asking me to do is against the law. Or does he want me to arrange for assisted suicide? Well, I can't help with that, either. Assisted suicide has to be prescribed by a physician, not a veterinarian." Jordan grasped her mother by the shoulders. "We've had our problems over the years, but he's still my father. My God, can't he see that?"

Annie blew her nose. "He said you do it every day—you put animals to sleep every day."

"I do *not* do it every day, and besides, it isn't the same thing as ending a human's life."

Jordan let go of her mother's shoulders and walked over to the kitchen sink. When she raised the shade covering the small window above the sink, she discovered the snow clouds had moved on, leaving behind a whitewashed neighborhood sparkling in the moonlight. Fattened and softened by billions of snowflakes, everything on the dingy lots had been transformed, creating a saccharine landscape where abandoned cars looked like giant cream puffs and roofs in need of repair were two-feet deep in frosting. She glowered at the Christmas card scene that would be gone in less than a week and lowered the shade.

"Does he really think I could do that to him, Mom? Does he think I'm heartless?"

"He said it would be quick and painless."

"That's not the point!"

Jordan whirled away from the sink and brushed past her mother, stopping in the doorway to stare at the man they were talking about, the man asleep in the oversized bed.

She wondered what they had done with the ratty old couch, and hoped they'd burned it. Her father owned one end of that couch, where he sat, day and night, eyes glued to the TV, rarely looking up or saying anything when she entered the room except to downplay her accomplishments, criticize the way she was dressed, or ask where she had been or where she was going.

Other than the couch being gone, the rest of the room hadn't changed in years. The three framed prints her mother bought at a garage sale still hung on the wall opposite the kitchen. Two broken down chairs, one green, one brown, flanked the front window and currently stood watch at the foot of the rented bed. A vinyl hassock with stuffing protruding from one of its seams moved around the room as needed for foot support or extra seating. That night it was tucked in the corner next to the floor lamp. There were no plants decorating the room, no colorful throw pillows, not even a basket of plastic fruit.

Inching toward the bed, Jordan tried to imagine what precipitated her father's outrageous plan. Had his pain become intolerable? Was he discouraged with the way his life had turned out? Was he tired of fighting his personal demons? She stood quietly watching him breathe. Each breath appeared to be an effort, and his lips made a puffing sound when he exhaled. She stepped back when he shifted under the covers to turn on his side.

After his breathing returned to a raspy but regular tempo, she moved closer and felt a chill when she saw how thin her father's face had become; how vividly his brown-black hair and heavy brows stood out against the whiteness of his skin. A lump formed in her throat, but she forced it down. Curious to know what pain medication he was taking, she took an empty prescription bottle out of the wastebasket under his bed and read the label: "Percocet, two tablets every four to six hours for pain."

As she studied her father's clean shaven face, at the deep creases in his cheeks that used to be dimples, part of her wanted to shake him awake so they could seriously discuss his condition while another part of her wanted to shake him till his teeth rattled.

You've got me cornered, haven't you, Daddy? If I do what you want, I'll be your good little girl, but spend the rest of my life with murder on my conscience. If I don't, and if I'm brutally honest with myself after it's all over, I'll always wonder if by doing nothing, I intentionally prolonged your death.

CHAPTER THREE

Jordan avoided the questioning look in her mother's eyes when she returned to the kitchen. She took a sip of the coffee Annie bought because it was inexpensive. It tasted like brewed wood chips, but she drank it anyway while scores of questions tumbled through her mind. *When did Daddy first learn about his illness? Has the cancer spread to his brain and altered his sensibilities? Does he think getting me to take his life is as easy as getting me to take out the garbage?*

"What does the doctor say, Mom?"

Annie rubbed her stub of a cigarette back and forth in the overflowing ashtray until the filter was a nub of white fluff. "He says it could be anywhere from a few weeks to a few months. He doesn't like to make predictions, especially now that the cancer has spread to Cooper's lungs." She paused. "I told you about that, didn't I?"

"No, you didn't tell me that—you didn't tell me anything!"

"I guess … I thought … I could handle it by myself." Annie heaved a sigh. "They say Coop probably won't see another winter."

"At least you won't have to listen to him complain about the weather."

"That's a mean thing to say."

"I came home like you asked me to, Mom, but please don't expect me to go all gooey all of a sudden."

"I know, Jordan, but you could lighten up a bit now that …"

"I'll try, Mom. I'll try."

A quick glance at her watch told her it was past midnight, so Jordan walked over to the kitchen sink, poured the rest of her coffee down the drain, and rinsed her mug.

"I don't know what I'm going to say to him tomorrow, but one thing's for sure; I have to make him understand that what he expects me to do is criminal. I also need to make him realize he's got me all wrong if he thinks I'll actually do it."

She bent down and gave her mother a peck on the cheek. "I'm beat. I think I'll sleep in the boys' room if it's okay with you. Do you mind if I open a window?"

Annie shook her head. "The bed on the left is already made up."

Jordan walked through the living room to the modest bedroom her brothers used to share. She opened the window a crack to freshen the air and undressed quickly, shivering when the cool fabric of her pajamas clung to her warm flesh. She slid between the sheets, pulled the covers over her head, and curled into a ball. In a couple of minutes, the warmth of her breath would make it comfortable enough to unfold her legs and stretch out.

When she was a young girl, and especially during her teenage years, she used her blankets like a cave where she could fume or cry over something her father said or did. Many a night she lay in her cave wishing he was dead, sometimes even contemplating how it might happen—an accident at work, perhaps, or a car crash on his way home from the tavern. But the brief feeling of satisfaction she got from such thoughts was always followed by a profound sense of loss when she tried to imagine life without him, and never in her wildest imaginings did she think he would one day ask her to pull the trigger.

She could hear Cooper's labored breathing through the flimsy wall that separated them, and pictured him lying there, alarmingly thin and smaller than she remembered, resting comfortably under a pile of blankets. Suddenly her mental picture changed to the much darker image of a white sheet covering an ice cold body. Was it a death due to natural causes, or one that had been hurried along in a mission of mercy?

Her thoughts turned to an even colder night less than a month before, when she had to leave the warmth of her apartment to handle an emergency for a client who had accidently run over her own dog. Arriving at the clinic that night, Jordan saw a mortally wounded Australian shepherd in the woman's arms and a haunting mixture of fear and unabashed supplication in the woman's eyes.

The most difficult part of the profession she had practiced for less than a year, was telling someone that his or her animal was beyond help. She never used the words, "put out of its misery," but there really wasn't a suitable way to verbalize the prognosis. Whether it was a dog, a cat, a parakeet, or a two thousand-pound bull, it was always a gut-wrenching experience for her as well as the animal's owner. Once the procedure was over, however, and the knot in her gut had subsided, she always felt she'd made the right decision.

She wondered if she would feel that same justification if she complied with her father's expectation. Thinking about it pragmatically, her father's solution wasn't exactly a quantum leap from euthanizing an animal. If it was acceptable to end the suffering of dumb animals, animals that don't understand the source of their pain or the consequences of their injuries, why was it wrong to do the same thing for an intelligent human being? Man is the only animal capable of reflecting on his own mortality. Man alone knows there are certain choices that can be made regarding the quality of life and even the manner and timing of death, so why shouldn't he have some say as to how and when it happens?

Jordan peeked at the digital clock next to her bed. The small bits of light forming the four numbers in 12:19 looked like pieces of rice to her, or tiny sausages, or better still, tidy rows of dead maggots. She tried not to blink so she could watch the maggots rearrange themselves from a nineteen into a twenty, but she was asleep before the numbers changed.

Near dawn, her sleep was interrupted by a nightmare. In it she was drowning in a swiftly moving river. Desperate for air, she tried to swim to the surface with splayed fingers and arms thin as toothpicks. An eight-legged calf tumbled through the swirling current, its legs stroking the water like cilia on a paramecium.

Cooper, sitting ramrod straight, floated by in his hospital bed. He had somehow attached one of his sheets to the foot rail, where it billowed in front like a spinnaker. His deep-set eyes were round as poker chips, and his black hair clung to the sides of his face. When he saw her, he cocked his thumb as if hitching a ride.

Bubbles the size of giant beach balls began bumping against her legs. She climbed onto one of them, hoping to ride it to the surface, but just when she was close enough to grab the rushes growing along the river's edge, the bubble popped, and she was back in deep water.

Jordan woke up clutching her pillow, relieved she hadn't drowned, yet dreadfully aware that the real nightmare was still to come. Lingering under the warm covers, she smelled the enticing aroma of coffee brewing—the kind of coffee that always smells good when it's perking but tastes terrible. She hadn't thought to bring her own French roast coffee when she left her apartment, and since her mother's coffee was better than nothing, she threw back her covers and dived into the chilly morning.

When Jordan entered the living room, Cooper was sitting in the green chair smoking a cigarette. His dark eyes reminded her of marbles on the face of a wooden doll—too shiny for his pasty demeanor. She was surprised to see he was wearing pajamas, pale blue ones with navy blue sailboats printed on them. The year she gave him pajamas for Christmas, he tossed them at her saying, "Only sissies wear pajamas."

"Good grief, Daddy," she cried, pointing at the cigarette dangling between his fingers. "Are you out of your mind?"

Cooper took a slow, deliberate puff. "Think maybe it'll kill me?" He laughed a wheezy kind of laugh that turned into a series of coughs.

Jordan shook her head and marched into the kitchen where her mother stood next to the stove stirring a small pot of oatmeal with a wooden spoon.

"Are you letting him smoke?" she whispered emphatically.

"Sometimes," Annie said, without looking up.

Jordan poured herself a cup of coffee. "Don't you realize that's making his condition worse?"

Annie banged the spoon against the rim of the pot to knock off a blob of oatmeal. Drawing her mouth into a tight line, she scooped a spoonful of hot cereal into a bowl. "Your father's dying, and I'm too pooped to argue with him anymore."

She sprinkled a teaspoon of brown sugar over the oatmeal and added a splash of milk. "You probably think that because you're a veterinarian you know all there is to know about death, but you don't."

Jordan started to protest.

"No … let me finish. Most deaths take a long time. You've never watched it happening, minute-by-minute, day-by-day." She snapped a TV tray together, carried it into the living room, and positioned it over her husband's knees. Cooper grasped her arm for support, and hung on so tightly the tips of his fingers disappeared into her flesh. He gritted his teeth while shifting to a more comfortable position, and then patted the back of Annie's hand when she set his breakfast in front of him.

The tender exchange made Jordan uncomfortable, so she got up and filled herself a bowl of oatmeal, even though she wasn't particularly fond of it.

"I'm sure you're wondering why I'm keeping him here," Annie said when she returned. "A lot of it's because of the expense, of course, but even if we had plenty of money I would still want him here, not in a nursing home, not even in a hospital."

She sat down next to Jordan. "When my dad, your Grandpa Parker, died, I visited him at the hospital every day. He had excellent care, but he was miserable there. He would point at the plastic name band on his wrist and say, 'See this? They put this thing on me the day I checked in. They might as well have stapled a tag in my ear. They keep me here so they can poke me and do experiments on me. Hell, I'm no better'n a steer!' Can't you just hear him?"

A hint of a smile appeared on Annie's face before she turned serious again. "He died there, you know. We were all with him: Grandma Leona, Carson, Doug, even Dad's sister, Sandy. It was such a spiritless place to die. As long as I can physically hold up, I'm going to keep your father right here." She looked Jordan straight in the face. "And if he wants to smoke, he can smoke. It's one of the few pleasures he has left."

Jordan ate a spoonful of oatmeal. "You're not letting him drink, are you?"

"Of course not. I know you're not supposed to mix alcohol with painkillers. You don't have to be a college graduate to know that!"

"Okay, okay, I was just checking." Jordan finished her cereal, and stiff as a robot, carried the empty bowl to the sink where she washed and dried it before putting it back in the cupboard.

"I don't know what to say to him, Mom," she said in a small voice. "Does he know you told me?"

"More or less."

Jordan sighed and took her mug of lily-livered coffee into the living room. Having finished his cigarette, Cooper was reinserting the oxygen plugs into his nostrils when she dragged the hassock in front of his knees and sat on it. For a minute she just looked at him, wondering whether she knew this man wearing pajamas. His gaunt appearance made her want to give him a hug; whereas memories of their volatile past kept her from sitting too close.

She cleared her throat and tried not to look too serious. "Mom said you wanted to talk to me."

Cooper fixed his polished marble eyes on her. "Is that so? Did you bring this snow with you?"

Jordan laughed nervously. "We got dumped on last night, that's for sure." She paused briefly, to give the empty churning in her stomach a chance to subside. "Mom says you're thinking about giving up the ghost … that is … hoping to get an early checkout." She took a sip of coffee.

Cooper came close to smiling. "That's a strange way to put it." He coughed several times—a deep, wracking bronchial cough that made his eyes water. "This isn't much fun, you know."

"I know, Daddy, I know." She paused, trying to think of something to say that wasn't as lame as the euphemisms she started out with. "Why are you asking me to get involved in this? Why don't you ask Dr. Sitkum to help you?"

"I did."

"What did he say?"

"He said he was trained to save lives, not end 'em."

Jordan took another sip of coffee. "Maybe he was being cautious. Even though we passed Measure 16, the opposition is still debating the legality of Death with Dignity and looking for some way to get the law thrown out. Our doctors are getting pressure from all kinds of special interest groups, and no doubt they're worried about encountering the same type of harassment that goes on at abortion clinics."

"I know all about that assisted suicide crap, and that's not what I want. Why should I go through that messy process, when you can take care of me in a few seconds? Just give me whatever you give the dogs, only more."

"That's euthanasia, Daddy. It's illegal. Even if assisted suicide becomes accepted everywhere in the country, doctors will never be allowed to commit euthanasia. The only thing Measure 16 allows a doctor to do is prescribe some life-ending drugs. It's up to the patient to decide if and when to take them."

Cooper switched off the oxygen and pulled the plugs out of his nose. His hands shook as he lit another cigarette.

Jordan grimaced. "I wish you wouldn't do that, Daddy. Besides making your cough worse, it's dangerous to be smoking around oxygen. You could start a fire."

"Good. Maybe I'll burn the whole damn house down. That would take care of things, wouldn't it, and I wouldn't have to listen to you make excuses." He started coughing again, so hard his face turned red and he began to gag.

"Mom! What do you do for him when he coughs like this?"

Annie was there in seconds with a handful of pills and a glass of water. "It's time for him to take these, anyway."

Jordan walked out of the room while her father swallowed the pills and caught his breath. When she returned a few minutes later, he appeared to have relaxed. Slouched in the green chair with his head bent to one side, he looked like a scarecrow hanging on a perch. A wave of sympathy washed over her when she sat on the hassock again.

"Daddy?" she cooed.

Cooper waved her off as if shooing a pesky fly. "Go away. And take your jerk-off excuses with you."

With some difficulty he lifted his head. His facial features shifted and rearranged themselves while he struggled for words.

"Why do you always, *always* disobey me, Jordan? That assisted suicide thing you're tryin' to talk me into is a crock of shit—I don't wanna die in my own puke." He paused to catch his breath. "I think you're using this legal mumbo jumbo on me, because you don't have the balls to do what I really want."

Jordan felt her lungs tighten. She quickly got off the hassock and stepped to one side.

"Or maybe you're enjoying this. Maybe you like watchin' your old man die. Does it get your rocks off, Miss Veterinarian?"

"That's enough, Coop!" Annie said. She looked apologetically at her daughter. "I think he could use a nap."

Numb with humiliation, Jordan put the hassock back in the corner and stumbled into the kitchen, where she stared at the floor, hugging herself. After Annie helped Cooper into bed, she walked to where her daughter was standing and wrapped her arms around her.

"I'm so, so sorry, sweetie pie. I never expected it to go this badly."

Jordan blinked back tears. "Why can't he see I'm just trying to help him?"

She pulled away from her mother's embrace to stand at the kitchen sink. "I'll do these dishes for you, Mom, and then I'm out of here. I know how hard this must be on you—that bothers me more than anything—but Daddy's never going to change. Not even at the bitter end."

CHAPTER FOUR

Leaning her head out the window of her Jeep, Jordan counted eight cars between her and the snowplow up ahead. Although she was back on the same snow-covered stretch of Highway 97 she had traveled less than twenty-four hours before, she felt it was better to be there than with a father who could expect her to euthanize him and insult her in the same breath.

As she neared Collier Park, the thirty-odd miles she had put between her and her father hadn't diminished the sting of his words, but she had to admit he was right about one thing—euthanasia was simpler than assisted suicide. The assisted suicide patient didn't just take a few pills and be done with it. The barbiturates prescribed were somewhat bitter tasting, and since they nauseated most patients, doctors prescribed anti-nausea medication as well. The total prescription amounted to a hundred capsules that the patient had to empty and stir into juice or pudding before he or she could get it all down.

The physician prescribing the approved drugs for the assisted suicide patient usually isn't present when the drugs are taken. With euthanasia, on the other hand, the person administering the fatal dose is involved up to his ears, and the way Jordan felt after that morning's unpleasant conversation with her father, she was beginning to give it some serious thought.

A shot of sodium pentobarbital would stop his heart in a minute. If his miserable soul is so anxious to be set free, let him frolic with the other mean spirits, and stop making life such a pain in the butt for everyone else.

Her family would never call for an autopsy, so the risk of discovery wasn't terribly great since her father's cancer was so advanced. But what if something went wrong? She had worked so hard, lived for years on practically nothing in order to become a veterinarian. Was she willing to bet her license or go to prison to obey her father's last command?

The line of cars ahead of her was poking along at less than twenty miles an hour, so Jordan listened to an Emmylou Harris CD and let her mind wander. She thought about the many obstacles she had to overcome before finally receiving her license and how gratifying it was to be in a position to treat and cure animals. She was aware her youthful appearance and slender frame were inconsistent with a James Herriot type of veterinarian, yet she resented the look she got from time to time, the raised eyebrow that begged to ask, "How could a cute little thing like you be a veterinarian?"

While she was still in training and someone asked such a question, she would usually blush and stammer something totally inane. When she learned women outnumber men at most veterinary colleges, she decided anyone asking such a question must be ill informed or gender biased or both, so she started injecting a few gory details into her replies meant to discourage her detractors.

"Why would a woman like me decide to become a veterinarian?" She always repeated the question to make it sound as stupid as it was. Then she would describe in great detail a teeming pustule of maggots she once discovered on the rump of a steer. For effect she liked to refer to the maggot discovery as a "life altering" experience. For good measure, she threw in a graphic description of what a live maggot looks like under a microscope.

Or if there was time, she would tell of a true experience that took place when she was nine years old, when her dog, Max, caught a jackrabbit and dragged it onto the front porch of her family's farmhouse. Max had chewed off one of the rabbit's forelegs, but the wretched creature was still alive, twitching and shrieking. Blood splattered her face and soaked the front of her shirt as she tried to pull the rabbit out of Max's jaws. There was so much blood on the porch it turned into a slippery mess as she and Max engaged in a tug of war for the rabbit.

Jordan won, but when she tried to protect the rabbit by holding it against her chest, it clawed at her with its feet until she dropped it. Max quickly caught it again, and this time broke the rabbit's back with one fatal chomp.

Occasionally, if the person questioning the young veterinarian's credentials also happened to be someone she didn't particularly like, she would casually mention that as a teenager she helped brand cattle at her grandfather's ranch. "I decided to become a veterinarian," she would say in all earnestness, "the first time my uncle handed me the knife at a calf nutting." That was usually a closer.

In truth it was the rabbit incident that started her lifelong interest in animals, but there was more to the story. After breaking the rabbit's back, Max proudly dropped his limp prize at her feet and looked up at her expecting praise. Instead, Jordan used her fists to beat the little brown and black mutt as hard as she could until he scooted down the porch steps and under a nearby tree, cowering there while Jordan tried to coax the rabbit back to life. She begged the rabbit to breathe or open its eyes, however no amount of petting or frustrated shaking would revive it. Covered with blood, she ran into the kitchen with the dead rabbit cradled in her arms.

"See what Max did!"

Only after she saw the shocked look on her mother's face did Jordan start to cry. After she told her mother what happened, Annie took the rabbit and dried her daughter's tears while explaining to her that many dogs were born to hunt, and that Max must be sad and confused over being scolded for doing his job. Through the screen door, Jordan could see the wirehaired dog eyeing the back door, still lying under the tree with his bloody muzzle resting between his paws.

She ran back outside to check on him, and Max pretended to ignore her at first. As she came closer, he looked up at her with a soulful expression in his eyes and frantically wagged his tail. When she reached out to pet him, he licked the back of her hand—the very hand she had beat him with a few minutes earlier. Even at the age of nine, the child knew this act of forgiveness was something extraordinary, and though it was naïve of her to attribute the unconditional love of her own pet to the entire animal kingdom, the incident kindled in her a determination to make animals the center of her life.

• • •

The leased farm where Jordan spent her early childhood finding out about dogs and rabbits and other warm and cold-blooded creatures, was located in the rural Henley district of Klamath Falls, a town in southern Oregon. Five acres in size, the farm was situated between a pig farm and a large-scale potato growing operation.

In the center of the five acres sat a two story house, more or less white on three sides, white peeling to gray on the south side. Poplars lined the long gravel driveway and grew along a pathway between the house and a sprawling, metal-roofed barn. A crumbling cinder block silo separated the barn from a single car detached garage, where the owner of the property stored his tractor. Since there wasn't room in the garage, Cooper parked his car in the gravel driveway next to a gigantic blue spruce.

A spacious wooden porch ran across the front of the old farmhouse from the kitchen to the living room. The door to the kitchen was the front door, since no one ever used the door to the living room. The kitchen, with its sitting area, wood stove, and dinette, was the family's gathering place. The small living room was rarely used.

On one wall of the living room, there was a photograph taken when Jordan was about three years old of her and her mother wearing matching peasant dresses. The two of them could have passed as hippies, and the Miller family did live a quasi-hippie existence the first few years they lived on the small farm. Annie raised a vegetable garden and gathered eggs from the half wild chickens that had the run of the property. She wove dandelions or clover into her own waist length auburn hair and spent idle hours reading stories to her daughter.

Jordan's father, Cooper, who moved to Oregon from Missouri when he was a freshman in high school, was a mechanic by day and a reluctant farmer before and after work and on weekends. He rose every morning at 4:30, and rarely went to bed before 11:00 o'clock at night. He wasn't crazy about the long hours, but the farm income helped stretch his paycheck, and when his wallet felt lighter than usual, he eased his woes by bragging to his friends that it felt great to be part of the anti-establishment, living in the country with his beautiful, free spirited wife and baby daughter. He was always quick to add, however, that it wouldn't be long before he'd have a son.

Sure enough, two-and-a-half years after Jordan was born, Annie gave birth to Jude, and fourteen months later Dusty came along. Cooper had his boys, and Annie, who quickly discovered she didn't have time for the earth mother crap she once thought was so cool, switched from paisley skirts to blue jeans. She kept a few mementos such as a Joni Mitchell poster that she tacked to her bedroom wall; otherwise, she packed up her long print dresses and took them to the thrift shop in exchange for children's clothes. She let her garden go to seed. She had her tubes tied.

She also cut twelve inches off her hair, though she never took the scissors to Jordan's auburn tresses which she brushed into a pony tail or braided into a thick plait that hung between her daughter's small shoulders. A braid was the practical alternative for this active little girl with a knack for getting her hair caught in barbed wire or coming home with it full of twigs and burrs.

As a child of nature's playground, Jordan spent a good part of every day outside, visiting the neighbor's hogs, catching small frogs and grasshoppers, playing with Max or exploring the farm's outbuildings. She knew every tree, anthill, snake hole, bird's nest, and hiding place on the property. If she happened to find an injured bird or small animal, she rescued it. With her mother's help, and if the animal wasn't too severely injured, she nursed it back to health.

She didn't even step on bugs if she could help it, with the notable exception of earwigs, those skinny brown bugs with pinchers on the ends of their tails. If she found one or more of those ugly bugs inside her house, she stomped it dead. She shrieked if she discovered an earwig on something she was wearing, and quickly got naked, personally inspecting every inch of her clothing before getting dressed again.

Whenever she opened the door to her beloved outside world, Max practically knocked her over in his excitement to go with her. Tail wagging, sniffing the ground in front of him, he would run ahead, race back to urge her on, and then run ahead again. He was determined to be the first one to arrive at whatever their destination. The only time he waited for her was when he wanted a pat on the head, and as soon as he got his reward, he was off to the next stump, fence post, or pile of dirt.

Her relationship with Max cooled when Jordan discovered there were cats in the barn. The family dog let her and her two brothers climb all over him, but he killed rabbits. There would be no kitty treats, she decided, after seeing Max chase an orange tabby under the tool shed.

Jordan became obsessed with the feral barn cats the first day she saw one sleeping on a bale of hay. She tried every quiet maneuver a six-year-old could think of to get close enough to touch one, but their lean bodies quickly slipped between the hay bales and out of sight. These cats weren't smooth and silky like her cousin Athena's black and white cat. They were dirty and scrawny with crooked tails and anxious eyes, and the orange tabby was missing half an ear, but Jordan thought she could make one of them her pet if she could just catch it.

One day, while her father walked from the barn, she asked him to help her with a feline rehabilitation project.

"I don't want you hangin' around them cats," he told her. "They're mean. They'll bite you."

"Please, Daddy, can't I have just one?" Her short, preschool legs could barely keep up as she trotted alongside her father pleading her case.

"No, I said. Them cats are wild." Cooper bent down until his face was just inches away from his daughter's. "Cats have to be raised around people from the time they're born or you can't tame 'em." His thick black eyebrows knitted into a frown. "Don't you go near those cats, understand?"

Reaching the front porch of the farm house, he sat on one of the shiny gray steps he recently painted. Max wiggled in beside him, and Jordan stood nearby.

"But they see you in the barn all the time, Daddy. Can't you get them to like you?"

"Well, maybe if I fed 'em or something, but I'm not about to start doin' that. I don't mind having one or two of 'em around here to catch mice, but if I fed 'em we'd be wadin' in cats."

He curled a muscled arm over Max's back. Panting lightly, Max held up his front paw for a chest rub, and Cooper obliged with five or six quick strokes.

"Couldn't you feed just one, Daddy? If you fed the same one, every day, it would get to like you, and then you could give it to me." Jordan sat down on the other side of her father, but not as close as Max.

"There's no way you can feed one at a time. If I put any food out there, those cats would fight like crazy over it."

"What if you caught one, and put it in a cage, and brought it back to the house? Then I could feed it, and the other cats wouldn't know."

Cooper walked to the top of the stairs. "Stop arguing with me, Jordan. *If* I could catch one of those devils, and *if* you could get it to come out of its cage, it would run all over the house and pee on things, and your mother would have a fit. I'm not gonna let you play with them wild cats, and that's final!"

Since she couldn't get her father to feed them, Jordan secretly began taking bits of food out to the barn when he wasn't around. She especially favored a gray tabby with gold eyes that allowed her to get a few feet closer than the other cats before it bolted. It took Jordan close to six weeks and several crusts off tuna fish sandwiches before the gray cat began to look upon the little girl as a food source. When Jordan arrived, food in hand, the elusive creature would emerge from the darkness and haltingly pick its way across the hay bales. It would rub its long, lean body against her legs and purr until she fed it, but run away as soon as the food was gone, or when she tried to pick it up.

Jordan took her pillow out to the barn so the gray tabby would have something softer than a hay bale to sleep on. When her mother asked where her pillow was, she brought it back. It was covered with cat hair, so she put on a clean pillow case and threw the dirty one in the laundry basket.

She was bursting with excitement over her new best friend, but couldn't share it with anyone, not even her cousin Athena. Her father had been quite clear—she was to leave the cats alone.

CHAPTER FIVE

Jordan's sixth summer of nonstop adventures in nature's playground ended in September, that bittersweet time in a mother's life when she sends her first child off to school. While she washed her daughter's hair, Annie remembered being Jordan's age and how excited she used to feel when school was about to start. Even new school supplies delighted her—the smooth, unblemished covers on the Pee-Chee folders, yellow-gold pencils waiting to be sharpened, a clean Pink Pearl eraser that looked good enough to chew, the waxy smell of a new box of crayons—old friends promising new adventures.

Thinking back, she allowed herself the luxury of wondering what life would be like if she hadn't gotten pregnant while she was still in high school. She might have gone to college; her grades were good enough. She might have married someone else, someone she met in college. She might not be pinching pennies to pay for bare necessities such as Jordan's school supplies. But when she looked down at her daughter whose eyes were squeezed shut to keep out the water and shampoo, her heartbeat snagged on a surge of love, and she resolved at that moment to do everything in her power to make sure Jordan didn't make the same mistakes she did.

"Are you finished, Mom?" Jordan asked, scrunching her shoulders to keep the water from dripping down her neck.

"Just about, sweetie."

While rinsing her daughter's hair, Annie felt several raised areas on the scalp where the hair was short as whiskers. "Have you been hacking at your hair with the scissors?" she asked.

"No."

"Well, you have some patches of extremely short hair on your head. I can feel them. Have you been playing beauty shop with your cousin, Athena?"

"No-o-o. Please hurry, Mom, I can't breathe."

Annie pushed aside a section of her daughter's hair to get a better look. Jordan's hair was so thick, it was difficult to know for sure, but there appeared to be several reddish areas where the hair was broken off close to the skin.

"This doesn't look right to me, sweetie," Annie said, drying Jordan's hair with a towel. The spots looked like some sort of a rash, so she wasn't alarmed, but thought it best to get a doctor's opinion to be sure.

Their family doctor, Dr. McLoughlin, was new to the community, anxious to build a practice and willing to take patients such as the Miller family who were slow to pay. He spent a long time looking at Jordan's scalp, and then asked Annie to remove her daughter's clothes so he could examine the rest of her skin. During the entire examination, Jordan chattered like a monkey about her first day at school.

"Is she okay, Doctor?" Annie asked.

Dr. McLoughlin adjusted his glasses. "Not exactly. I need to check on something. I'll be back in a minute."

Annie caught some fabric in the zipper as she helped Jordan get dressed in the clothes she wore for her first day of school—a new green and white striped dress Grandma Leona bought for her, white stockings, and freshly polished white shoes.

When the doctor returned, he got right to the point. "Mrs. Miller, your daughter has ringworm in several places on her scalp."

Annie opened her mouth, then bit her lip and looked over at Jordan who was sitting in a chair with her legs sticking straight out in front of her. Her daughter's eyes were round with worry, and after the doctor's thorough scalp examination, her kinky, unbraided hair was sticking out in all directions, making her look like a frightened mermaid.

Dr. McLoughlin straddled a stool and rolled over to where Annie sat. "Ringworm is a highly contagious disease," he told her. "Anything coming into contact with the lesions needs to be sanitized, disinfected, or destroyed. I'm going to prescribe a combination of an oral drug, which attacks the disease from inside, and an antifungal preparation for you to apply directly to the affected areas. The lesions are only on her scalp. I didn't find any on the rest of her body."

"How in the world did she get ringworm?"

The doctor shrugged his shoulders. "That's hard to say. We usually blame it on cats—especially feral cats. In truth, almost any animal can carry ringworm, and it can even be found in the soil. The fungus thrives on dead skin cells, so any host animal will do, and you don't have to see it on an animal's hide for it to be present. It's probably no comfort to you at this point, but ringworm isn't as prevalent as it used to be." He cleared his throat. "Head lice are much more common."

Annie shuddered at the thought of parasites living on her daughter's scalp. "Will I have to cut her hair?"

"Actually, you'll have to shave it down to the scalp. It's the only way you can keep the lesions dry and prevent the fungus from spreading." Still seated, Dr. McLoughlin rolled his stool over to a large cupboard where he withdrew a package wrapped in plastic.

"Your daughter seems excited about starting school. Since ringworm is contagious, she will have to wear one of these caps until the lesions have completely healed." He pulled off the paper covering and held up a white cotton elasticized head covering that looked like a shower cap. "She has to wear one of these, or she can't go to school. I'll give you this one. They're simple to make, if you don't want to buy more. Make them out of sterile cloth and use plenty of bleach when you wash them."

"How long will it take her to get back to normal?"

"Figure ten days to two weeks. Using a combination of oral and topical treatments will speed things up." He scribbled out a prescription. "Do you have any questions? You look perplexed."

"No. I'm just having a hard time with the part about cutting her hair. Look at her. I can't imagine my little girl with a bald head."

"I suppose that will be a bit tricky," he acknowledged, before turning his attention to Jordan. "Have you been in contact with any cats lately, young lady … or any other animal?"

Jordan shifted in her chair. "Yes," she answered, averting her eyes. "I play with our dog every day, and sometimes I pet Peaches, our cow."

The doctor leaned closer and pushed his eyeglasses back in place on his nose. "But no cats?"

Jordan looked down at the shoes her mother polished for her first day at school. Shrinking from the doctor's penetrating expression, she squeaked, "I found a cat in the barn."

• • •

That evening, Cooper, armed with a .22 caliber rifle, entered the barn on a cat quest. The cats were quicker and more elusive than he expected, especially after the frightful first blast. It took him seven rounds to kill three of them—a calico, an orange tabby with half an ear, and a gray tabby. While searching the barn for more strays, he found four kittens in the loft. They were so small that a rifle would have blown them to smithereens. He considered wringing their necks, but put them into an empty fertilizer sack, closed the sack with a piece of baling wire, and tossed it into the backseat.

He headed toward Lost River in the old station wagon he detested. Even after sprucing it up with a free paint job, he thought the Chevy wagon was just plain ugly. He wanted a truck so badly he could taste it, but there wasn't enough room in a pickup to hold his wife and kids, and there was no way they could afford two vehicles.

He could hear the four kittens mewing and hissing at one another in the back seat, and the closer he got to the river, the more uncomfortable he felt about drowning them. When he imagined their frantic last minutes—cold and wet, clawing at one another in the dark with no way out of their burlap death chamber—he drove into town instead. He left the bag of kittens at the Riker Veterinary Hospital near the Big Y Junction. Whoever opened up the next morning could decide what to do with them.

On his way home, Cooper stopped at Mac's Store for a can of beer, which he drank before he got there. By the time he wheeled into the driveway, he was so worked up over the fact his daughter had disobeyed him, that he was ready to give her the licking of her life.

• • •

Inside the farm house, Annie and Jordan remained relatively calm until they heard the first crack of Cooper's rifle. They both jumped with each blast, and trying to keep their emotions in check, neither one spoke.

While Cooper got rid of the cats and kittens, Annie cut Jordan's hair, and after a heart-wrenching ten minutes of cutting, a lustrous heap of hair covered the floor. If it hadn't been tainted by ringworm, Annie would have gathered it into a clump, braided it one last time and saved it.

Tears rolled down Jordan's cheeks while the hair clippers buzzed over her scalp, but she didn't make a sound. When Annie was finished with the razor, she daubed a foul smelling fungicide on the patches of ringworm now clearly visible on her daughter's scalp. Gazing in dismay at her bald, miserably contrite daughter, she could no longer hold back her own tears. When Jordan saw her mother crying, she broke down and sobbed. Annie held her for a long time before the sobbing stopped.

"I hate Daddy," Jordan blubbered. "Why did he have to shoot my cats?"

"Don't talk like that, Jordan. Daddy had to get rid of those cats to protect you and the rest of us from getting infected. Ringworm is a disease and a hard one to get rid of."

"Why couldn't we just give them some of my medicine?"

"It doesn't work that way."

"But he killed them! I don't think we should ever kill animals."

"Animals are killed for a number of reasons. Your grandfather butchers cattle to provide meat for the hamburger you like. We shoot a horse when he breaks a leg, because the poor animal can't be taught how to use crutches." She began sweeping up the hair on the floor. "Cats don't understand illness or injury, either. If we put medicine on a cat's ringworm, the cat would lick it off for sure." Annie screwed up her face. "And this stuff stinks. Imagine how bad it would taste."

Annie took the skullcap Dr. McLaughlin gave her and stretched it over her daughter's bald head. The plain white cap looked so clinical, she decided to doll it up with a ruffle or some ribbon before Jordan wore it to school.

"Can I see myself in the mirror, Mom?"

"You look fine, sweetie pie, and don't worry—your hair will grow back. I'm sorry about the cats, but let's not talk about them any more tonight, okay? It's time for you to go to bed, and if you still want to talk about this tomorrow, please don't ask me whether the cats would rather be bald than dead."

CHAPTER SIX

One Saturday, not long after her tenth birthday, Jordan was up and dressed before dawn. It was branding day at the V-Bar-J ranch, the ranch owned by her grandparents, and she had been looking forward to this day ever since the snow melted and the pussy willows got fuzzy. She didn't know what role her Uncle Doug had in mind for her, but instead of watching between the boards of the corral, this year she was going to be part of the action.

Every Memorial Day weekend, Annie's family congregated at the ranch she grew up on for a food fest and to brand the winter-born calves. Rounding up the cattle scattered around Stukel Mountain and branding the new calves took the better part of a day. All ages and genders participated in the process, if only to open gates, run errands, or eat their share of the food.

Jordan's great grandparents, who died before she was born, bought a section of land in 1912 at the base of Stukel Mountain, more a humongous hill than a mountain when compared to the peaks in the Cascade Range. Josephine and Vernon Colton worked every day except Sunday for eighteen years, clearing the land, building a house, erecting a barn and outbuildings, setting posts, stringing barbed wire, and putting in an irrigation system. They raised cattle, grew alfalfa, hay and potatoes, and were able to expand their holdings from 320 to 1500 acres by leasing, then buying more property as they could afford it.

Along the way, they also raised a family—three boys and a girl. One of their sons was killed during World War II and another, Austin, who didn't like getting his hands dirty, went to college and became an accountant. He got his degree from the University of Oregon in Eugene and never moved back to the Klamath Basin. Their only daughter, Sandy, married Wilson, a well-to-do rancher who owned a sizeable spread near Pendleton.

That left one son, Parker, Annie's father and Jordan's grandfather, to continue ranching and farming on the Colton homestead. Parker thrived on ranch work, especially raising livestock; however he wasn't as able a money manager as his father. When blight ruined his potato crop three years running, he had to sell off a large portion of the land his parents had worked so hard to acquire.

Parker worked the 800 remaining acres with his sons, Douglas and Carson, who would inherit the land, if they showed an interest, and more importantly, if they could keep their old man from losing the ranch.

"Is it time to go?" Jordan asked, as she raced through the kitchen for the umpteenth time since breakfast. Annie was washing the dishes and waiting for her Jell-O salad to set.

Jordan opened the refrigerator and jiggled the salad. "I think it's ready, Mom." She took the salad out of the refrigerator and carried it over to her mother where she jiggled it again. "See?"

Jordan turned her attention to her younger brother who sat at the breakfast table in his pajamas. Slim, shaggy-haired Jude was trying to see how many soggy Cheerios he could slide onto the tines of a fork.

"Hurry up, Jude," she ordered. "You're going to make us all late."

Jude pretended, as usual, not to hear his older sister.

Cooper stepped into the kitchen from the adjoining bedroom. "Listen, everybody, I told you to be ready by nine. Dusty's in the car, and I'm leaving in fifteen minutes, with or without you." He slapped open the screen door and pounded down the porch steps.

Jordan grabbed a sweater and ran after him. The spanking she received after the ringworm incident not only warmed her butt, it gave her a permanent understanding that when her father said something, he meant business.

"I'm ready, Daddy," she beamed, before hurrying to the station wagon and jumping into the backseat with Dusty.

It was warm for a Memorial Day, and though the Miller family arrived at the Colton ranch at 10:00 o'clock, the pile of pop and beer buried under ice in red plastic coolers was already beginning to disappear. Cooper grabbed a can of beer and sat by himself on a bench at the far end of the deck.

Most of the Colton women were inside the house, sharing family news and making preparations for dinner, while the men played cards at one of the tables set up on the lawn. A few of the younger cousins were tossing horse shoes. The four older cousins, under the supervision of Parker's sons, Carson and Douglas, were on horseback rounding up the cows and calves. It would be two or three hours before the cattle crew returned.

There were two houses on the Colton property. Leona and Parker Colton lived in the main house, the older and larger of the two structures. Douglas, and his wife and daughter, Athena, occupied the other house. Big dinners and family gatherings always took place at the main house, which was the original homestead house.

Carson and his son, Davey, lived in a doublewide mobile home permanently parked between the barn and his brother's house. Carson's ex-wife, who preferred painting horses to riding them, left Carson, Davey, and the V-Bar-J ranch when Jordan was still a baby.

"You're here!" Cousin Athena cried out, when Jordan popped into Grandma Leona's roomy kitchen. Filled with aunts and cousins, the kitchen was a popular gathering place where enticing smells bubbled from pots on the stove, and salads, pies, and homemade rolls covered the countertops.

Twelve-year-old Athena grabbed her favorite cousin by the hand and raced for the back door. "There's something I want to show you," she said, pink with excitement.

Running toward the corral, Athena tossed her long, sun-streaked hair from side to side, whipping it across her shoulders like the mane of a cantering palomino. Jordan tried to imitate her cousin, but couldn't produce the same dramatic effect with her own chin length auburn hair. After the ringworm healed and her hair grew back, her mother kept it cut short.

Athena called for Duke, the designated kids' horse, a retired cow pony that sat as many as four small riders at a time. Duke flicked his ears and swished his tail before plodding over to the fence so the girls could climb onto his bare back.

Athena climbed on first with Jordan sitting behind her. They headed for the water hole halfway up Stukel Mountain, and since Duke knew the way, the girls relaxed and chatted amiably as they wound through the juniper trees, manzanita brush, and wild plum bushes that grew on the sloping hillside.

When the two cousins reached the water hole, they dismounted and sat in the shade of a small stand of trees. Jordan had been trying to get Athena to disclose her secret during the entire ride, but her cousin just teased her with wait and see responses.

"Now can you tell me?" Jordan asked after Duke ambled over to the pond.

Athena checked to make sure no one else was around before lifting the front of her t-shirt. "See my new bra," she announced.

Jordan's hand flew to her mouth. She couldn't take her eyes off the white cotton undergarment, so white it seemed to glow in the shade of the junipers.

"It's … very pretty," she gushed. She looked at the front of her own totally flat shirt, hoping to detect a change in contour. "When did you get it? It looks tight."

"It feels great. It's kind of hard to fasten, so I hook it in front, then switch it around to the back. I'm growing pretty fast now, so you'll probably get this one when I'm through with it."

"I don't need your dumb bra," Jordan sputtered. "I mean … I can get one of my own." She was usually happy to receive Athena's hand-me-downs, but this bra business was different. "I'm sure Mom will buy me one."

Athena reached for the hem of Jordan's shirt. "You don't need a bra, do you?"

Jordan backed away. "Stop it. I don't have to show you, and I don't want to see yours anymore, either."

Athena grinned. "You're jealous."

Jordan glared at her cousin. "I am not!"

But it was hard not to be jealous of a cousin who possessed everything Jordan wished for and didn't have. Athena's father called her honey and treated her like a princess. She was already in middle school. Her hair was as long and thick as a horse's tail. She had a beautiful black and white cat named Silky, and now she had a bra!

BRUTE HEART

Jordan pulled a handful of berries off a juniper tree and began throwing the slate blue missiles, one at a time, as far as she could. When her hand was empty, she led Duke from the water hole to the low hanging juniper branch she and Athena used for the remount.

"I promised Mom I would take Jude and Dusty for a ride after lunch," she said. She gave her cousin a sidewise glance. "You can come, too … if you want."

Athena tossed her beautiful blond mane and said, "You go ahead. I can ride Duke any time I want.

• • •

Just past noon, the roundup crew returned with the cows and calves they gathered from the less traveled parts of Stukel Mountain and the outer reaches of the ranch. When Jordan saw animals filling up the pasture, she dashed to the corral where her uncles were in the process of separating the calves from their mothers, driving the calves into a large corral and keeping the uneasy cows in an adjacent field. Separated by the corral fence, the cows could see and hear their calves, but couldn't interfere with the branding process.

Jordan could hardly contain her excitement as she climbed up the boards of the corral fence to sit next to her Grandpa Parker. Parker Colton sat on the top rail of the corral with the heels of his boots hooked two boards down. The wiry patriarch, with just a hint of a paunch resting on his V-Bar-J belt buckle, shaded his eyes with his hand to block the afternoon sun. When he scanned the backs of the bawling calves, he saw more rust-red hides than black.

"How many?" he asked his younger son, Carson, who sat astride his horse on the other side of the fence.

"Thirty Herefords and eighteen Angus. Not as many as last year, but they all look healthy." Carson took off his dusty Stetson to smooth his bronze hair. "About two-thirds bulls by my count."

Parker's face brightened at the bull count. On average, steers brought five cents a pound more on the market than heifers. "Good job. Tell your brother I said so."

Carson smiled broadly and accepted the praise as if he had sired the lot himself.

From across the corral, his brother, Douglas, waved his hat in the air and bellowed, "Yo! Carson! The cows are trying to rush the corral. See if you can spread 'em out."

Taller and slightly darker than his brother, Douglas was on foot, pushing through the crush of calves to get to the fire barrel. Sleeves rolled to the elbow and jeans caked with dirt, he waved his hat again, this time at his nephew, Billy.

"Hey, Billy, wait for me before you start that fire." He skirted several more calves before reaching the teenager.

"Got scout juice?"

Billy pointed to a can of charcoal lighter. "Right here."

Douglas grinned and patted his nephew on the back. "Good man. I guess a true Boy Scout wouldn't approve, but it's a heck of a lot quicker than kindling."

He and Billy rolled the beat up, blackened oil barrel toward the calf table. The barrel shielded the fire from the wind and kept the coals red hot. Several ventilation notches sawtoothed its base, and a small square window had been cut out of one side. The window served as an opening for the branding irons inserted into the coals in the bottom of the barrel. Several V-Bar-J irons were buried in the hottest coals and rotated so at least one iron was always hot enough to burn a readable brand.

The rectangular corral where the calves were being kept was roughly twenty-five yards across. A fenced chute, slightly wider than the animals that would soon be passing through it, connected the holding area to the calf table, a contraption with a wooden table on one side where the calves would be vaccinated, ear tagged, dehorned, castrated, and branded.

Douglas and Billy set the branding barrel close, but not too close, to the calf table. By the time the fire inside the barrel was roaring, Jordan and the rest of the helpers were gathered near the calf table listening to their Uncle Doug issue instructions.

"Keep the calves coming," he said, "but don't rush them. And watch your hands and arms while you're near the chute. There's not much room between the boards of the chute and the calf's sides, so it's easy to smash a bone in there. That's your bone I'm talking about, not the calf's."

Douglas checked his duty roster. The bawling of the cows and calves was deafening, forcing him to shout his instructions. Billy was charged with keeping the fire hot and rotating the branding irons. Two of the older and stronger nephews were assigned the task of flipping the calf table. While the calves were restrained, Aunt Sandy would give them their vaccinations and tag their ears. Carson and Douglas would do the castration and branding.

After all of the duties had been assigned, Douglas put his list in the back pocket of his jeans and walked to the end of the chute. Since Jordan hadn't heard her name called, she tugged on her uncle's sleeve and asked, "What about me?"

Douglas smiled down at her. "Did I forget you? Well, there is one more job I haven't filled, and that's somebody to hold the calf's tail."

Jordan puckered her brow.

"That might not sound to you like an important job, but it is. You've got to keep the tail *up* and out of my way when the calf is being castrated, and hold the tail *down* when it's being branded." He still had to shout for her to hear him. "Don't forget that last part, Jordan. If you don't hold the tail *down* when the calf's being branded, you could end up with a blast of recycled alfalfa in your face."

"What's that?"

Carson let out a whoop. "Cow shit!"

Jordan felt a warm glow spread across her face.

"You got that right," Douglas hollered, "and watch your step today, all of you, 'cause there's lots of it out here."

He checked his list again. "Is everybody cool with their assignments?"

"D-a-a-d," Athena whined from the back row of helpers.

Douglas walked over to his daughter and curved an arm around her shoulders. "Athena, honey, I was thinking you could be our runner. That's another important job, because once we get started, we can't stop what we're doing unless there's an emergency. If we need something simple—beer, water, pop—you can be a big help by getting it for us. This work makes us awfully thirsty, you know, especially on a sunny day like today."

Athena looked as if she had just taken a bite out of a lemon. Jordan pressed her lips together to keep from giggling.

After a few mistakes at the start, Doug's bovine assembly line began to function the way he planned. As each calf got to the end of the chute, two of the strongest of the teenage cousins flipped the calf table on its side and held it in place. Next, Carson's son, Davey, secured the calf's head with a metal restraining bar. Sandy injected a multi-purpose vaccine into the calf's shoulder and stapled a V-Bar-J ear tag onto its ear. If it was a bull calf, one of the boys spread the animal's legs apart while Jordan forced the tail up and Douglas neatly incised the scrotum. Using a razor sharp knife, he completed his part of the process by reaching inside the fresh incision to cut the cords attached to each testicle.

Eyes wide, Jordan watched every move of the operation. She used her shirt sleeve to wipe the perspiration off her forehead. "It's so loud," she yelled to no one in particular.

After her Uncle Doug daubed antiseptic on the incision, she held the tail down while her Uncle Carson carefully positioned the smoking hot V-Bar-J brand on the calf's right rear flank. It took about three seconds to burn through the hair into the flesh. At that point, the calf's ordeal was over, and it could run back to its mother for a comforting suck.

It was a good thing everyone involved understood their role, because once the operation was in full swing, the bellowing of the cows calling for their calves and the calves bawling over their predicament made it impossible to hear anything anyone was saying.

• • •

As the work neared completion, the pasture next to the corral was full of newly branded V-Bar-J calves, all of them sticking close by their mothers. When the noise subsided, the old-timers—Parker, his brother, Austin, and brother-in-law, Wilson—sauntered over to the fire barrel.

"Looks like you've got everything under control here," Parker said to his sons.

Douglas and Carson grinned and exchanged glances. The chute and calf table and been their idea. They hadn't lost a calf to infection in the three years since they began using it, and it sure beat branding in the dirt.

Austin pointed the tip of his shoe at the bucket of calf's balls near the calf table. "Who's taking care of the treats?" he asked.

Douglas wiped his brow with the back of his hand. "To tell the truth, we've been too busy." He looked around for his daughter. "Athena—will you please go up to the house and get the iron skillet? Ask your mom for some salt and pepper and some Tabasco sauce, too. Make it quick, honey."

"And some oil," Wilson added. "You know … salad oil or such."

Austin picked up the bucket of balls and set it next to the fire barrel. "Somebody besides me needs do the cooking," he said. "I'll be happy to eat my share, but I'm no cook."

"That's okay, Austin, I'll do it," Wilson volunteered. "Lord knows I've had plenty of practice."

Athena returned with the cooking supplies, and handed them to her grand-father. Parker put the heavy black skillet on top of the hot branding barrel and poured half a cup of Wesson Oil in it. When the cooking oil started to pop, a small crowd of men and boys gathered around the fire barrel.

Wilson peeled the membrane off one of the fresh testicles. "I need to cut this sucker into smaller pieces," he said. "You macho types may eat 'em whole, but I cut mine up. The calf's, that is." Someone laughed. "A whole one's more than a mouthful," he added, prompting a few more chuckles.

When she saw her Great Uncle Wilson toss some of the dollar-sized pieces of calf testicle into the hot oil, Jordan stood on her tiptoes to peer inside the pan.

"Is that to eat?" she asked.

"Sure is, darlin.' Bet you haven't had a Rocky Mountain oyster before, have you?"

Jordan eyed the dark pink flesh sizzling in the frying pan.

"We call 'em Stukel Mountain oysters over here," Carson said.

Wilson nodded approvingly. "Hell of a good idea. Maybe we should call 'em Battle Mountain oysters back home." He used his knife like a fork to turn the pieces over and brown the other sides. "Who wants the first one?"

Sandy, who was counting the used syringes, locked eyes with her brother. "I think Parker should have it. It's his herd."

"Thanks, Sis," Parker replied, "but I think I should share this first batch with Doug. He deserves most of the credit for everything going so well today."

After a hectic, sometimes bloody afternoon, Douglas was more than ready to crack a beer and savor his juicy reward. He ate a few more oysters after his trophy bite, but the calves' balls were disappearing so quickly, he had to wait his turn for those.

Jordan watched with fascination as her grandpa, uncles, and some of her cousins ate the fried pieces of meat that only a short time ago had been attached to the calves. She wandered over to where Athena was standing and asked if she was going to eat one.

Athena wrinkled her perfect nose. "No way. I tried one two summers ago, and it was yucky!"

"What did it taste like?"

"I don't know—like kidneys maybe. Ever eat kidneys?"

"No."

"Well, it tasted to me like kidneys, and they make me barf."

Jordan pondered her cousin's words for a few seconds before walking back to the fire barrel. "Can I try one?" she asked.

The crowd around the burn barrel watched as Wilson gave his little niece a sizzling piece of oyster. She smelled it. It smelled okay. She licked it. It tasted salty. She blew on it to cool it down, and then nibbled the edge. When she realized she was all of a sudden the center of attention, she stuffed the rest of the oyster in her mouth and chewed vigorously before swallowing it. After she licked her fingers, she got a round of applause, and her Uncle Carson gave her a high five.

CHAPTER SEVEN

Cooper and Annie missed their daughter's "coming out party." Annie was helping in the kitchen, and Cooper, who spent the better part of branding day drinking beer, was passed out on the living room floor in front of the television set. When it was time to leave, Annie insisted on driving, but Cooper grabbed a cup of coffee and parked himself in the driver's seat while she was rounding up the children.

During the first mile of the trip home, nobody said a word. Arms folded in frustration, Annie stared straight ahead. Jude and Dusty were horsing around on their side of the backseat, giggling and trading farts. Jordan sat next to them, shushing her brothers from time to time and elbowing Jude, who sat in the middle. She could tell her father was drunk and her mother was upset. Her brothers, however, seemed oblivious to the emotions simmering in the front seat.

When Annie's composure finally melted, she uncharacteristically lashed out at her husband in front of the children. "I can't believe how much beer you drank today. Do you know how humiliating it was to find you lying there, drooling on the carpet?"

Cooper was driving slower than a bike rider pedaling in the dark and not as straight. Jordan coughed gently to remind her parents there were little ears in the backseat, and at least two of them were listening.

Annie heard the cough but chose to continue. "What were you and Lewis trying to prove, anyway—who could drink the most before he puked?"

Cooper tried to light a cigarette and spilled hot coffee down the front of his shirt. This elicited a string of curses, and when he grudgingly acknowledged Annie's rebuke, he spoke as if he had a mouthful of mashed potatoes.

"Look, Annie, I din't even want to go over there today. I don't like them people. They don't like me, neither. They look at me like … they got a belly ache or somethin'."

"Don't be ridiculous," Annie huffed. She set her jaw and stared at the center line for a slow half mile before sounding off again. "Why is it, Coop, we were both eighteen when we got married, but somehow I've turned twenty-seven while you're still eighteen. Maybe even younger, when you act the way you did today."

"That don't make any sense," Cooper said, tossing his half smoked cigarette out the window.

Annie took a hard look at the man sitting next to her. "Why can't you grow up and be a real father to our kids … and a son-in-law, or a brother-in-law? Stop being so selfish with your time, and for God sake, stop drinking so much. We've got three kids to raise, and I can't do it by myself."

Cooper pounded his fist on the steering wheel. "God damn it, you're not raisin' 'em by yourself!" He dropped what was left of his coffee, grabbed the wheel with both hands, and pounced on the gas pedal.

Annie pressed her spine against the seat back and fixed her eyes on the road ahead as the fence posts along both sides of Merrill highway began flying past them. The car began swerving back and forth across the centerline, and in a panic, Annie reached for the steering wheel. Cooper grunted something, and tried to push her away, but Annie held on to the wheel in spite of a hard blow to her ribs.

She let out a scream as the headlights of an oncoming car suddenly appeared directly ahead of them. Using every ounce of a mother's determination to protect her children, Annie jerked the steering wheel back on track, narrowly avoiding a collision.

Jordan squeezed as much of herself as she could into her corner of the backseat. Annie's scream caught the attention of the two boys who sat up straight, eyes round. First Dusty, then Jude turned around and stood on their knees to look out the back window at the taillights of the barely missed car, the howl of an angry horn trailing behind it.

"You'll get us all killed!" Annie cried, as the battle to control the car continued. Wailing like an animal caught in a trap, she hung onto the wheel with both hands until Cooper gave her a shove that knocked her against the door on her side of the car. Satisfied he had made his point, he finally eased up on the gas. He let Annie cry for a few seconds before grabbing her by the arm and dragging her back across the seat next to him.

"Listen to me, Annie. You wanna know what it's really like to raise these kids by yourself? You keep this up, and by God you'll find out!"

By the time Cooper finished his rant, the besieged little family was home, and as soon as the car stopped next to the blue spruce, Jordan ran upstairs and jumped into bed and hid under the covers. She always got a knot in her stomach when her parents argued, but she had never seen them get physical, and it had never happened in the car where she couldn't escape, and any knot she may have experienced in the past was nothing compared to the fear of dying.

Buried under her blankets, Jordan listened for more yelling. She heard the door to her parent's bedroom close followed by the muffled sounds of the TV, but nothing more. The TV was still on, and her mother was asleep on the couch when Jordan got up the next morning.

After a silent breakfast, Cooper and Annie exchanged hugs. The rest of the week Annie smiled a lot and cooked her husband's favorite foods including the dreaded liver and onions that Jordan and Jude hated. Cooper made amends by playing catch with his sons and taking them fishing on Lost River. Occasionally he took Jordan fishing with them, although he never included her in their ball games or rough housing on the lawn.

Jordan was certain her father liked Dusty best. Dusty had their father's cavernous dimples, warm brown eyes, dark, almost black hair, and the same not-so-tall but athletic build. She wondered why it was such a big deal to look like your father and wished people would stop mentioning it whenever they saw Cooper and Dusty together.

Jude, on the other hand, with his fair skin and cinnamon stick hair, resembled Jordan and Annie. He even had their delicate bone structure, which contributed to his gangly appearance. He was on the quiet side, spacey at times, whereas Dusty was loud and aggressive, and though he was a few inches taller than his brother, whenever they competed against one another, Dusty usually won.

It seemed to Jordan that their father picked on her and Jude, but looked the other way when Dusty got into trouble. He would laugh and pump his fist whenever Dusty ran farther, or hit a ball harder, or did just about anything better than she or Jude could do it, and if she or Jude *did* win a race, bring home a ribbon, or get a good grade at school, the best they got was a grunt of satisfaction.

Since she couldn't compete with her brothers when it came to catching fish or winning races, Jordan decided to make her mark with perfect behavior, something Jude and Dusty never quite got the hang of. She learned to cook simple things like scrambled eggs and grilled cheese sandwiches so she could lighten her mother's load. She always made her bed and kept her upstairs bedroom pristine. To ward off fights or other forms of confrontation between members of her family, she assumed the role of peacekeeper by picking up after her brothers or hiding her father's empty beer cans in the bottom of the garbage can so her mother wouldn't see how many there were.

Jordan also made an effort to relate to her father. She watched TV with him, paying attention to his favorite programs so she could ask questions about them. He would respond with one or two-word answers, or tell her to be quiet if she asked too many.

One July evening, she decided she might make some points if she volunteered to help him milk the cow. Surprisingly, he accepted the offer and gave her one of his rare smiles when he picked up the aluminum milk pail and headed for the barn.

Jordan chattered incessantly while she and her father walked around the shed to the barn. "I know I can do it, Daddy. Peaches likes me. I'm not afraid of her, either."

"It helps if Peaches likes you, but milkin's harder than it looks. You have to imitate the way a calf sucks by using your hands in just the right way. I'll show you. Then I'll let you try."

Peaches was waiting by the side door when they reached the barn. Cooper led the cow to her stall, fit the stanchions around her neck, and scattered some alfalfa into the hay bin directly in front of her. He cooed and clucked as he washed her udder and readied her for milking.

When it was time to start, he switched on the transistor radio that hung from a nail on the barn wall. Cooper milked his only cow twice a day in eight or nine minutes, or about the time it took to listen to three songs on KLAD. Peaches flicked her ears as a Statler Brothers song began to play. The sound quality produced by the cheap transistor radio was tinny and scratchy, but the part time farmer believed it was the country/western music that made his cow such a good milker.

Cooper placed a small stool next to Peaches, and then straddled the stool, tucking his knees under her belly. He sat so close he could rest his forehead in the hollow of the cow's flank. Peaches stood perfectly still as he gently stroked her bag.

Jordan watched her father take two of the cow's teats in his hands and squeeze them evenly and quickly, pulling ever so slightly as he pointed two streams of warm milk into the pail. After ten or twelve squirts he stopped and showed Jordan the exact finger rotation he used to stimulate the flow. His fingers were thick, and the black that was always under his fingernails looked even blacker when his fingers were curled around the pinkish white teats.

He transferred one of the teats into his daughter's right hand. "You try it. Go slow. Make sure you're holdin' it right."

Jordan investigated the teat's shape, turning it upwards to peer at the hole where the milk came out, and her eyes widened with wonder. "It's so soft," she said.

She curled her fingers around the teat and slowly squeezed it the way her father showed her. Nothing happened. She squeezed harder, but still couldn't get anything to come out. She repeated the finger sequence over and over until her hand started to cramp. Frustrated, she gave the teat a hard jerk. Peaches lifted one of her back hooves, held it suspended momentarily, then lowered it.

"Don't yank on it. It hurts her when you pull too hard. You'll figure it out. I didn't get any either, the first time I tried."

Jordan whispered a few words of encouragement to herself as she practiced the finger rotation. After several more attempts, a thin stream of milk hit the wall of the pail. "Oh!" she chirped, surprised at the sound it made. "I did it!" She jumped to her feet and began dancing around Peaches who promptly kicked the milking stool on its side.

Cooper righted the stool and returned to milking. "That wasn't bad for a first try, but I'd better finish or we'll never get out of here. Maybe you can practice some other time." Peaches took a mouthful of hay as familiar hands began pulling in a steady rhythm.

"Why does a cow have four teats, Daddy?" Jordan asked, looking at her father with newfound admiration.

Cooper shrugged. "I don't know. Maybe two are for milk and two are for cream." He chuckled to himself. "I'm just kiddin'. All I know is, you've got to make sure all four of 'em's empty."

Jordan held her father's free hand while he carried the full pail of milk back to the house. The sun hovered just above the horizon, and with the cool approach of evening, the mosquitoes were looking for blood. When they began whining around Jordan's ears, she let go of her father's hand to swat at them.

"We'd better hurry," she said, walking faster. "Thanks for the lesson, Daddy. I did pretty good, didn't I?"

"Not bad. Not bad for a little squirt."

• • •

It was the only milking lesson Jordan received. By the end of summer, Cooper was back to his old pattern of leaving every night after dinner to hang out with his friends. Sometimes he would go to his best friend Perry's place to work on a '55 Chevy he was restoring. More often he, Perry and one or two of their coworkers met at Buck's, a Klamath Falls tavern where they drank beer and watched whatever sporting event happened to be playing on the ceiling-mounted TV.

Buck's was a smoke filled, blue collar tavern that specialized in shots and beers. In fact, the owner proudly boasted there wasn't a wine glass in the place. Popcorn in paper bowls decorated the few tables randomly scattered around the room. Pretzels with mustard, hardboiled eggs, and pickled Polish sausages were for sale at the bar.

The décor at Buck's hadn't been updated in forty years. There were no windows, just glass blocks where windows might have been before the retail space was converted to a tavern. The ceiling and the top half of the walls were white yellowed by cigarette smoke. A narrow strip of molding separated the top half of the walls from the bottom half, which was painted dark brown. The brown half had numerous gouges and scrapes in it and a few gaping holes. No one could remember when Bucks was last painted, but it was usually so dark inside the tavern it didn't matter.

Nobody hassled Cooper when he was at Buck's. He could talk about whatever interested him, or sit and say nothing if that's what he felt like doing. The guys who hung out at Buck's didn't judge him by what he did for a living or what he owned, which gave him the freedom to relax. Most of the time, he relaxed too much, drank too much, and went home with a snoot full.

Every night, while Cooper was at Buck's unwinding with his friends, Annie sat at home, worrying he might wreck the car, hurt himself, spend too much money, or get into some other kind of trouble. She knew the tavern's phone number, but not wanting to appear needy, never dialed it.

While Annie fretted away the hours Cooper was gone, Jordan lay awake upstairs listening for the sound of his car. When the night dragged on with no sound of him, she would get out of her bed to stand by her bedroom window and watch for headlights. If she stood at just the right angle, she could see part of the main road that intersected with their driveway. Her hopes rose with every set of headlights that came around the curve, and sometimes she would make wishful predictions such as *Daddy's car is going to be one of the next five.* If none of the next five cars turned out to be his, she would predict it would be the next five, or the next ten. Most nights she gave up and went back to bed, falling asleep as soon as she heard the crunch of tires on gravel.

One night during her self-imposed vigil, Jordan heard her mother crying and mumbling to herself in the kitchen below her bedroom. Hoping to find out what was wrong, she crept downstairs and hid behind the pantry door, leaving the door open a crack so she could see into the kitchen.

She hadn't been in her hiding place more than two minutes when the back door opened. She sucked in her breath as her father staggered in. If he discovered she was out of bed at this time of the night, she would be in big trouble.

Cooper took off his jacket, and trying to drape it over the back of a chair, it fell on the floor. When he wandered over to the kitchen table where Annie was sitting, she blew her nose and wiped her eyes, but didn't look up.

"We can't go on like this," she said, staring at the pile of papers in front of her. "Pacific Power is threatening to turn off the electricity. School starts again in two weeks, which means the kids are going to need clothes and supplies, and I can't keep asking my parents to bail us out. They're not rich, you know."

Cooper used the kitchen counter to steady himself as he lurched into a chair. He hung one arm over the back of the chair and turned toward Annie.

"Then why don't you get off your ass and go to work?" he said, taking a drag from the cigarette that dangled between his fingers.

"I'm going to," Annie said, her voice quavering. "I won't make much, but I can take care of a few of these bills."

She began crying again. "We'll have to move into town. The way you go through money, we still won't be able to afford two cars which means I'll have to walk to work, and I can't do that from here."

The ash dropped off the end of Cooper's cigarette. "Suit yourself."

Having heard more than enough and none of it good, Jordan tiptoed upstairs and climbed back into bed. A lump formed in her throat the minute she laid her head on her pillow. She quickly decided it was her father's fault they had to move, and she hated him for it.

I wish he would leave some night and never come back. Then Mom wouldn't cry, and we wouldn't have to move.

The anger and blame quickly morphed into guilt, and the lump in her throat got bigger until it finally dissolved into a trickle of tears that ran down the sides of her face, wetting her hair and forming puddles in her ears.

CHAPTER EIGHT

Moving is not the most traumatic of life's changes, but to a young girl leaving the only home she had known, it felt as if planet Earth had blown apart, even though the house she was moving into was only eight miles away. Convinced she would never be happy again, she sulked for days and found one more reason to envy her cousin, Athena, who didn't have to move at all.

Cooper gave Peaches to Grandpa Parker, hoping to pay back part of what he owed his in-laws. The timing was perfect, since Parker needed a productive dairy cow to suckle a pair of orphan calves he'd been bottle feeding. Jordan was there when the calves got their first taste of the real deal. Calm as usual, Peaches accepted the frisky calves despite their vigorous sucking and occasional head butts.

Cooper and Annie butchered the chickens, which meant chicken dinner every night for nearly two weeks. Jordan was never able to make a pet out of one of the free range hens, and the roosters scared her to death, so she accepted the demise of the chickens without complaining. What she did hate to leave were her friends at school, Peaches, and the neighbor's pigs, especially one she called Stinky. She climbed her favorite apple tree one last time and said goodbye to the barn, the pasture, and the wild flowers that grew along the irrigation ditch—even the purple-headed thistles.

The house she and her family moved into was an 800-square-foot, two-bedroom rental near an abandoned lumber mill in one of the older sections of Klamath Falls. The mill had been closed for years. Over time, vandals had broken or shot holes in every one of its windows, and noxious weeds covered what had once been the parking lot. A huge wigwam burner, used for burning scrap wood when the mill was thriving, had never been dismantled. By far the tallest structure in the neighborhood, the giant fortress could be seen for miles, a rust covered billboard advertising the plight of its surroundings.

Time and tenants had taken their toll on the once bustling neighborhood. The small houses fell into disrepair when the timber ran out and the mill closed. Originally owner-occupied, the mill houses gradually became rentals, shabby little boxes in a hardscrabble neighborhood marked by shift work, sweat work, or no work at all.

The house Annie and Cooper decided they could afford was one of the area's smallest. Since there were only two bedrooms in the house, Jordan spent her first three weeks sleeping on the couch while her parents converted a utility room into a tiny third bedroom. They didn't own a washer and dryer, so Annie and Cooper removed the utility room's stained concrete sink, capped the pipes, and cobbled together a room that would have been small for a nursery let alone a girl's bedroom.

When her room was ready, Jordan begrudgingly moved her few possessions into a windowless cubicle less than half the size of her previous bedroom with just enough space for a twin bed, a four-drawer dresser, and a makeshift closet with a shower curtain for a door.

Jordan was so miserable over the move, the house, the neighborhood, and her cell-like room that she didn't even thank her parents for their efforts. Annie knew her daughter was intrigued by the fact she had been born during the Woodstock music festival, so she bought a cheap frame for the Joni Mitchell poster she'd held onto since her quasi hippy days, and hung it in Jordan's room. That simple, decorative item hanging by her bed finally elicited a hug and a fragile smile.

Other than Annie getting a job at a nearby convenience store, there was little to celebrate in a rundown neighborhood with no place to roam. The five members of the Miller family now shared half the space they lived in before, and since there wasn't a fence around their house, Max, who was still healthy for a nine-year-old dog, had to stay inside most of the time.

Finding her new world to be cramped and chaotic, Jordan escaped whenever she could into books she checked out from the county library. Jude turned inward and spent most of his days and nights curled up next to Max on the living room floor. True to form, Dusty made two new friends the day he moved into the neighborhood. Joseph and Angel Blanco, along with their four brothers, lived in a similarly small house next door. After Annie met Dora Blanco, a stay-at-home mom, she asked her new neighbor to keep an eye on Jordan, Jude and Dusty while she was at work.

When Jordan found out the woman next door was going to be her babysitter, she stood on the tips of her toes and whined, "Jude and Dusty need a babysitter, Mom, but I don't. You know I won't get into any trouble." She volunteered to peel the potatoes that evening, and searched until she found the peeler without having to ask her mother where to find it.

"You're only ten years old," Annie replied. "I trust you, but I'd like to find out more about the kids in your school before I let you loose in this neighborhood." She counted out five potatoes and gave them to Jordan. "Let's wait for a few years. Then we'll see."

"But, Mom, I don't want to be the only girl." Jordan took several deep swipes of potato skin off one of the potatoes. "There are six boys next door plus Jude and Dusty make eight."

"You should be used to being around boys by now. Just ignore them. And don't take so much potato off with the peel—it's wasteful."

Jordan sighed dramatically. "What if I make a new friend? Can I at least go over to her house?" She wrapped the potato peels in newspaper and placed the soggy package in the garbage bucket under the sink.

"You can probably do that once in a while. Just make sure you tell Dora your friend's name, and especially her telephone number."

Annie wiped her hands on a towel and picked a stray thread off Jordan's yellow sweatshirt. "So tell me, have you met anyone special at school?"

Jordan's face lit up. "There's this girl named McKenzie. She sits next to me in art class. She and her sister are friends with another girl named Kimberly. I ate lunch with all three of them today."

"Why don't you ask them to stop by the house so I can meet them?"

Jordan's smile disappeared at the thought of her newfound friends coming to the house. What would they think when they saw her dinky bedroom, and what if they found out she had a babysitter! Even worse, what if they came over when her father was drunk?

"I think I'll wait, Mom. They're awfully busy."

The move into town ended Cooper's ten-year stint as a part time farmer, but he was inwardly pleased to be rid of of the headaches. At first he put the extra time this gave him into the move, as he and his friend, Perry, handled the heavy stuff, including the construction of Jordan's room. After his family was settled, however, Cooper began spending more time than ever at Buck's, which was now a lot closer to home.

Every evening and most Saturday afternoons, when Cooper came home from the tavern, he almost immediately fell asleep on the couch. This rendered him harmless enough, but left two lumpy chairs or the floor for the rest of the family or anyone else who happened to drop by. When he woke up, he usually had the living room to himself, because the children had made sure to be someplace else.

During the years they lived in the Henley district, Cooper rarely got involved in his children's lives unless it meant doing something fun. This changed after he moved into town as he went from being a part-time farmer to being a full-time nitpicker. Rules and censures sprouted daily, and though the rules weren't in writing, the Miller children were expected to know what they were and act accordingly.

Some rules such as "your skirt can't be shorter than two inches above the knee," applied to just one child. Others such as "lights out and in your beds by 9:00 o'clock" were universal. There were rules concerning maximum minutes per phone call, who could call him Dad and who should call him Daddy, where to sit at the kitchen table or in the living room, the right way to open and close the front door, when to talk, when not to talk, the pecking order for using the bathroom, how often they could spend time with their friends, and so on. All rules were strictly enforced—no exceptions, no complaining, and never, ever ask why.

• • •

For the first five years she lived in town, Jordan never invited her friends to come inside the house if she suspected her father was home. If she miscalculated, and her friends happened to walk in on her father while he was sleeping off a recent trip to the tavern, she made up stories to explain why he was taking a nap. Luckily, when the four girls got together, it was usually at Kimberly's house. Kimberly had a large purple and white bedroom, her own telephone, and a fluffy, blue-eyed malamute.

One evening during her fifteenth summer, Jordan and her three friends, who had been swimming at the municipal pool that afternoon, dropped by her house to get what she needed for a rarely allowed sleepover at Kimberly's. Jude and Dusty were playing outside. Cooper was gone, as usual, so Annie was the only one in the house. The four girls were laughing and talking in Jordan's room when the phone rang. There was no such thing as privacy in the Miller household, so Annie's side of the conversation could be heard throughout the house.

"Again? Where's the car?" Her words were clipped and icy. "I'll have to figure out a way to get down there. How much is it going to cost us *this* time?"

Jordan closed her bedroom door and tried to divert her friends' attention by talking louder than usual about a cute boy they saw diving off the high board that afternoon. It didn't work.

"Maybe I can get Dora to take me," Annie continued. "Jordan can watch the kids for an hour or so."

Jordan stopped talking and leaned against the closed door so she could listen in earnest to what might be happening to her own plans for the evening.

"You're not sorry about what matters," she heard her mother say. "You're just sorry you got caught. I'll get there as soon as I can."

Annie hung up without saying goodbye, and within seconds there was a tap on Jordan's door. She looked at her girlfriends, who were being way too quiet, and told them she'd be right back.

"Please wait," she said, gesturing for her friends to sit wherever they could find a spot.

She followed her mother into the kitchen. Averting her eyes, Annie told Jordan she was going to ask Dora to take her to where Cooper's car was stalled. It was a pathetic lie, but Jordan pretended ignorance.

"That means you can't go to Kimberly's tonight," Annie said, picking a cigarette butt out of the ashtray and lighting it. "I need you to keep an eye on the boys, the Blanco boys, too, until Dora and I get back. We won't be long." She spoke calmly, as if a stalled car was a common occurrence.

Jordan's friends were speaking in hushed tones when she returned to her room.

"I have to *baby*sit tonight," she told them, trying not to cry.

Her friends put on gigantic fake smiles and began gathering their things to leave. She was certain the three girls heard everything her mother said, so she closed the door behind her and took a deep breath, ready to face the music that was far from her favorite song.

"Do you guys have a sec?" she whispered. "There's something I really need to talk to you about."

Kimberly was sitting on Jordan's twin bed, her long white legs crossed at the ankles. Sisters, Morgan and McKenzie Scott sat cross-legged on the floor with their canvas tote bags in their laps. Morgan was a year behind her sister in school, but the two girls were tight as twins.

Morgan eyed her sister. "We can stay for a minute or two, can't we McKenzie?"

McKenzie shrugged her shoulders. "I guess so. What's up, farm girl?"

Jordan stood against the door with its knob pressing into her lower back. "I don't know how to say this," she began, "but there's something I haven't told you guys." Her legs felt weak, so she put her hands behind her back and hung onto the door knob. "I didn't tell you, because I was worried you might not want to run around with me anymore if you knew about it."

"We wouldn't do something like that," Morgan said.

McKenzie moved the tote bag off her lap and onto the floor so she could sit on it. "You're talking about your dad, aren't you? We kind of knew there was a problem."

Jordan tightened her grip on the doorknob. "I'm totally embarrassed to tell you ... you probably already know ..." She hesitated. "My father drinks too much!" Her mouth was so dry, the words stuck to her tongue. "I think he's an alcoholic, but I'm not sure."

Kimberly's pale eyes softened as she gestured for Jordan to come sit beside her on the bed. "How can you tell? That is, how can you tell he's an alcoholic, not how can you tell he drinks too much."

Jordan sat on the bed next to her friend, then picked up her pillow and hugged it to her chest. "I don't know. I wish there was a way to know for sure."

Kimberly put an arm around Jordan's shoulder. "It doesn't really matter. You're not an alcoholic, so we don't care how much your dad drinks. Well… as long as he doesn't drive us anywhere."

McKenzie cracked her gum. "Did he get picked up for drunk driving?"

The bluntness of the words, "drunk driving" stung Jordan somewhere behind the breastbone, and she felt the red flush she hated creep all the way to her hairline.

"Yes," she whispered, "I'm pretty sure that's what happened." She looked at her three friends. "I wish like crazy I could go with you guys tonight, but I have to stay here and make sure my brothers don't get into trouble." She scooted off the bed, tears stinging her eyes. "Maybe I can come over later."

Morgan and McKenzie stood up and sandwiched her in a hug. "It's okay, Jordan," McKenzie said. "Shoot, our dad has a few too many once in a while."

Morgan nodded.

Kimberly joined the group hug. "Mine does, too. Both my parents do."

• • •

The house was eerily quiet after Jordan's friends said their goodbyes. Sitting alone in the living room, her ears picked up an occasional shout from her brothers and the Blanco boys who were playing ball in an empty lot across the street. Their voices sounded hollow and distant, lower than young boys' voices. She wondered how long she should let them stay out there, now that it was getting dark.

Through the back door came the sound of a neighbor's rainbird sprinkler going *chick, chick, chick, chick, chick, chick* in one direction, then *chicka, chicka, chicka, chicka, chicka, chicka* when it reversed. The rainbird's mantra repeated over and over while Jordan waited inside an empty house for her parents to come home.

CHAPTER NINE

Dora gathered the empty soft drink containers, napkins, and McDonald's bags piled on the front seat and tossed them into the back of her minivan. Annie climbed in, and the two women engaged in light conversation as they drove to the county jail to pick up Cooper.

In order to reach the gas pedal, Dora had to press her chest against the steering wheel and stretch her neck to see over it. The buttons on the front of her shirt strained against the pudgy roll around her middle, and her stretch pants were pulling apart at the seams. Surprisingly unruffled for a mother of six boys, there was a smile on her shiny round face, in fact, Annie had never seen her frown.

"How 'bout this warm night?" Dora said. "Almost like Chico."

"It feels good," Annie said, lost in her own thoughts. "We don't get many nights like this."

"Your daughter okay with the kids?"

"Yes, I trust her completely. We shouldn't be gone long."

Annie rested her forearm on the open window frame and let the warm air roll across her skin. As she sat wondering what to say to her husband after she bailed him out of jail again, it dawned on her that this was the first time she had gone anywhere with Dora. They spoke almost daily, took turns watching the children, borrowed an egg or two once in a while, but they never went shopping, to a movie, or out to lunch the way lady friends did.

"I really appreciate your doing this on such short notice. I'm ashamed to have to ask."

Dora shrugged. "I seen worse things than this. It could be drugs, you know." She paused briefly before adding, "Be happy your husband go to the job every day. My Joaquin go one day, then he get drunk and lie around the house and lose the job. But what does he think, when he don't go to the job for a week?"

"I guess I shouldn't complain, Dora. There are many days when Coop doesn't feel well, but he always manages to drag himself to work. If only he would put that same effort into being a good husband and father."

They waited for two red lights to change before Annie spoke again. "You mentioned drugs. Do you think Joaquin is into drugs? You don't have to answer that if you don't want to, Dora."

"I s'pose I say too much, but you I trust. Drugs are worse than booze, you know. My husband, he could go to prison. Drugs is 'spensive, too. Sometime I think maybe Joaquin stealing. Where else he get the money? But I don't say nothing, 'cause, you know, I got six boys. Thank God you give me money to watch your kids. He don't know you pay me."

The two women fell silent for a few blocks. Then out of the blue Dora asked, "Why you no get a divorce? You got the job an' all."

Although Annie sometimes asked herself that same question, she didn't think someone she barely knew would have the nerve to ask it.

"I don't make that much money, Dora. I think Coop would help out, but he doesn't make a whole lot, either, not enough to support two households. Besides, he really does love our kids, even though he doesn't show it. I think he really loves me, too, for that matter."

"Do you lub *him*?"

Annie exhaled audibly. "Ho boy—you ask tough questions, lady. Right this minute I'd like to choke him." She felt inside her purse for the checkbook. "I've been through this before, though, and after a few days I start thinking maybe it was partly my fault. Then he gives me that shy smile of his, and … well, it just kills me."

"He very handsome man," Dora giggled. "Nice … what you call?" She used her index finger to bore an imaginary hole in one of her cheeks.

"Dimples. See! That's another reason why I'm not leaving. Women still find him attractive, and I couldn't handle seeing him with another woman, so I keep hoping he'll change. He's such a sweetheart when he's not drinking."

Annie looked at her watch. "I do worry about the kids, though. I often wonder how much they know, and what's going on in their minds. I hope their father's drinking doesn't screw up *their* little lives."

. . .

Dusty threw a worn out sneaker across the short distance between his bed and that of his brother, hitting him square in the back. As usual, Jude was trying to lengthen the night while Dusty was up with the sun.

"C'mon," Dusty yelled. He threw the matching sneaker. "We're supposed to go swimming in the canal. Joseph and Angel are waiting for us. You always make us late."

"Leave me alone," Jude groaned, his face planted firmly in his pillow. Just gimme ten more minutes."

"No. I'm not waiting for you this time. You can stay here and rot for all I care. You stink, anyway. You stink, fart face!"

"Okay, okay, don't get excited."

Jude peeled his gangly frame out of a tangled sheet and sat on the edge of his bed. He looked malnourished even though he ate practically everything put in front of him. "See, I'm awake, dumb ass."

He began rummaging through the pile of clothes, shoes, magazines, candy wrappers and miscellaneous junk that littered the floor of the crowded bedroom. "What'd you do with my cutoffs?"

"I didn't touch your stupid cutoffs." Dusty retrieved the sneakers he tossed at his brother. "The mice must have carried them away. The mice probably used them for a nest." His brown eyes danced with glee as he laced up his sneakers. "Ha! Or the *stink* bugs took 'em."

Jude found his cutoffs near the bottom of the junk pile and put them on in a hurry. He stepped into his own sneakers without stopping to tie them, and raced to the bedroom door with Dusty on his heels. When Jude stopped suddenly, Dusty ran into him.

Dusty began pummeling his older brother on the back. "Open the door, asshole!"

Jude turned around and gave his brother a shove. "Shut up for a minute, you little creep. Before we go swimming, we need to talk about what happened last night. Did you see Dad when he came home?"

Dusty put his hands on his hips, and stuck his chin out. "We don't have time for this. Let me outta here!"

Jude pressed against the door and dug in his heels while he scrutinized his brother's face. "No, we have to talk about this right now." He licked his lips and made himself look dead serious. "Dad's an ex-con now, you know."

Dusty's eyes widened, then narrowed. "He is not. He didn't commit no crime."

Words burst from Jude's mouth like exploding pop rocks. "Then how come the police picked him up? They made him get out of his car. They wouldn't even let him drive to the station. Mom had to go get him. When she got there, Dad was in jail—locked up."

"I don't believe you."

"It's true. I heard Jordan talking on the phone after Mom and Dad got back. Jordan was mad because she couldn't go over to Kimberly's. You know how she scrunches down between the wall and the stove when she's on the phone? Well, she was talking real low, but I could hear her. She was crying and blabbing all about it."

"How come she found out?"

Jude shrugged. "Mom tells her everything."

Dusty chewed on this news for a minute while attempting to burn a hole through his brother's chest with the intensity of his glare. "I don't care. I'm going swimming." He pushed Jude aside, ran through the living room and out the front door, slamming it hard. Annie called after him to come back and eat his breakfast, but he kept on running.

• • •

"Heard about last night, Coop," Perry said. He ran a hand across his nearly bald head, and slid onto the barstool next to Cooper, his butt draping the seat like a giant mushroom cap. "They give ya' any trouble?"

"That cop was out to get me. He must've been watchin' this place for days. I hate those bastards!"

Perry whistled at Kerby, Buck's bartender of few words. Catching Kerby's eye, he pointed at his friend's nearly empty glass. "Let me get you a fresh one, Coop. You could probably use it, right?"

"Does the pope shit in the woods?" They both laughed even though they used this same mangled cliché every chance they got.

Kerby sat two frosty glasses of draught on the bar, wiped his hands on his apron and waited for Cooper to finish the beer he was drinking when Perry walked in. Perry chugged half his own beer with the first quaff, smacked his rubbery lips, and celebrated the end of the workday with a satisfied "a-a-h."

"Whatcha gonna do now?" he asked, wiping his mouth with the back of his sleeve. "You know, so they don't getcha again." He grabbed the nearest bowl of popcorn and began shoveling it into his mouth.

"Hell, I don't know. I'm one of the best damn drivers there is." Cooper scanned the small group of patrons sitting around the bar, looking for consensus. "There wasn't any traffic on the road or nothin'."

"This is your third time, ain't it?"

Cooper nodded. "The wife won't speak to me. We can't afford the fine. I'm in deep shit."

A young man with bumps on his forehead sat on the stool next to Perry, listening intently to the Buck's regulars. "Sorry to butt in," he said, "but there was a cop car outside when I got here."

"Where at? I didn't see one." Cooper peered at the glass blocks that substituted for windows. "How 'bout you, Perry. See a cop when you came in?"

"No, but I wasn't lookin', neither." He waved his empty popcorn bowl at Kerby. The dour bartender dumped the last of the popcorn from a five-gallon can into Perry's bowl. There was more left in the can than the bowl could hold, and Kerby came close to smiling when Perry tried to corral the overspill.

The pimply-faced man leaned into the conversation. "The cop wasn't on this side of the street. He was parked in Albertson's parking lot, right in the middle of the customers' cars."

A small cloud of gloom settled over Cooper's end of the bar. He, Perry and the young stranger watched in silence as the last batter struck out in the bottom of the sixth inning of a Mariner's game. When the game ended, Cooper drained his glass and stood up.

"Think I'd better go while the gettin's good." He fist bumped the back of Perry's fuzzy head. "Thanks for the beer, bud."

Cooper drove home that night as carefully as a sixteen-year-old taking his driver's test. He checked Albertson's parking lot as he drove by, but didn't see a cop car. He kept an eye out for a car with lights on top while he drove down South Sixth Street to a mini mall near the Alameda Bypass. He checked out the cars parked in the mini mall, then squared his shoulders and walked inside the liquor store. A beer drinker, he wasn't sure what to buy, so he settled on a fifth of the cheapest whisky on the shelf.

"Takeout," Cooper said, handing the clerk a twenty dollar bill. The store clerk smiled politely and slid the bottle of whisky into a slim paper bag. Cooper twisted the top of the bag around the bottle's neck and tucked it under his arm as he walked out the door.

CHAPTER TEN

Kimberly's parents bought her a car for her sixteenth birthday—a silver 1978 Chevrolet Monte Carlo with a candy apple red interior. Seven years old, the car had a couple of dents, and the metallic shine of the factory paint job had dulled, but to Kimberly and her friends, the car was their silver chariot.

Most weekend nights the silver chariot could be found cruising north on Main Street and south on Klamath Avenue, checking out who was dating whom or looking for new faces. The whole boy-girl scene was still somewhat foreign to Jordan; due to some extent because she hadn't been allowed to date until she turned sixteen. That momentous birthday came and went, and she still hadn't gone somewhere with a boy unless one of his parents was driving. She occasionally made out at parties, mostly because that's what everybody else was doing, but she shied away from the in crowd boys or anyone from an affluent family.

One fall night during Jordan's junior year, she and her friends were in Kimberly's car, making their first trip up Main Street when Morgan spied someone interesting.

"Look," she exclaimed. "It's that guy ... what's his name? He graduated last year. You know who I'm talking about, McKenzie, the guy in our Spanish class."

"You're seeing things," her sister remarked. "Try cleaning your glasses."

Morgan, who was riding shotgun, pointed at a white GMC pickup two cars ahead of them. "I know that's him. He used to wear a cowboy hat to class every day."

Kimberly moved into the left lane. As the silver chariot drove alongside the white pickup, the four friends got a good look at the driver who had on a black cowboy hat and was wearing a white t-shirt even though it was chilly outside. He planted a tanned forearm on his open window frame and winked at the four sets of eyes gawking at him.

Jordan let out a squeak, scooted off the backseat, and crouched on the floor behind the driver's seat. McKenzie rolled down her window, moistened her lips and flashed her foxiest smile. The boy in the pickup scanned the occupants of the Chevy and smiled back.

"He's hot," McKenzie said after the pickup pulled ahead.

Morgan turned around and smiled at her sister. "He has dreamy eyes don't you think? Kind of sexy looking."

Still sitting on the floor with her chin on her knees, Jordan asked if the boy winked at them again. McKenzie grabbed her by the arm and pulled her onto the seat. "You are so lame. You'll never meet anybody if you keep hiding down there."

Jordan straightened her shirt. "As if sitting up here is going to make a difference."

"Don't be so negative all the time," Kimberly said. "You've got a lot going for you, Jordan. You've got a darling face, and your grades are to die for. You're fun, too, and a good basketball player for being so short. I'm sure glad I don't have to play against you."

Jordan blushed. "Thanks, Kimberly. Too bad you're not a boy."

McKenzie twisted one of her dark brown curls around her finger. "Speaking of boys, did I tell you guys I got Todd Crane to be my locker partner?"

"No, but that doesn't surprise me," Kimberly said.

Morgan leaned forward and looked out the windshield. "I've got to pee, you guys. Is there anywhere around here you can pee for free?"

"You've got the bladder of a chipmunk," McKenzie teased. "Better hold it, though, or you'll take the fun out of riding shotgun. And don't make her laugh, you guys, whatever you do."

As the four friends neared the end of Main Street for the third time, they saw a long, green car parked on Third Street near the Klamath County Library. Someone inside the car was motioning for them to stop.

"I think that guy wants us to pull over," Jordan said.

The old Plymouth Fury had at least five, maybe six boys in it. Someone wearing a red sweatshirt was leaning out the back window.

"Who's that?" Kimberly asked.

"Troy Powers," Morgan and McKenzie answered in unison. "He's supposed to be having a party tonight," McKenzie added. Her brown-black eyes flashed with excitement. "I heard some kids talking about it after school. Did you hear about it, Kim?"

"No … Jordan and I were at basketball practice."

"Well, supposedly his parents are out of town. Somebody said he's got a keg."

"How'd he get a keg?"

"Who cares," McKenzie huffed. "If they invite us, should we go?"

Morgan pulled a mirror out of her purse and checked her lipstick. "Okay, but not till I take a pee."

"I have to work tomorrow," Jordan sighed.

McKenzie gave her a friendly nudge. "Don't be a party poop."

Kimberly wiggled her fingers at the boys in the Plymouth. "Well, I'm pulling over. I don't want them to think we're not interested."

"I have to be in bed by nine," Jordan said. "We'd barely get to the party before I had to leave."

Morgan tried to be helpful. "Can't you stay out later if you call and ask?"

"You don't know my father."

"Won't he be asleep when you get home?"

"Wouldn't that be nice? He waits up for me whenever I go anywhere at night. When I walk in the door, he doesn't even say hello. Instead he looks at me like I'm a piece of crap. I feel like crawling through the living room on my belly when he does that."

"Why would you need to crawl?" McKenzie asked, giving her backseat companion a playful shove. "Have you been doing something to feel guilty about, farm girl? Is there something you haven't told us about?"

Jordan grinned and shook her head. "I wish. But sometimes I'm not sure I want to go out on a real date. If I did, my father would make me pass inspection when I got home. I mean, what if I'd been making out? Even if I combed my hair and put on lipstick, I'd never be able to hide what I had been doing."

Kimberly parked next to the curb before turning around to join in the fun. "What if you did something your father would *really* be upset about?" she asked, raising her eyebrows.

"You mean ... ohmygod! If I ever went all the way, I'd never be able to walk into my house again. I'd have to tell the guy I was with to keep on driving. Keep on driving, buster. Maybe to Mexico."

They joked and teased one another about real and imaginary sexcapades until all four of them were laughing hysterically.

"Okay, you guys, now I've *really* got to pee," Morgan whined.

Troy Powers leaned so far out the back window of the Plymouth Fury he almost fell out. "Hey! What's so funny?" He waited expectantly while the giggling in the silver chariot continued. "Want to go to a party?"

• • •

Jordan had trouble falling asleep that night. Separated from her friends and the fun she knew they would be having, she was angry at her father for being so rigid and upset with her mother for not getting him to change. She was sick of being imprisoned while her friends were going to parties, meeting boys, and getting more popular every day. Nobody even knew she existed.

But when she got past the sour grapes she chewed on when she went to bed most nights, she wasn't sure being left out of the dating scene was such a bad thing. It had taken months to work up the courage to bring her girlfriends home, so when she pictured introducing a boy she liked to a father who might be drunk or verbally abusive, she decided her snug little room might be a safe haven instead of a prison ... until she heard the familiar sounds coming from the kitchen.

Every night except Sunday, Cooper bought a fifth of cheap whisky and brought it home in a brown paper bag. He never bothered to use a glass or add ice cubes; he drank straight out of the bottle. The kitchen cupboard he stashed his whisky in had a squeaky door hinge that announced every drink he took. In such a small house, it was impossible to escape the sequence of sounds—door squeaking, paper crinkling as the bottle came out of the bag, cap being unscrewed, a stretched out pause while Cooper took a drink, cap being screwed back on, paper crinkling again, and then a final squeak when the cupboard door closed.

Jordan was aware of the derogatory words used to describe alcohol abuse—drunkard, boozehound, lush, wino—terms that clearly reflected social stigmatization, and she winced whenever she heard one of those terms, even if the reference was directed at someone other than her father.

If, for some reason, she had to explain her father's behavior, she tried not to act like it bothered her. She found it was best to simply say, "My father's an alcoholic" and let it go at that. Afterward, she would drop her eyes and drop the subject, hoping the person she was talking to hadn't linked her to the sins of her father, a father who was drunk most of the time, mean, unreasonable, uncaring, and someone she tried to avoid.

• • •

The following morning, Jordan's negative thoughts were gone, replaced by the thrill she felt every Saturday as she headed for her job washing dogs at Pretty Pet, a grooming shop located downtown. She needed the money, of course, but what she really enjoyed about her job was being around dogs again. Max died when he was eleven, and she missed having an animal in her life.

The sunny, mid-October morning was brisk yet warm enough to walk to Pretty Pet. Annie worked most Saturdays, so Jordan had to depend on her father if she wanted a ride to work. The weather had to be terrible before she would ask him, and since she played basketball every school day and jogged three or four times a week, a two-and-a-half mile walk was practically a stroll.

That Saturday she was running late, so she had to jog part of the way to work. Her mother gave her a running bra for her sixteenth birthday, but Jordan only wore it when she played basketball. She often wondered how it would feel to have large, womanly breasts bouncing against her chest when she ran up and down the basketball court. Although ever since junior high she had been hoping her breasts would get bigger, it appeared she would have to buy her bras, if she wore one at all, in the junior department.

When she arrived at Pretty Pet, the shop owner, Mrs. Sherwood, was fighting with the key that unlocked the door. Droplets of perspiration glistened on her upper lip and the flab under her arm jiggled when she twisted the key back and forth. After the lock gave, she bumped the door open with her hip and sent Jordan to her car for a box of supplies.

Mrs. Sherwood cut all of the dogs' hair, leaving the prep work to her young helper who was also responsible for organizing supplies and keeping the shop clean. Jordan always brought a change of clothes to work because she usually ended up soaked and muddied from wrestling some of the larger, dirtier dogs in and out of the bathing sinks.

"I don't think we'll be real busy today," Mrs. Sherwood said, still slightly out of breath when Jordan returned with the supplies. "Things are usually slow this time of year. Should pick up again over the holidays."

She took off her man-sized cardigan sweater and hung it over the back of a chair. Her flip flops pounded the concrete floor as she rocked from foot to foot to lessen the pain in her arthritic knees. "Probably only need you till noon," she said, after checking the appointment list.

Jordan's face fell. "That's okay, Mrs. Sherwood, don't worry about me."

"I won't. It's a business, you know, not a charity."

Jordan turned around quickly, hiding her chagrin behind the box of supplies she carried to the back of the shop. She carefully emptied the box and stacked the contents on a shelf. Next, she cleaned the shop's two large dog washing sinks, checked the water temperature, wiped down the portable kennels, and swept the spotless floor.

It seemed like an eternity before the first customer arrived and Mrs. Sherwood's attitude improved. When her shop was busy, she joked with the customers, hummed a lot, and talked baby talk to dogs of all sizes. Like magic, she could calm the feistiest dog into letting her snip, comb, shave, fluff, or cut its toenails.

At 10:30, a man arrived with a kitten he found eating out of a dumpster.

"She's a sweet little thing," he said, "but I'm not sure how clean she is. I don't want my children touching her if she has worms or bugs. Can you check her out for me?"

"We don't deworm," Mrs. Sherwood stated. "You'll have to take her to a vet for that. We can wash her and dip her for you, though. That should get rid of any bugs. We'll also check her for ear mites." She yelled to the back of the shop, "Did you hear that, Jordan?"

"Yes, Mrs. Sherwood."

Jordan could barely contain her excitement. People seldom brought cats to Pretty Pet, however when they did, Mrs. Sherwood usually assigned them to her. Jordan hadn't said a word to her parents or anyone else about cats being part of her job. After the ringworm episode, her father threatened to knock her socks off if she ever touched a cat again, any cat—wild or tame.

"I'll take good care of her," she said, smiling like the Cheshire Cat when she reached for the kitten. After the man left, she unlatched the door to the cat carrier containing a gray kitten with yellow-green eyes. When she picked the animal up, her hand closed around a heart that was beating sixty miles an hour. The kitten's pink tongue was sticking out as it breathed rapidly through its open mouth.

"I didn't know cats panted," Jordan said to herself, stroking the kitten in an attempt to calm it.

Mrs. Sherwood asked to see it before she wrote "wash cat, trim nails" in her appointment schedule. She flipped the kitten over and looked under its tail. "It's a male. Be sure and tell the fellow that when he comes back."

"How old do you think it is?"

"Barely old enough to be weaned." She rubbed the kitten under its chin. "It seems to have been around humans, though, and it's small, so it shouldn't give you much of a fight." She handed the kitten back to Jordan and turned her attention to a nervous cocker spaniel that was dancing on her worktable.

All hell broke loose when Jordan put the kitten through the wash and rinse cycles, but he seemed to enjoy being blow dried. Clean and dry, the kitten looked so adorable Jordan snuggled her face in its fluffy hair. She rested it on her shoulder and listened to it purr as it nuzzled her ear lobe and suckled the skin on her neck. The sucking tickled like crazy, but Jordan was so happy to be holding the little fur ball that she didn't try to stop it.

By noon, the kitten was on its way home to be with its new family, and an hour later, Mrs. Sherwood told Jordan she could go. Feeling broke and low as a snake's belly, she headed for home. There wouldn't even be an animal to comfort her when she got there, and she promised herself that as soon as she was on her own, she was going to get a cat. If her father didn't like it, he didn't need to come to her house, and she probably wouldn't invite him anyway.

• • •

Taking the long way home, carrying her dirty dog washing clothes in a grocery bag, Jordan had only walked three or four blocks when she had a strange feeling there was a shadow creeping up her back. This was odd, since she was walking on the sunny side of the street, so while waiting for the crosswalk signal to change, she looked around to see if anyone was behind her. There were two boys on skateboards, and half a block away, a girl with a shopping bag, certainly nothing unusual.

When the signal changed, she walked across the intersection to the next block, and nearly jumped out of her sneakers when a horn honked. She looked around again, and this time her heart leapt to her throat and her feet glued themselves to the sidewalk. It was the boy in the white pickup.

CHAPTER ELEVEN

Jordan's heart was beating so fast it felt as if there was a sparrow trapped inside her shirt as she clutched her bundle of dog washing clothes to her chest and powered ahead, legs churning, eyes focused on the cracks in the sidewalk. She couldn't talk to a boy, especially that boy, with her hair such a mess and no place to hide the dirty clothes she was carrying, so she hoped the boy in the white pickup would drive on by.

She was about ready to look over her shoulder again when he pulled along-side.

"Hey," he said in a loud, manly voice. "Your sneakers are starting to smoke."

Jordan heard him chuckling to himself as he drove close to the curb, matching her pace. "Need a ride?"

"No thanks," she said, still avoiding eye contact. "I need the exercise."

"Can't you stop for a minute? I need to ask you a question."

Jordan slowed, and then stopped. The boy driving the truck stopped, too, but kept his engine running. When she looked into the pickup cab, all she could see of him was square, white teeth and the whites of his eyes since his face was shaded by the brim of his hat.

"Okay," she said, "Go ahead and ask. I probably won't know the answer, though."

The square, white teeth grinned at her. "Why were you were hiding on the floor last night?"

Jordan giggled when she thought how silly she must have looked hunched between the front and back seats of Kimberly's car. She inched closer, and when she saw him full face, she felt a tickle start somewhere in her midsection and travel all the way to the top of her head.

"How did you see me?"

The boy turned off the engine and scooted over to the open window on the passenger side of his truck. This gave Jordan her first good look at him and the black muscle shirt drawing attention to his well toned arms.

"I can see everything from up here," he smiled. "It's one of the benefits of cruising around in a truck. What were you doing down there, anyway?"

Jordan took a measured breath. *This boy is way too good looking to be talking to me.*

"Nothing," she stammered. "Not hiding … nothing at all."

He poked the underside of his hat brim with his index finger to move his hat back on his forehead. "So if I asked you where you were heading so fast, would you say nowhere?" He spoke slowly, looking her up and down as if measuring her for a band uniform.

Jordan's lips felt as if she had just eaten an entire Popsicle. She didn't know why this magnificent hunk was paying attention to her, but she was flattered and curious, and since she didn't have to work the rest of the afternoon, and because one of her friends might see her driving around with him—that would be cool—she opened the door, stepped onto the foot rail, and hopped into the front seat as if she did this sort of thing all the time.

"Where you headed?" he asked.

Jordan's hands were shaking so hard she had trouble fastening her seat belt. "Do you think we could just drive around for a while? If you have time, that is."

He gave her a friendly smile. "Got all day."

He turned his pickup down South Sixth Street, and since they were heading in that direction, Jordan led him to Highway 39, and then to the V-Bar-J ranch. She didn't know exactly why she ended up taking him there, but it was a sunny October afternoon, and she hadn't been out to the ranch all summer. They arrived just in time for a late lunch consisting of potato salad, roast beef sandwiches, freshly canned pickles, and homemade chocolate chip cookies.

Jordan couldn't stop smiling when she introduced handsome young Riley Palmer to her grandparents and her cousin, Athena.

Listening to the others talk while they ate lunch, Jordan found out her uncles now had full responsibility for the ranch, which meant Grandpa Parker was officially retired. Grandma Leona said she would like to retire, too, but retirement was something men did. "Women keep on working till they die," she said with a twinkle in her eye.

Athena, who graduated from high school the previous June, still lived at home. She worked at the county courthouse as an administrative assistant and proudly announced she had a new boyfriend. "You've probably seen him around town." Athena said. She turned to Riley. "Drives a red Taurus, almost new."

When it was time for Jordan to say something about her own family, she saw Grandma Leona's mouth tighten into a small, dried up strawberry. Jordan felt like an actress muffing her lines as she rambled on about the family's activities over the last several months. She made sure not to mention Jude's poor grades or Dusty's two-day suspension for fighting. She didn't say a word about her father, either, because he hadn't changed for the better, if that was what her grandma was hoping to hear.

After lunch, Jordan showed Riley around the ranch. When she spotted Peaches on the far side of the pasture, she ran over to the fence for a closer look. Riley grabbed a handful of hay to coax the cow closer, and when Peaches trudged over to where the young couple was standing, her huge udder with its pendulous teats swung from side to side barely clearing the ground. Although her hooves were splayed and her hipbones jutted out at odd angles, the old cow was still a good milker, according to Grandma Leona. While Peaches chewed on the hay, Jordan scratched her behind the ears and told her she missed her. Peaches nudged the girl's arm for more hay, but showed no sign of recognition.

When the two young people walked inside the barn, Jordan breathed in the sweet smell of the alfalfa and sighed as she plopped down on one of the hay bales. She motioned for Riley to sit across from her, and when he did, he was so close their knees almost touched.

Riley looked around the barn while Jordan twiddled with a piece of hay.

"Nice barn, he said. "I've always wanted to live on a ranch. I'd be a cowboy if the work wasn't so hard and it paid worth a damn."

The sound of his baritone voice saying, "worth a damn" made Jordan's heartbeat quicken. She tried looking him in the face, but when his eyes met hers, she blushed and looked at her hands again.

They walked back to the ranch house so Jordan could thank her grandparents for lunch, then drove back to town, chatting like old friends. She asked him where he worked, and he told her he was a cook at the best Italian restaurant in town. He asked her how tall she was, and when she said she was five-foot-two, he laughed and called her a munchkin. When he told her he was living at home to save money for college and hating every minute, she wanted to hug him.

After giving Riley her phone number, she fairly floated into her house, and couldn't wait to tell her mother about her amazing afternoon. Unfortunately, Annie wasn't home, so she sat in her mother's spot on the couch to wait for her. Cooper sat at the other end of the couch with four empty beer cans lined up on the floor like tin soldiers waiting for their marching orders.

"Where's Mom?" Jordan asked, as calmly as she could.

"At work," Cooper mumbled, looking at the TV screen. He finished a fifth beer and lined it up with the rest of the empties. "You work all day?"

"Just till one."

He frowned. "What did you do for the rest of the afternoon?"

Even though her brain told her to keep her mouth shut, Jordan was so giddy with excitement she couldn't keep the words from tumbling out of her mouth.

"This cool guy gave me a ride out to the ranch, and we had lunch with Grandma and Grandpa."

Her father didn't say anything more, so Jordan pretended to be interested in the football game he was watching. The football uniforms, the bands, the cheerleaders, the banners and bright clothing worn by the fans spilled across the screen in a blur of colors. She didn't have a clue who was playing or winning, nor did she care.

She had a feeling her father wasn't watching the game either, which was unnerving. *Why is he staring at me? I haven't done anything to be ashamed of. I'm sixteen. I can go out on a date.* She groped for something to say.

"Peaches is still alive," she squeaked.

Still no word from the other end of the couch.

"I think the guy I met today is going to ask me out." She assumed that bit of news would surely break the ice, at least produce some kind of a wise crack. When her father didn't respond, she took a quick peek and saw he was indeed staring at her.

Suddenly, he scooted across the couch toward her, his boots scattering the neat little army of beer cans he had assembled. "That's what I thought," he snarled.

He grabbed Jordan by the arm and yanked her toward him. "How'd you get that hickey on your neck?"

"I don't have a hickey." Jordan shook her arm out of his grasp, thinking he was drunk out of his mind. Riley hadn't even kissed her let alone given her a hickey.

Cooper stood up and grabbed her by the arm again, this time using it to pull her off the couch. He led her into the bathroom and shoved her against the sink so she could see herself in the mirror. When she looked into the mirror, she saw two faces reflected there, one white with fear, one red with fury.

"You think I'm stupid?" He pulled Jordan's shirt collar down. "That's a hickey if there ever was one, you little tramp."

Jordan felt as if she was going to faint. Staring into the mirror, she was stunned to see what certainly looked like a hickey just below her left ear. Was it a bruise she got at basketball practice? Could it be a smudge of dirt? She wet her finger and rubbed the troublesome spot.

"That's not gonna get rid of it." He turned his daughter around and shook her. "Admit it!" he hissed, shaking her harder.

She scrunched her shoulders in an attempt to make her neck disappear inside her shirt collar. "Daddy, it's not what you think. Please let me figure out where this came from."

Suddenly he slapped her, full on the cheek. The impact caused her hair to swing wildly against the side of her face where some of it caught in the corner of her mouth. She spit the hair out and tried to get away, but she was trapped between the sink and the bathtub.

"Don't you lie to me!" He slapped her once more, and this time she burst into tears. He glowered at her for a second then left, slamming the bathroom door behind him.

Jordan sank to her knees and sobbed. Her father hadn't laid a hand on her since she was a child, and except for the ringworm spanking it was never more than a swat or two on the bottom. She rested her throbbing cheek on the bathtub's cool porcelain edge, then pulled some toilet paper off the roll and pressed it against her eyes. "Why doesn't he believe me?" she blubbered.

She thought she heard a tap on the bathroom door. She sucked in her sobs and heard it again. "Who is it?" she asked, praying it wasn't her father.

"It's me, Jude. I gotta go. What's all the yelling about?"

Jordan blew her nose and wiped her face with a washcloth. She took another look in the mirror at the small purplish mark on her neck, and rubbing it with the back of her hand, looked around for something to take the sting out of her enflamed cheek. Seeing her mother's pink chenille robe hanging on the bathroom door, she buried her face in it. The robe felt so soft and warm against her cheek, almost as comforting as … *the little gray kitten! The kitten I washed and dried this morning must have given me that hickey when it suckled my neck.*

Jordan yanked open the door and dashed by Jude, stopping short when she realized, *I can't tell Daddy I got that hickey from a kitten.* She stumbled to her room in a daze, and threw herself on her bed, sobbing in frustration.

Her father grounded her for two weeks—no basketball, no social activities, no phone calls. She was so distraught she didn't even tell her mother what happened, so as far as Annie knew, her daughter got a hickey, lied about it to her father, and was probably in need of some discipline.

Every night for two weeks, after washing the dinner dishes, Jordan stayed in her windowless room, doing her homework or reading a book before going to bed. Several times after the phone rang, she heard her mother, sometimes one of her brothers, telling somebody, she was sure it was Riley, that she wasn't allowed to come to the phone.

• • •

Jordan didn't come face to face with Riley again until almost a year later when she saw him coming out of the Emporium. He was alone, so she followed him to his car, an old Volkswagen Beetle he ended up with after selling his truck for the last of the cash he needed for college. While he unloaded an armful of purchases, she begged him to let her explain what happened, and in less than thirty seconds she told him about the kitten, the hickey, and how her father grounded her for two weeks, which meant she couldn't take phone calls, and that she hoped he wasn't still mad at her.

When finished, she held her breath, waiting for Riley to say something out of one of her daydreams. Any scenario would do, ranging from telling her he hadn't been able to stop thinking about her as he took her in his arms and kissed her in front of God and everyone, to a simple, "Okay, I'll call you."

Instead, he chucked her under the chin and said, "Too bad, munchkin, I thought that love bite was for real."

CHAPTER TWELVE

It was not yet dawn, black as midnight inside the cluttered tent as Jude fumbled with the buttons on his shirt. He could hear the other hunters moving about the campsite, their boots crunching on the frozen ground. Fragments of their conversation filtered through the tent wall, reminding the thirteen-year-old that if he wanted to play with the big boys, he needed to shake a leg.

In a blind hurry, he slid his skinny butt into jeans so cold they made his legs ache, and after rummaging through a tangle of four sleeping bags and four sets of assorted belongings, he found his jacket. Dressed for the cold, he stepped outside.

The three early birds—his brother, his father, and his father's friend, Perry—were standing next to the remains of the previous night's campfire. Even on tiptoe, each step Jude took crackled the dry, frost covered grasses and pine needles that blanketed the forest floor. There was no way he could just sneak up and pretend he had been there all along.

The small hunting party had set up camp in a dry swale between two ridges, generously forested with seventy-year-old pines and chest high Manzanita bushes. Their campsite was about two miles off Highway 140 near Doak Mountain. They had the landowner's permission to hunt there, so Cooper and Perry never considered hunting anywhere else, especially since one of them had bagged a deer there eight of the last ten hunting seasons.

Breakfast consisted of coffee and a bag of greasy donuts. When Jude approached the other hunters, Perry, who the Miller kids called "Uncle," was feeding small pieces of donut to an eight-week-old golden retriever puppy that was zipped inside the front of his jacket with just the tip of its nose sticking out.

"Well, if it isn't Sleepin' Beauty," Cooper said to Jude when he joined the group.

Jude ignored his father's taunt and shoved his hand into the oil stained bag of pastries. Uncle Perry and Dusty had a good laugh over the Sleeping Beauty remark, and their delight at Jude's expense burst forth in a tandem of small white puffs as their chuckles hit the cold air. Jude stuffed half a donut into his mouth, then quickly ate the other half plus three maple bars, washing them down with a cup of lukewarm coffee.

As dawn began to break, deep shadows still permeated the swale where they were camped, although the faint glow spilling over the eastern ridge gave the four hunters a sneak peek of the sunny day ahead. Jude wondered who he would be hunting with and listened intently while the two men on the other side of the fire pit swapped strategies. Cooper and Uncle Perry were close to the same height, however his father's lean body was half the width of Uncle Perry's beefy frame. Both men gestured excitedly as they shifted their weight from one foot to the other.

They're pumped, Jude thought, as he allowed a ripple of excitement to flow through his own veins.

Dusty checked the rifles that were propped against a stump with their barrels pointing skyward. He and Jude, with rifles borrowed from their Uncle Carson, had spent several weekends shooting beer bottles off fences, learning to sight these new weapons and get used to the recoil. Cooper taught his sons to pace off the distance of their shots until they were able to accurately estimate 100, 150 and 200 yards. He warned them never to try for a target, especially a moving target, over 200 yards away.

"You'd probably end up with a wounded animal, not a dead one," he told them. "That won't make you no hero to me."

He also showed his boys how to shoot from different positions: crouching, standing, lying flat on their bellies, and even using the wrong hand.

While waiting for Dusty to select a rifle, Jude mentally rehearsed the shooting instructions he had been given. During their practice sessions, Dusty naturally turned out to be the better shot, but Jude decided he wasn't going to let that ruin his first deer hunt. It was bound to be a good weekend, he thought, since the weather was so nice and his father never mixed alcohol with guns.

Jude smiled to himself when he remembered something that happened the week before, when his dad was drunk and his sister came home with a hickey. *Jordan should have known better than to hang around Dad when he's drunk. I wonder how come she gets such good grades.*

Jude was surprised when it turned out he and his father were paired for the day, but after giving it more thought, he decided it was probably to make sure he didn't screw up. He kicked a pinecone as hard as he could, then picked up his rifle and followed his father into the woods.

Cooper was standing next to a patch of bitterbrush, waiting for him. "Stay clear of the brush," he told his son. "The deer can hear it scrape against your clothes. And try not to step on any dry twigs or branches. Pretend you're an Indian or Davy Crockett or somethin'."

While the two hunters hiked down the eastern side of the ridge, Jude, the greenhorn, quickly discovered that deer hunting was a juggling act requiring him to simultaneously look and listen for deer, keep his mouth shut, balance the extra weight from his backpack, hang onto his rifle, keep away from low hanging branches, watch for snakes, and try not to fall over the blow-down trees that littered the forest floor.

It was slow going for the first half-hour, but as Jude and Cooper descended to a lower elevation, the evergreens thinned and blended with scattered stands of yellow leafed aspens. The tall meadow grass growing around the base of the trees was dry as raffia, and the florets on the frost-killed rabbitbrush had shriveled into brownish clusters.

Cooper pointed at the trunk of a quaking aspen that had been partially de-barked by antlers. "See that?" he said, trying to keep his excitement in check. "Deer like this place. They've got plenty of meadow grass in the spring, and then they go and eat the farmer's grain all summer. That's why the deer from around here taste so good."

At 8:30, they came upon a barbed wire fence surrounding a stubble field twenty acres or more across. A flock of Canadian geese peppered the middle of the field, their broad gray bodies with black and white markings a stark contrast to the pale stubble. When Jude walked over to the fence for a closer look, the flock took off helter-skelter, hundreds of wings flapping simultaneously and honking cries piercing the air.

"How much farther?" Jude asked, squinting at the geese until they became a V of specs in the distance.

"See that clump of bushes up ahead? The deer bed down there during the heat of the day. We'll follow the fence to where those bushes grow over it. Then we'll hang a left and go up the hill a ways."

Jude lingered a while in the parched meadow grass before falling into step behind his father. The sun warming the back of his navy windbreaker was beginning to make him sleepy. His feet hurt, but he knew it would be nearly dark before he could take his boots off and get some relief for the blisters that were forming on the backs of his heels.

The two hunters took separate stands inside thick groves of ponderosa pines. Cooper picked a spot about twenty yards from the fence and sent Jude up a gentle slope another fifty yards away. Camouflaged by the mottled shade cast by the pines, both hunters had a 180-degree view of the bed-down area.

"Remember what I told you," Cooper said to his son when they parted. "Aim for the high part of the shoulder. If you hit the deer there, it's instant death."

Relieved to get the weight off his hot, sore feet, Jude found a spot where he could sit with his back against the trunk of a tree. The meadow was quiet except for the ringing sound made by thousands of insects fanning the air. He watched an ant run across his foot. The first ant was joined by another, and the two of them darted back and forth across the instep of his boot. He checked the lunch his mother packed and decided he would share some crumbs with the ants when he finished his sandwich. He kept his eyes on the bed-down area for what seemed like an hour before checking on the ants again. In less than a minute his eyelids grew heavy and his head fell to his chest.

He awoke to his name being called from someplace far away. He heard his name again, closer this time followed by, "Shoot, damn it, shoot!"

Jude grabbed his rifle and jumped to his feet, shocked to see a mule deer the size of a small horse crashing through the brush, a flash of amber and antlers running so fast its feet barely touched the ground. "Here we go," he said to himself, as he held his breath and raised his rifle to his shoulder.

"Shoot the damn deer, Jude!"

Jude's heart was pounding and sweat prickled his armpits. He aimed for the deer's shoulder, steeling himself for the kick that would come when the gun discharged, but when he squeezed the trigger, he heard the sickening, impotent click that told him the safety was still engaged.

"You idiot!"

He quickly removed the safety and aimed again. When he pulled the trigger the second time, the rifle exploded, and in spite of the many times he practiced bracing for the kick, he flinched. A small puff of dust marked his miss to the deer's left, and the terrified animal changed direction in mid air.

Sweat glistened on his upper lip when Jude took aim for the third time, tightening his finger on the trigger and tensing for the recoil. Although the blast was deafening, the rifle didn't slam into his shoulder the way it should have, and when he lowered it, he saw the deer fall to its knees less than thirty yards in front of him. He rubbed his eyes and wondered how the deer could be down when he couldn't remember pulling the trigger.

He threw his rifle to the ground and backed away from it as if it might buck and snort and fire on its own. His rubbery legs somehow carried him to the fallen animal, and as he stood watching it, one of the deer's hind legs jerked. After that, the three-point buck lay perfectly still. It was a clean kill, just as his father said it should be.

"Get back," Cooper yelled, and running up the slope, he reached the deer in a matter of seconds. It wasn't moving, but he touched the deer's exposed eyeball to make sure it was dead.

"I had to take your shot," he said, somewhat out of breath, "or we'd of lost 'im." He scowled at his hunting partner who was standing next to the deer with his mouth agape. "What in hell happened to you? After all that time we spent practicin', couldn't you get the job done?"

Jude's tongue felt thick. "I had him," he stammered. "I had the perfect shot. You must have shot him just before I pulled the trigger."

The disappointment on Cooper's face was almost palpable. "What took you so long? I hollered at you four times."

Jude could barely make his lips form words. "I wanted to be sure, Dad." He looked down at his boots. "It won't happen again."

Cooper brushed his son aside and took a sharp knife out of his backpack. He had Jude brace the deer's legs apart while he made a shallow cut from the animal's pelvis to its sternum, deep enough to sever the belly skin without puncturing the intestines or bladder. Next he separated the two halves of the deer's abdomen and cut away the membranes connecting the digestive track and inner organs.

Jude felt the heat of life rising from the animal's carcass when his father opened it up. The smell of hot blood and entrails nauseated him, but he didn't dare let on after his pitiful shooting performance. He winced as a dozen or so yellow jackets swarmed into the body cavity to feast on the fresh meat. The voracious wasps were tenacious, and one of them stung him on the ear lobe when he swatted at it.

Cooper carefully removed the deer's liver, wrapped it in newspaper and put it in his backpack. "Send a signal, Jude. We're gonna need some help packin' this big fellow back to camp. He must weigh close to two hundred pounds."

. . .

As the sun went down, the wind picked up, and the pleasant afternoon air was replaced by a bone-chilling cold. The four hunters sat around the campfire while a fresh deer liver sizzled in an iron skillet resting half on, half off the coals. Uncle Perry poured each boy a cup of freshly made coffee before he ducked inside the tent, emerging a moment later with a bottle of bourbon. He took the bottle over to where Cooper was sitting, poured a healthy portion of bourbon into two red plastic cups and topped them off with hot coffee. Jude sneaked a quick look at his brother to see if he had noticed the booze that all of a sudden had joined the party.

Dusty sat on a stump, sporting a kiss ass grin, acting as if he hung out with the guys this way all the time. He couldn't wait to tell how he and Uncle Perry first stalked a porcupine, then a stray heifer, thinking they were onto a deer each time.

"Good thing we didn't shoot," Uncle Perry said, his round face reddened by the fire. "That farmer'd never let us come back here if we nailed one of his cows."

Jude listened to the day's stories and tried to laugh when everybody else did. Thankfully his father didn't tell the others that his oldest son had choked that morning. They simply thought Cooper had done what he did almost every year—bag a deer the first weekend of hunting season.

While their stories got longer and crazier, the two men continued filling their red cups with coffee and bourbon. They started swapping bloopers from past hunting and fishing trips, and soon the two of them were snorting and giggling like school boys.

When Dusty asked how the liver was doing, Cooper swore and pulled the frying pan off the fire with his bare hands. "The liver's ruined." He swore again and blew on his burning fingers, cursing his own stupidity as he stomped around the campfire.

Uncle Perry wiped his knife on the leg of his jeans. "It don't look so bad. Maybe a little crusty on this part here."

Breathing heavily, he bent over the pan and sliced the liver into four sections. He picked up one of the larger pieces with his fingers and ate a third of it in one bite. "Oh, man, you're gonna love this," he said, smacking his lips.

Dusty reached into the frying pan and took the smallest quarter. He blew on it, and then began eating it with his fingers like Uncle Perry. "M-m-m-m. Try it, Dad. It's not ruined."

Sure, Dusty, you little suck up.

Cooper muttered something under his breath and dropped his portion of liver onto a paper plate. He ate his quarter with a knife and fork and didn't say a word. When he was finished, he set his bloody plate on the ground for Perry's puppy to lick.

"The rest is yours, Jude. Better hurry before it gets cold."

Jude looked into the frying pan. Charred black on one side and semi raw on the other, the dreaded chunk of meat sat in a pool of bloody juice and oil, reminding him of the rank, nauseating smell of warm guts, the dark red cavity that held the deer's liver, heart, and intestines, and how the walls still twitched in a few places even after the insides had been removed.

I don't even like regular liver. Why do I have to eat deer liver?

The deer's carcass—skinned, gutted and wrapped in an old sheet to keep the bugs off—hung from a rope in a nearby tree. When the wind blew, the rope made a creaking sound as the carcass swung back and forth. With its head removed, the deer was about the size of a small man, and in the growing dark, its sheet-covered carcass looked like a ghost hanging from a gallows.

Jude's head began to spin. Three faces grinned at him from across the campfire, their gruesome mouths growing larger, then smaller, then larger again while they chanted, "Eat! Eat!" The liver in the pan was a horrifying lump of black and red meat that had been part of the deer's guts when it was alive. Now the deer was dead, its carcass swinging back and forth from a tree branch going "creak, creak, creak, creak."

Jude jumped off the rock he was sitting on and threw up next to the tent.

"Oh, gross," Dusty groaned. "Make him clean it up, Dad."

"Jesus, Jude, what's the matter with you? You won't even take one bite of the best liver in the world. You can't shoot. Why'd you even come? Go get the shovel."

Jude crept behind the tent to look for the shovel. While his eyes were adjusting to the dark, he listened to the others discussing the fate of the remaining piece of liver.

"Hand me that pan," he heard his father say. "Anybody else want some?"

"I'll have a bite," Uncle Perry volunteered. "Better put it back on the fire, though. The cold air's turnin' the bacon grease white. I don't want to bite through a inch o' grease to get to the liver."

Jude felt his throat seize again, and he practically choked trying to hide the sound of vomiting from the others. His father yelled at him to move his ass, so he wiped his mouth on the sleeve of his jacket and picked up the shovel. When he rounded the tent, his father was pointed at him with his red cup.

"I'm thinking maybe we brought a princess with us after all," he said, nudging Uncle Perry with his elbow.

Cooper tried to stand up, but lost his balance. He grabbed onto his big friend for support, and they both fell to the ground, clutching one another, kicking dirt and pinecones into the campfire and laughing themselves silly. Yipping with excitement, the golden retriever puppy jumped on Uncle Perry and began licking his ear.

Dusty smiled triumphantly as he ate the last piece of liver.

Jude hurried with the shovel. The thick layer of pine needles covering the ground was spongy and easy to lift, so he got rid of his stinking pile of shame in seconds. He leaned the shovel against the side of the tent and crept inside, where he climbed into a cold sleeping bag with his clothes on. He was hungry and shivering from his toes to his teeth. His ear lobe throbbed where the yellow jacket stung him. He had blisters on both feet, a terrible taste in his mouth, and a huge aching hole in his heart.

CHAPTER THIRTEEN

McKenzie looked at the formaldehyde-soaked cat on Jordan's table and asked, "Where's the penis? Mine's supposed to be a male, but I can't find its thing. Didn't you say yours was a male?"

"Yes, do you want me to show you what it looks like?" Jordan pushed aside a clump of wet hair on her cat cadaver to expose a tiny, hairless bump. "That's it. Did you think it would be pointing at you?" The two girls snickered and exchanged grins.

"Why are you trying to find it, McKenzie? We haven't even started studying that part."

"Yeah, well, knowing Miss Abbott, we'll probably never get there. Can you imagine her saying, penis in front of the whole class?" McKenzie rolled her eyes. "We'll never even touch the reproductive organs." She cracked her gum and grinned.

"Sh-h-h, look behind you."

Miss Abbott, wearing a black knit dress with hair dyed to match, looked disapprovingly at the two young women chatting about their cats. "Go back to your table, McKenzie. Jordan's not your lab partner, Clark is."

"Talk to you after class," McKenzie mouthed to her friend. She gave her curls a toss as she walked back to her assigned table.

At the beginning of their senior year, when Jordan and McKenzie signed up for advanced biology and learned that one of the requirements was to dissect a cat, her fearless friend had said, "Cool beans," whereas Jordan fretted about it for months. In Biology I, as a sophomore, she dissected a frog without feeling a single pang of sentiment, but frogs were cold blooded and didn't have eyelashes, and even though cats and kittens meant trouble for her, she still adored them.

The day she and her lab partner received their cat cadaver, Jordan looked at the stiff carcass for at least a minute before pulling it out of its plastic storage bag and laying it on the table. She poked the cat's rib cage. She pushed up the skin on one side of the cat's mouth to look at its tightly clenched teeth. She pried open an eye. Even before Miss Abbott passed out a sheet with instructions and warnings, Jordan had established a clinical relationship with her cadaver.

Over the next several class periods, she got to know her cat inside and out. Using a scalpel, she made an incision along the entire length of the under belly. Next she carefully peeled back the cat's skin and muscle layers to expose the major internal organs and arteries. Gradually, she and her partner located everything on their list, labeling the body parts with tiny flags mounted on long pins. They only goofed once, when they couldn't identify the pancreas.

Jordan was amazed at how detached she felt during the dissection process. It was fascinating to look at the various parts of the cat's anatomy and learn their scientific names. The only negative was the smell of the formaldehyde, and it didn't take long to adjust to that.

"So, did you locate your cat's penis?" Jordan asked McKenzie after class was over.

"I don't think so, and Clark's no help. He called me a perv, so I told him to go to hell."

Jordan laughed. "The more I think about it, McKenzie, it might be better if you didn't find it. That way you can't do something weird with it. I mean, you're the only one in either of Miss Abbott's advanced biology classes who sewed a zipper into your cat's stomach."

"Hey, that was cool. Bet you wish you'd invented it."

The two friends locked arms. McKenzie gently bumped against Jordan's shoulder and Jordan bumped back. They were laughing and zigzagging down the hallway when they met up with Morgan at the top of the cafeteria stairs.

"Hurry up, you guys, I'm starved!" she said, as the three friends raced for the lunch line. Kimberly would have joined them if she hadn't been on B schedule.

Still a junior, Morgan wasn't taking advanced biology, however she didn't want to be left out when that day's lunch topic was a continuation of the penis discussion. After McKenzie complained about her cat's missing penis, she, too, was curious why her sister was making such a fuss.

"I still don't know why you're so interested," Jordan teased. "There's not even a flag for it."

"Jeez, Jordan, I just want to see what it looks like. You know—what color it is. How big. It can't be very big or I would have found it by now."

She slurped the mostly ice left in her Coke. "Did you ever see a horse's penis, farm girl? I hear they have big ones."

Jordan laughed. "They do … huge ones … scary even."

The Scott sisters shrieked with laughter. Jordan tried to act cool, but couldn't keep her lips from spreading into a grin.

McKenzie leaned closer. "Like, how big? Show me. You'd like to know, too, wouldn't you, Morgan."

Morgan nodded enthusiastically.

Jordan held her hands out in front of her, two feet apart. By then she was grinning like a hyena.

"No way!" McKenzie squealed as she bopped Jordan with her notebook. The three friends laughed so hard they were still wiping their eyes when the bell rang for class.

• • •

That afternoon Jordan was scheduled to meet with her senior advisor about what she planned to do after she graduated. From the time she attended middle school, Jordan's teachers and counselors had urged her to go to college. She never let on that she was interested in college at all, because talk of college lead to talk of family finances, which always made Jordan squirm. Although her grades were outstanding, especially in math and science, she couldn't afford to go to college, especially not for the eight or more years it would take to become a veterinarian, the career of her dreams.

Her friends had already made their plans. Kimberly was awarded a basketball scholarship at George Fox University and McKenzie was pre-enrolled at Southern Oregon College. Jordan found it hard to imagine life without McKenzie and Kimberly. Would they stay in touch? Would she feel funny palling around with Morgan, the quieter Scott sister? Would Kim and McKenzie think she was stupid and unsophisticated because they were going to college and she wasn't?

Senior advisor, Harriet Davis, was sitting behind a desk piled high with books and catalogs when Jordan walked into her office. In the middle of a telephone conversation, she motioned for her to take a seat, so Jordan picked up a magazine and began leafing through the pages.

"I'm more than a little concerned," Mrs. Davis began, after the call ended a minute later, "that your name isn't on the list to take the SATs. Next Friday is the absolute deadline if you hope to enter college this fall."

"I know. I know," Jordan sighed. She set the magazine aside. "I've told you before, Mrs. Davis, there's no way I can afford to go to college. I can't even afford to take the tests. I'll probably go someday after I save up for it."

"I admire your optimism," Mrs. Davis said, eyeing her reluctant protégé, "but most young people find it extremely hard to get back into the educational mainstream once they leave." Scooting forward in her chair, she pressed her matronly bosom against the desktop. "They get married and start a family, or they spend every penny they earn, or they simply lose interest after a while. You're an excellent student, dear. You should be going to college before many in your class, and I think I've figured out a way you can do it."

She picked through the stack of catalogs on her desk. "I'm almost positive we can come up with the money to cover tuition, fees, books, and part of your room and board. If you are willing to work to cover the rest of your expenses, you could start college this fall."

Mrs. Davis waited for Jordan to say something. When she got no response, she handed her a thick catalog and told her to open it to page 577.

Flipping through the pages of the catalog, a herd of hurdles stampeded through Jordan's mind. *My parents never even graduated from high school. I don't have the right clothes. I'm not as smart as the kids from Portland. Most of the kids going to college don't have fathers that hang out in taverns.*

She closed the catalog. "Not everyone is meant to go to college, Mrs. Davis."

The senior counselor folded her arms. "Tell me, dear, do you have a job in mind that will utilize your intelligence and pay you enough to make a decent living? Or maybe you would rather hitch your wagon to some local fellow's star and let *him* determine your future. Perhaps you think some hotshot construction worker will whisk you away in his half ton truck and all your problems will be solved."

Jordan hunkered down and tried to think of an excuse to go back to class.

Mrs. Davis left her desk and sat down in the chair next to her. "I'd like to see you do something with your life," she said, softening her tone. "You've got the brains and the work ethic to be one of the few of your classmates to be successful. Don't let your parents' circumstances drag you down." She paused. "Do you really want to end up like your mother?"

Jordan's face reddened at the sudden realization her teachers might know a lot more about her personal life than she thought. She wanted to yell at Mrs. Davis that she was wrong to criticize her mother. It was her father who had the problem.

"What kind of work would you like to do," her counselor continued, "if money was no concern, if nothing was holding you back, if you could go anywhere in the world you wanted to go?"

Jordan opened the catalog again and absent mindedly turned page after page while trying to think of a good answer. The truthful response would be to share her dream of becoming a veterinarian. Avoiding the letdown such a reply would surely produce, she decided instead to focus on the "anywhere in the world" part of her counselor's question.

"Maybe I could join the circus," she ended up saying. "That way I could work around animals, which is what I like doing most." She had never thought about joining a circus and rather liked the idea. At least it would get her away from home.

Mrs. Davis raised an eyebrow. "If it's the animal part of the circus that interests you, have you ever considered working at a zoo?"

Jordan had never been to a zoo. She had seen pictures of zoos with many species of animals and birds in cages or locked behind bars. She went to the Shrine circus once and was fascinated by the exotic beasts in the animal acts.

She could still recall the pungent smell of elephant dung mixed with saw-dust.

She shook her head. "No, not a zoo. I never even thought about a circus before you asked me that question. What would I do at a zoo, clean cages? I can't see how I'd need a college education for that."

Mrs. Davis walked back to her desk mumbling to herself, "You may be an A student, Miss Miller, but you don't need to be a class A jerk." She shuffled through some papers before finding the right brochure. "Have you ever considered becoming a veterinarian?" she asked, forcing a thin smile.

Jordan held onto the seat of her chair as if sitting on a flying carpet.

"Read this. Just the first three paragraphs."

The brochure Mrs. Davis handed her was from Oregon State University. What Jordan read on the first page gave her goose bumps.

Becoming a Doctor of Veterinary Medicine is much like becoming a Doctor of Medicine with the primary difference being that a veterinarian must apply his or her skills to members of the animal kingdom as opposed to that elite group of mammals known as homo sapiens.

A Doctor of Veterinary Medicine has to successfully complete course work similar to that of the medical profession, including such subjects as microscopic anatomy, virology, anesthesiology, pharmacology, even public health, and then apply their learning to fish, reptiles, birds, hamsters, dogs, cats, sheep, pigs, cows, horses and anything else that the homo sapiens decide to domesticate.

A veterinarian's duties can be as simple as removing a splinter from an animal's paw or as technically complex as determining the genetic makeup of the howler monkey. He or she might choose to travel country back roads attending to sick or injured livestock, serve as wet nurse to a newborn panda in a municipal zoo, or spend countless hours over a microscope searching for a way to eliminate e coli from the food chain.

"Miss Abbott tells me you're her best biology student, Jordan. I've also heard positive comments from some of your other teachers. Do you really think joining a circus is such a wise thing to do?"

Jordan studied the brochure in her hand. "If I went to college, I would have to compete with Portland kids, plus kids from California, and other kids who might have gone to private school."

"That's what the SATs are for, dear. Your score will be compared to scores from all over the country, including Portland and California. If you score poorly, we may have to talk again, but I have a feeling you will do just fine."

Jordan squirmed in her chair. "I'm sorry, Mrs. Davis, I just never felt I could afford to go to college. Do you really think there's a way?"

"Let's start over. Are you ready to look at that catalog I gave you, the one that's about to fall off your lap? Turn to page 577. This is a wonderful scholarship, dear. I think it might be just what the doctor ordered."

CHAPTER FOURTEEN

The early morning rain made soft pit pat sounds as it sprinkled the dormitory windows of Jordan's third floor room. Looking through the raindrops at the sidewalk below, she saw a couple of early risers sidestepping puddles on their way to wherever they were going at such a ridiculous hour. She would need an umbrella again, same as yesterday, and the day before that, and nearly every day since November. Enormous potbellied rain clouds seemed to hover forever over the town of Corvallis. Day or night, outside or inside, the air was always damp and her sneakers permanently soggy.

It was the beginning of spring term. She had overcome the freshman jitters and made it through two grading periods with flying colors. She still felt lonely and out of her element at times, but thank God for Mrs. Davis. She thanked the senior counselor over and over, gave her an effusive handmade thank you note at the KU class of '87 graduation party, and made sure to visit her during Christmas break.

Expense-wise, Jordan was keeping her head above water, however there was no room in her budget for pop from the Coke machine or a hamburger at the Memorial Union. The financial aid Mrs. Davis helped her secure was a work/study grant that covered her tuition, books and fees, and gave her a job that paid for her room and board. By walking, taking buses, sharing rides, even hitchhiking once in a while, she had been able to get along without a car.

She also received assistance from some surprising sources back home. Mrs. Sherwood, pleased with Jordan's decision to major in animal science, was sending her ten dollars a month for poop around money. The other surprise came from Uncle Perry, her father's workmate and drinking buddy. She nearly fainted when Perry dropped by Pretty Pet the Saturday before she left for college with a check for five hundred dollars. He made her promise not to tell anyone, especially her parents. He said he would send more when he could, because Coop was his best friend, and she and her brothers were the closest thing he had to a family.

The Saturday morning Jordan left for college, Annie had to work, so her father drove her to the Greyhound bus depot. He helped her with the canvas sided suitcase her grandparents gave her as a graduation present plus two cardboard boxes tied with rope. The other passengers waiting to embark were a ragged lot, so Jordan and her father blended right in—she in a t-shirt and sweatpants and he in a frayed denim jacket and oil stained jeans.

Cooper smoked one cigarette after another while he and Jordan waited for the bus. Neither spoke for what seemed like an eternity even though the bus arrived in twelve minutes. When it was time to board, Cooper touched his daughter on the arm and pressed a piece of paper into the palm of her hand. It was an awkward moment for both of them—no hugs, just a quick goodbye before Jordan hurried onto the bus.

After she took her seat, she was astonished to find that the piece of paper in her hand was a twenty dollar bill. She scooted over to the window and saw that her father was still standing where they said their goodbyes.

"Look up, Daddy," she cried.

Cooper couldn't hear her over the roar of the bus engine so she pounded on the window. When he saw her face pressed against the bus window looking down at him, he smiled shyly and blew her a kiss.

She held the bill against the window and mouthed "thank you," grinning and waving at him until the bus left the station. When he was out of sight, she sat back down in her seat and cried all the way to Chemult.

• • •

Jordan's rectangular dorm room came furnished with twin beds separated by a four-foot walkway. There was a built-in desk at the head of each bed and a small closet at the foot. The wall flanking the desks had two large windows in it, which was a welcome change, but she still shared a bathroom, a very large bathroom, with the rest of the women living in the same wing.

Although her dormitory room was larger than her cubbyhole at home, she didn't live there alone. Her roommate was from a prosperous Lake Oswego family, and Wendy brought so many clothes with her she had to use half of

Jordan's closet. Every day she spent hours on her private phone or studying at a table in the MU where she could socialize with her friends. Jordan, on the other hand, made good use of the built-in desk at the head of her bed.

Their first day as roommates, Wendy insisted they spiff up the room with some posters and matching bedspreads. When Jordan explained she couldn't afford it, her new roommate went ahead and decorated the room anyway. After she had the room looking the way she wanted it, she made sure Jordan understood that she would be taking everything with her at the end of the school year.

Jordan's assigned job, the job Mrs. Davis helped her get, was working three shifts a day, six days a week in the Snell Hall cafeteria. The first shift started at 6:00 a.m. It was still dark at 5:30, and Wendy's earliest class started at 9:00 o'clock, so Jordan had to dress every morning without making a sound or turning on a light. She glanced at the raindrops on the dorm room windows. At least the weather matched her mood that morning.

As she loaded her backpack with the books and notebooks she would need for the day, Jordan wondered what her high school friends were up to. McKenzie was rooming with another girl from Klamath Falls, so she didn't have to adjust to someone new. Jordan hadn't heard a word from Kimberly, didn't even see her at Christmas, but Kimberly's gentle nature would win over anybody. Jordan's roommate, on the other hand, barely talked to her. The cold shoulder she got from Wendy and the disdain she felt from others when they learned she worked in the cafeteria, did nothing for her self esteem.

After a wet, six-block walk, Jordan arrived at Snell Hall. She tucked her hair into an oh-so-attractive paper shroud and donned a pair of clear plastic gloves. Her first task every morning was to cook a big pot of oatmeal. After that, she made dozens of sandwiches, wrapped them in plastic wrap, and stored them in the cooler for lunch. She was boiling water for the oatmeal when Jenny, the dishwasher, walked over and asked, "Did you see the new guy?"

"I just got here. Did they hire somebody to replace Kirk?"

Jenny nodded. "He started today, and he's a beaut. Go take a look, and remember—I saw him first."

Jordan strolled over to the cook's station. The new cook was spreading a gigantic mass of hash browns on the grill, and he was a beaut all right, the beaut who three years earlier ran over her heart with a white pickup.

"Is that really you?"

Riley's mouth dropped open then slowly widened into a wolfish grin. "It is I, your one-of-a-kind, overqualified, underpaid campus cook. How are you doing, munchkin?"

During the next few days, Jordan asked Riley as many questions as she could without looking like a lovesick puppy. She learned his mother had passed away in January, and being her closest relative, he had dropped out of college to settle her affairs. He said it was no big deal, because he hated studying anyway. He didn't want to lose his college friends, though, so he came back to Corvallis and was working as a cook until he found something better.

Jordan's schedule allowed almost no time for socializing, but one evening, when Riley asked her to have a cup of coffee with him after the dinner shift, Jordan said yes, even though she had a test the next morning. Lingering over café mochas, they talked about their families, their friends, their favorite songs, what made them laugh, where they wanted to live someday, and it was as if they were back in his white pickup, driving home from her grandparent's ranch.

Riley put his arm around Jordan's shoulder as he walked her to her dorm. After saying good night, he started to leave, then turned around and kissed her. It was a bold and confident kiss, not sweetly sensitive the way she always imagined it would be. She wrapped her arms around his neck and kissed him back, exhilarated by this new excitement coursing through her body. Surely this was a one-time occurrence, she thought, and before she said goodbye, she had already begun preparing herself for the burst of the bubble.

The next morning, she was more than a little apprehensive about going to work. Riley's kiss wasn't just a friendly peck; it was a full blown, put up or shut up kind of kiss, so what was she supposed to say when she saw him? The new cook, who liked to tease his coworkers, broke the ice by making her his target that morning.

"Hey, Jordan—did you get caught in the rain, or do you always look like a drowned rat?"

She blushed and shot back, "Where's *your* hair net, turkey."

Then she decided to lob a spoonful of egg salad at him. She aimed at his shoulder, but the yellow glob landed square on his butt. She laughed when she realized she actually hit him, and rushed across the room with a wet towel.

"M-m-m-m, rub harder," he urged, when she was wiping the egg mixture off his butt.

Jordan giggled, too embarrassed to speak.

"You'll pay for this, you know," Riley warned, when Jordan went back to making sandwiches.

After the breakfast crowd cleared, Riley brought his coffee over to the empty table where Jordan was eating a plateful of pancakes and sausage. He spun a chair around and straddled it around to face her. Jordan looked up briefly, and then continued eating, partly for something to do while he ogled her and partly because her 8:00 o'clock class was going to start in fifteen minutes.

"Got to get to class," she said between bites.

"You sure look better without that stupid hair net," he said, boldly appraising her. "In fact, you look gawjuss this morning, if you don't mind my saying so."

Jordan took a bite of pancake and tried not to turn purple. "I've got a pretty good arm, don't you think?"

Riley smiled. "You've got a good arm all right." He blew on his coffee. "Too bad you don't have any tits."

Jordan almost choked on her food. Crimson flooded her cheeks as she vigorously chopped her link sausage into bite-sized pieces. "I can't believe you said that." Stabbing a piece of sausage with her fork, she waved it in his face, "You pig!" Her face felt so hot she was sure the glow could be seen all over campus. She quickly finished her last three bites of breakfast, got up from the table and disposed of her tray.

Riley called after her. "I told you I'd make you pay, didn't I? Now we're even."

Don't look at him, she told herself as she hurried toward the exit. *Don't you dare look at him.*

CHAPTER FIFTEEN

A week after the egg salad caper, Jordan went out on a date. Most of the people she knew, and all of her coworkers, were attending college on a budget, so when she and other students got together on the weekend, which wasn't often, they went places as a group, sharing expenses, not dating in the traditional sense.

Riley met her in front of her dorm in his older than dirt Volkswagen Beetle. The bug's light blue exterior had no shine whatsoever, and some of the dings had rusted into holes. There was a large dent on the passenger side, and the interior smelled like dirty socks, but it was paid for, and got thirty miles to the gallon. Jordan was over the moon when she opened the car door to take a seat next to the young man she had been fantasizing about for years.

Riley spent the entire week after insulting her, trying to get back in the munchkin's good graces. He left a fresh cinnamon roll at her workstation every morning. He kidded her about not being able to take a joke while showering her with compliments. He gave her space when she seemed to need it. He finally bought her a long stemmed rose, and looked so sweet and innocent when he gave it to her that her heart did flip flops.

The weather improved along with their relationship, and a week of warm spring days turned the typically wet Corvallis campus into a dreamscape of pastel blooms. The freshly sprouted blossoms on the trees and bushes were so delicate, so perfectly formed that they appeared to be fashioned from pink silk, white lace, or lavender organza. Dressed for spring, the rhododendron bushes, ornamental fruit trees, azaleas, and wisteria competed for the eye's attention like contestants in a Little Miss Oregon pageant. Jordan had to admit, spring was never that lush and intoxicating in Klamath Falls. Maybe all the rain she'd been putting up with was good for something after all.

Riley ordered two giant 7-Ups at the Burger King drive thru and headed for a wooded area outside of town where families picnicked on sunny days. He parked next to a grove of birch trees about a quarter of a mile off the highway and rolled down his window.

"I've got a surprise for you." He took her cup of 7-Up and held it under the dashboard. When he pushed one of the knobs on the dashboard, a clear liquid squirted into her cup. He pumped the knob back and forth several times, then handed the icy mixture back to her proclaiming, "Riley the bartender—at your service."

"Wow, is this what I think it is?"

Riley used the same knob to sweeten his own drink. "Let's drink to a renewed friendship," he said, grinning broadly when he touched his cup to hers, "and peace in the kitchen."

Jordan took a sip and rolled the liquid around in her mouth to investigate the taste. It tasted just like 7-Up, so she relaxed and drank deeper.

Riley explained in great detail how he had converted the reservoir meant for windshield wiper fluid into a secret place to hold booze. He told her how lucky he was to find what he needed for his invention, since his VW was so old and the parts had to be brand new. After he found the right parts, he drilled a hole in the dashboard and repositioned the flow tube so the reservoir could be accessed from inside the car.

"If the police stop me, they can't ticket me for driving with an open container. Cool, huh?"

Jordan raised her cup in a mock salute. "Brilliant. Can I try it?"

Holding the knob between her fingers, she pumped a thin stream of vodka into her cup. She took another drink, and when Riley leaned his head back, she did, too. While they listened to several songs on a soft rock radio station, she thought about what it was that attracted her to this brash young man. Besides his good looks, she liked his self assurance—a bit forward, she conceded, but not intimidating. He wasn't a well heeled preppie, whose parents took him out to dinner on weekends, and that was a bonus. She was sure the preppies she met in class or elsewhere on campus laughed at her behind her back, or worse yet, pitied her, when they saw her working in the cafeteria.

Riley refilled both of their cups and got out of the car. "There's supposed to be a waterfall on the other side of that hill. Let's see if we can find it."

He put his arm around Jordan's waist as they walked along a path that eventually led to a fast-moving stream where they discovered a short stretch of rapids, but no waterfall. The beauty of the lush, mixed growth forest fascinated Jordan. The thick tangle of evergreen and deciduous trees embraced every imaginable shade of green, from the green-black undersides of the fir boughs to the chartreuse velvet moss that wrapped around the tree trunks and clung to the tops of rocks in the streambed. Vine maples, with sleeves of new green foliage, stretched across the rapidly moving water, their arms so long they sometimes entwined with those from the opposite side of the stream to form a leafy canopy.

Goose bumps prickled her arms and legs. "Thank you for bringing me here," she sighed.

She finished the last of her drink and sat the empty cup on a rock. The new grass growing in every direction smelled almost as sweet as alfalfa. Grabbing a fistful of her long skirt in each hand, Jordan fanned it out on either side of her body and ran through the grass like a fledgling trying to fly. She whooped and twirled, dancing solo to the music of the rushing water and the chorus of crickets singing backup.

"Hey, wait for me," Riley said, running after her. "You need a partner."

Grabbing her in his arms, they began dancing a clumsy sort of polka, flattening the grass beneath their feet as they turned circle after circle. With Riley holding her close, she looked down the front of his collared shirt and saw light brown chest hairs begging to be touched.

The two dancers stopped when their feet became entangled, continuing to hold one another while they laughed and caught their breath. Jordan was never sure who kissed whom, but they moved quickly from the dance position into a full embrace. Riley's eager, searching kisses made Jordan feel deliciously dizzy, free and invincible.

"Lie down," Riley murmured, his lips on her forehead.

He lowered her onto the tall grass they trampled when they danced. Jordan unbuttoned Riley's shirt and buried her face in his chest hair. She felt a tingling sensation move from her lungs into her throat, then down through the center of her body when he moved his hands over her breasts, braless under a cotton t-shirt.

"It's okay," Jordan whispered, when Riley covered her body with his. She surrendered her mouth to his kisses, luxuriating in her own ecstasy as he began undressing her. *This is the way it's supposed to be*, she thought, as a luscious glow spread from her ear lobes to her knee caps.

About the time she was wiggling out of her panties, an unwelcome nausea began percolating in her stomach. It rose to her throat in seconds, turning the warmth and comfort of Riley's bare chest into a slab of suffocation. When the sick sensation hit, it hit hard, and suddenly her lover's body felt like a boulder. Her hands and feet were cold as ice and her butt was numb.

She pulled her mouth away for a gulp of air. *I can't stop now*, she said to herself on the verge of panic. *Please hurry, Riley. If you don't, I'm going to barf!*

The ringing in her ears muffled her lover's moans, and she didn't even know it was over until he rolled onto his back. Jordan lay perfectly still in the rumpled bed of grass, making no attempt whatsoever to retrieve her clothes or cover herself. She was vaguely aware of coldness and dampness and her own white flesh glowing in the moonlight, but she had such a bad case of the whirlies, she didn't dare move, not even a little finger.

When Riley cozied up to her and nuzzled her ear, it was the only warm spot on her body. He kissed her cheek and lightly stroked her hair, but she didn't sigh, didn't giggle, didn't open her eyes, didn't move a muscle except to swallow and swallow and swallow, promising her soul to the highest bidder if she just didn't heave.

CHAPTER SIXTEEN

Although Jordan lost her virginity that night, she didn't lose her cookies, and she quickly learned the difference between getting a buzz on and being slammed. She also learned sex could be terrific when her brain and her stomach were working properly. Sex with Riley was quick and fierce. He liked it rough. He liked to bite. He expected her to submit to his every whim, and Jordan was so crazy about him, she would have made love upside down and backwards if he asked her to. She was even pleased when he asked her to buy his condoms. As long as he paid for them, she was happy to spare him the embarrassment.

Riley, who was known around campus as the cowboy, never said no to a party. Jordan went with him as often as she could, somehow maintaining a 3.0 average and her scholarship, but not the high marks she made her first two terms.

Jordan and Riley drank beer on Friday nights then switched to the hard stuff on Saturdays, since they didn't have to work the next day. On weekends, after partying harder than they probably should have, the young couple spent the night in Riley's studio apartment, waking up with morning after disease and its classic symptoms of headache, cotton mouth, cracked lips, and a raging desire for sugar. Their cure of choice was sweetened coffee and toast slathered with peanut butter and honey. Breakfast was usually in bed.

"You're a messy eater, Riley" she joked one morning, while she picked toast crumbs out of his chest hairs one at a time.

"Well, I'm not the only one." He grabbed her, and pinning her against the mattress, licked the spot between her breasts where a drop of honey landed. Still holding her down, he rubbed his sandpaper chin on her face and neck until she shrieked with laughter.

Riley loved every inch of his little munchkin's body, but constantly ridiculed her for spending so much time studying, especially if she studied with her classmates. His party friends were clearly impressed they had a future veterinarian in their midst, and a cute one as well; however behind her back, Riley told them he didn't think she would make it. Sometimes, even while she was standing next to him, he would say things like, "Don't be bringing your pups to her until she proves herself."

Six months after their first date, Riley quit his cooking job. He collected unemployment for a while before landing an entry level job selling printers for Hewlett-Packard. For this white collar job he had to give up his cowboy hat and dress professionally, and the first time Jordan saw him in a shirt and tie, she wondered how long it would be before he dumped the kitchen wench who mashed eggs and cleaned tables every day. She liked him better in his hat.

Riley's HP job required some travel during the work week, so that gave Jordan a chance to study, and the young lovers still spent every weekend together. Jordan told her mother about Riley when she went home for Christmas vacation, even going so far as to say she was in love with him. Annie was pleased to see her daughter so happy, but expressed concern when Jordan told her Riley didn't like her friends and wasn't exactly crazy about her becoming a veterinarian.

It was the summer between her junior and senior years before Jordan asked Riley to meet her parents. Kimberly was getting married in June, and Jordan was going to be part of the wedding. She couldn't wait for Riley to see her in the backless purple taffeta dress Kimberly chose for her bridesmaids. She imagined him mentally undressing her during the wedding ceremony, pressing his body against hers while they slow danced at the reception, eager to get his hands on her yet knowing he would have to wait until they were alone.

When the day of the wedding arrived, Riley was supposed to pick her up at noon. At a quarter to twelve Jordan sat on the edge of her bed, hands folded in her lap waiting for him to arrive. Her neatly trimmed fingernails sported a fresh coat of clear polish, and her purple satin shoes, a half size too small, sat side by side on the floor, ready to step into as soon as Riley knocked on the door.

She looked at her watch. Her father was probably at Buck's, so if Riley arrived on time, he could meet her mother, chitchat for two or three minutes and leave without having to meet the man of the house. Hearing a car approach, Jordan listened intently, hoping it was Riley. Riley's Honda Prelude didn't have a whiney engine like his old bug, so she couldn't tell if it was him or not. Then the back door opened, and in the time it took her father to walk from the back steps to the living room, she had switched from hoping Riley would be on time to praying he would be late. In twenty minutes or less, her father would be asleep, and she and her date could leave without having to go through awkward introductions.

Jordan had stopped discussing anything of a personal nature with Cooper after the punishment she received over the false hickey. He knew she had a ride to Kimberly's wedding, but the guy coming to pick her up was, according to what he'd been told, just a friend. There would be hell to pay if her father found out her escort was the same young man who had supposedly given her that hickey. Well, her relationship with Riley had gone way past hickeys, and he must never find out about that.

Jordan sat bolt upright when she heard a knock at the front door. Her heart raced at the prospect of seeing Riley for the first time that summer, but her freshly shaved armpits started to sting when she realized a quick getaway was out of the question. She took a deep breath, smoothed the front of her dress, grabbed her purse and poked her feet into the purple pumps.

"Hi there," was the best she could come up with when she swished into the living room in all her purple glory and saw Riley standing there with his mouth agape. She had to admit, the deep purple color of the dress brought out the green in her gray-green eyes. The tight fitting bodice emphasized her delicate proportions, and the deep cut of the backline was dramatic and sexy.

"You look gawjuss," Riley exclaimed, and Jordan, although pleased, wanted to stuff a sock in his mouth.

During the short time it took to make introductions, a discomforting flush spread from her face to her shoulders. Her hands and feet were freezing, so she wondered if all the blood in her extremities had suddenly migrated to the parts of her that were blushing. Riley, looking like a suntanned California poster boy in his yellow shirt and beige sport coat, walked over to where her father was sitting and held out his hand. Cooper wasn't a bit subtle about looking Riley over from head to toe, the same way he'd been scrutinizing Jordan's bare back. He grunted something unintelligible, and halfheartedly shook hands before turning his attention to the TV.

Annie tried to make up for her husband's rudeness by talking to the young man about his drive from Corvallis and the depth and color of Klamath Lake before Jordan nudged her escort toward the door.

"Bye, Daddy," she said, faking a carefree mood, wishing her father would show some sign of friendliness. Silent and glassy eyed, Cooper looked up briefly when Jordan opened the door and gave the young couple a perfunctory wave.

As soon as she stepped onto the front porch, Jordan began to feel blood flowing in her hands and feet again. The young couple walked across the weeds to where the Honda was parked, and Riley bowed like Cinderella's coachman when he opened the car door for her. Jordan giggled and made sure all of her purple skirt was safely inside the car. After he closed the door, and no one except Riley could hear her, she let out a totally unconstrained, decidedly unfeminine whoop of joy.

• • •

Later that evening, still deliriously happy, Jordan stood in the Elks Club dining room with McKenzie and Riley, sipping the champagne that remained in her glass after the wedding toast.

"Isn't this the most fabulous wedding you've ever been to?" McKenzie gushed. "I've never seen this many people at a wedding in my life. Doesn't Kimberly look beautiful?"

For the wedding, Kimberly wore a strapless gown of white organza and a fingertip veil that she removed when she got to the reception. Her normally straight hair was curled in a platinum cascade that grazed the tops of her shoulders. Her shoes were white, her skin was white, just about the only thing about her that wasn't white was her pale blue eyes.

"Did you see Miss Abbott?" McKenzie asked. "She's the only woman here wearing black. Does she even own anything that isn't black? Look at her hair. It's positively stapled to her head with bobby pins."

Riley, who usually kept Jordan to himself, decided to check out the bar.

As he left, he lightly ran a finger down her bare spine, and she tingled with pleasure while her handsome hunk blended into the crowd around the bar.

"Weddings are a great excuse to get smashed, don't you think?" McKenzie said, eyeing Riley. "Suppose this will do the trick?" She took two glasses of champagne off the waiter's tray.

Jordan led McKenzie to a table away from the dance floor. "Let's sit down for a minute. My feet are killing me."

With a rustle of purple taffeta, the two bridesmaids seated themselves at a lavender-draped table. The previous occupants left their empty glasses, along with a crumpled *Kimberly and Hunter* cocktail napkin. A large blob of cake frosting sat in the middle of an oily ring on the tablecloth. McKenzie took a swipe of the icing and sucked if off her finger.

"How can you stand that stuff," Jordan asked, screwing up her face. "It's nothing but sugar and lard."

McKenzie scooped up the rest of the frosting and noisily sucked it off her finger. "It's the frosting on the wedding cake. It should be a sin not to like wedding cake."

Jordan picked up the wrinkled cocktail napkin and folded it into a triangle. "Where's Morgan? I haven't seen her since Kim and Hunter cut the cake."

"She was in the ladies lounge a few minutes ago. I think she's tired … and bored since she can't drink for another three months."

"How's she feeling?"

"She feels like Moby Grape tonight. Otherwise she's fine."

"And what about you, McKenzie?" Jordan kicked off her shoes. "When are you going back to SOU?"

"I'm not. My job at the attorney's office is kind of interesting, and Mom and Dad say I can stay with them as long as I want. 'Course I'm not planning to live with them forever. After all, a girl needs her privacy." She cocked an eyebrow. "Know what I mean, jelly bean?"

CHAPTER SEVENTEEN

After the guests consumed three tiers of a four tier wedding cake along with several cases of champagne, and Kimberly and her new husband had been given a proper sendoff, Jordan and Riley sneaked away to the motel room she reserved for them. Hanging onto one other for support, they unlocked the door and staggered into the room where they quickly, albeit clumsily, stripped off their clothes and almost made it to the bed.

When they hit the edge of the mattress, they slid onto the floor where their lovemaking was swift and frantic. In the middle of a barrage of kisses, Riley bit Jordan's lip. She drew her head back, then plunged back in, craving the closeness, eager to bury her face in the familiar scent of his cologne, wanting to feel like the most beautiful girl in the world for one magical night. Still entwined on the motel floor, they fell asleep.

Four hours later, Jordan stumbled into the bathroom. Although she wished she could be lying next to Riley when the sun came up, it was 2:00 a.m., and she needed to get home. Her father no longer expected her to be in by midnight, but he would be furious if she stayed out all night.

With some difficulty, she got Riley up, dressed, and back in the car. Parked in front of her house for what Jordan thought would be a quick goodbye, a few smooches turned into deep kissing, and she didn't try to stop him when he slipped her purple dress off her shoulders.

Despite being lost in the moment, she saw the porch light flick off, then on again.

"I've got to go," she said, pushing against Riley's chest. "My father's still up."

Riley held her tighter. "You can't go now, munchkin. I'm up, too, if you haven't noticed."

His hands covered her breasts. "Perky," he called them, which turned her to mush every time he lingered there.

"Besides, you owe me. This is the only time I'll see you all summer."

"Okay," she whispered, "but we'll have to hurry."

Riley reclined the seat as far back as it would go. It took him some doing to get through several layers of tulle and taffeta, and just as he bared her thighs, Jordan saw the silhouette of her father approaching the car. She gasped and shoved Riley so hard his head hit the door frame. She was frantically trying to get back into her dress when the door on her side of the car flew open.

"Well isn't this a pretty sight." It was too dark to see Cooper's face, but Jordan could imagine his expression. "Get out of the car, tramp."

"I'm sorry, Daddy, just let me …"

"I said, get-out-of-that-car."

He grabbed her by the arm and yanked her off the front seat. Her arm felt as if it was being pulled out of its socket as he dragged her across the yard toward the house. She made an effort to cover her naked breasts with her free hand, and heard a tearing sound when the skirt of her bridesmaid's dress snagged on a rock. One of her shoes fell off as she tried in vain to twist her arm out of her father's grip. She yelled to Riley for help, but her gallant escort wasn't there to hear her. In less than ten seconds he had raised the front seat, started his car, and fled the scene of the crime.

Realizing he couldn't drag his daughter up the front steps, Cooper dropped Jordan's arm. He looked down at her, half dressed, totally exposed by the porch light and boomed, "Put that whore of a dress back on and get inside!"

Jordan didn't know whether to scream or cry. She slid her arms through the straps of her dress and rocked back and forth hugging herself while her father stood on the threshold holding the door open. She rubbed her sore shoulder and walked inelegantly into the living room, where she removed the one purple shoe that miraculously stayed on her foot during the trip across the front yard. She had sobered up some, but still wasn't steady on her feet, even without shoes, when she lowered her head for the ax she expected to fall.

Cooper shut the door and stood in front of her with fisted hands, his face black with anger. He opened his mouth, but nothing came out. It was a long minute before he said, "Piss on it," and told her to get out of his sight.

Surprised and relieved, Jordan slunk to her room where she hung up her damaged dress and put on a cotton nightgown. Glancing at herself in the mirror, she was appalled to see hair that looked as if it had been combed with an egg beater and badly smeared mascara. Her entire right arm and shoulder ached, and there was a lump in her throat the size of a basketball.

She crawled onto her thin mattress and closed her eyes, praying sleep would carry her to a happier place. Her afternoon and evening with Riley had followed her imaginary script to perfection—the sexy dress, the wedding, the champagne, the slow dancing, making love in the motel. She could still feel the warmth of his skin against hers, still smell his cologne, but after the wonderful evening they spent together, she couldn't understand why he left her to face her father's wrath alone.

Sleep was being stubborn, and as she lay there, trying to relax, she heard the squeaky kitchen cupboard open and close. The third time she heard the dreaded succession of sounds, she covered her head with her pillow, and she must have fallen asleep shortly after that, because the next thing she knew, her pillow was gone and her father was standing next to her bed.

"Thought you had me fooled, din't you."

The harsh disruption of sleep coupled with the champagne she drank earlier in the evening gave Jordan an instant headache, and when she realized her father was in her room, she began to tremble. Expecting the worst, she cradled her head in her hands and cried out in pain when he dug his fingers into the flesh of her shoulders to pull her out of bed.

"I know I raised you right, so why can't you act like it?"

He shook Jordan hard, and then cuffed her with the back of his hand, not once or twice, but in rapid succession. When she held up her arms to protect herself, he slapped them as well. Her head jerked back with each stinging blow, and she heard herself screaming in pain and disbelief.

Suddenly Annie wedged herself between them. "Are you crazy?!" she cried. She shoved her husband against the dresser next to Jordan's bed, sending books and basketball trophies crashing to the floor. "Don't you lay another hand on her, or you and I are through."

Jordan scooted away from her parents and cowered in a corner.

"Your daughter is a slut, Annie, and I don't want her sleepin' under my roof if she's sleepin' around!"

Jordan started to cry. It was a soft cry at first, barely a whimper, until years of pent up anger and frustration turned the whimper into a howl. All her life she had weathered her father's insults and censures without saying a word, never arguing, never questioning his authority or his unreasonable decisions, wanting to scream at times, but always biting her tongue. That night she let it all out, bawling and beating her fists on the floor until he backed out of the room.

The next morning, Cooper stayed in bed until noon. Jordan was standing in the middle of the kitchen, using a spoon to eat peanut butter out of a jar when he walked in and poured himself a cup of coffee. He was showered and shaved and looked as if he was about to leave. She took the jar of peanut butter with her when she slid behind the table to get out of his way.

"Listen, Jordan," he finally said to her. "You've got to be more careful. You think you're all grown up now, but you can still make mistakes."

He leaned against the kitchen sink sipping his coffee, while Jordan used her spoon to scrape the last of the peanut butter out of the jar. When the stalemate went on too long, he said, "You don't get it, do you? Well I'll be damned if I'm going to apologize."

He set his coffee cup in the sink and walked out the back door. As soon as she heard her father's car start up, Jordan picked up the phone.

CHAPTER EIGHTEEN

When Jordan called Riley, she thought he would ask her to move in with him. Instead, he asked her where she would go if she left home.

"Anywhere, she sighed. "My brother Jude moved out before he even graduated from high school. He's living in a dump with four other guys, but I'll bet you couldn't pay him to move back here."

Hoping Riley's shoulder would be one she could cry on, their brief phone conversation just added to her blues. Not only did he squash her dream of moving in with him, he didn't apologize or even acknowledge speeding off while she was being dragged through the dirt, and when she told him her father had slapped her silly, he said he used to get the same or worse when he lived with his stepdad.

The following day, Annie took command of the situation, and soon Jordan was moving her few belongings into her Uncle Doug's ranch house, feeling like a squatter as she unpacked her clothes and hung them in what used to be Athena's closet. Athena's sunny upstairs room was three times the size of hers, with muslin curtains on the dormer windows, a bright floral quilt on the full size bed, and Avon sachets in the dresser drawers. She should have been delighted with her cheerful new surroundings, but found it disheartening to be on the receiving end of her cousin's hand-me-downs again.

Athena and her husband lived about ten miles from the V-Bar-J ranch on a farm they purchased shortly after getting married. Her husband of three years worked for Burlington Northern, and Athena was a stay-at-home mom who took care of their baby girl and raised rabbits for the commercial market. She made more money selling rabbits than she did working at the courthouse, and she could do it without having to hire a babysitter. She explained to Jordan that lean white rabbit meat was becoming more popular now that people were trying to lower their cholesterol levels. Skinned and dressed, a rabbit didn't *look* like the Easter bunny, and after it was cooked, it tasted better than chicken.

With her baby daughter strapped to her chest, Athena showed Jordan around her rabbitry. The neatly stacked hutches were filled with rabbits of many colors, napping in the clean straw, playing, wrestling, or copulating, all happening so quickly Jordan couldn't always tell the difference. Athena unlatched one of the hutches and pulled out a large gray and white rabbit.

"We've spoiled this one. Scratch her between the ears. She loves it."

Jordan threw herself wholeheartedly into whatever needed to be done around the Colton ranch. There were sprinkler lines to move, trips into town for fertilizer or other supplies, animals to feed, and she took her turn driving the mower or the baler when the alfalfa was ready to cut. The 250 acres her grandfather planted in alfalfa usually produced three cuttings between May and September.

Over the course of the summer, Jordan was surprised at the number of times her uncles attended to their own animals' ailments without calling a vet. She asked her Uncle Doug about it when she helped him treat a cow with pink eye. Jordan held the cow's head while her uncle squirted a dropper of medication into one inflamed eye. She watched in amazement as he sewed the Hereford's top and bottom eyelids together with a needle and catgut. When he finished, the bawling, one-eyed animal made a beeline for the rest of the herd.

He chuckled when he caught Jordan's bewildered expression. "I sewed her eyelid together to keep the sun out. When the cat gut dissolves in a few days, that eye will open up and be just fine. We do this sort of thing all the time."

"Why didn't you call The Doc?"

"The Doc? I can see where you're coming from, but if we called a vet every time we had an ailing animal, we'd have to build him a bunkhouse and put him on the payroll." He put an arm around her shoulder as they walked back to the house. "In fact, me and Carson are hoping you'll teach us a thing or two down the road—help us save even more."

"Oh, I will, Uncle Doug. I promise."

The hot days and cool nights raced by quickly, and summer melted away.

Riley was too busy to come for another visit, although he called once a week. She thought about him constantly, especially after showering the day's dirt and sweat down the drain and climbing into bed. It wouldn't be long before she would be tangled in Riley's sheets again and a different kind of sweaty.

One Sunday in early September, Annie came out to the ranch. Jordan hurried from the barn when she saw her drive up. Her mother and Grandma Leona were on the back porch when she got there, and before rounding the corner of the house, she decided to stop and listen to what they were talking about.

"He's sorry, Mother, I know he is. He hasn't used those exact words, but he did tell me to ask her to come home. He's hardly been drinking at all this summer. He knows he was wrong."

"So he's cut down on his drinking again?" Leona sniffed. "Well, say what you will, I won't let her leave until it's time for her to go back to school. Parker wouldn't want her to go, and neither would your brothers. Why does Cooper want her to come home so badly, so he can hit her again?"

Jordan covered her mouth with her hand.

"You seem to think Coop is some terrible ogre who beats his children, and you're just plain wrong."

"Has he ever hit *you*? We see you so seldom, you could be covered with bruises and we wouldn't know it."

Annie laughed nervously. "Really, Mother, I can't believe you would ask such a thing. Coop and I argue once in a while, and sometimes he yells at me, usually when I say something I shouldn't."

Leona picked a dead rose off the bush spilling over the porch rail. "What in the world has happened to you, Annie? You used to chase deer out of your garden with a fly swatter and kill rattlesnakes with a shovel. How did you get to be such a dishrag?"

"I am *not* a dishrag. You don't know every little thing that goes on in my home. We're a lot more normal than you think."

"Like a poor people's soap opera, you're normal," Leona muttered.

Jordan decided it would be awkward at this point to make an appearance, so she went around to the front of the house and entered from the kitchen. When she opened the screen door and walked onto the porch, her mother hugged her for a long time.

"You're so tan," she said, beaming at Jordan while holding her at arm's length. "Don't get too much sun, though. It causes wrinkles. Your Grandma Leona says you've been a big help this summer. Do you like it way out here, or are you ready to come home?"

Leona glared at her daughter. "That's dirty pool, Annie."

"Daddy said he didn't want me living under his roof," Jordan said, trying not to sound like she was complaining.

"He didn't mean that, sweetie. He didn't really want you to leave in the first place. I was frazzled by what happened that night and rushed you out here before he had a chance to make amends. He hasn't been drinking for over a month, and things are good right now. You'll see."

Leona stood with her hands in her pockets, shaking her head.

"I could come home, Mom, but the alfalfa is ready to cut again. After we finish with that, it will be time to go back to school." She smiled at her grandmother. "It's been a wonderful experience. Really, Grandma Leona, I can't thank you enough."

"We're going to pay you something, Jordan. It won't be much, enough to buy yourself some new clothes though."

"Please don't do that, Mother. You know how Coop feels about taking money from you and Dad."

"I don't care. Your daughter worked like a hired hand all summer." She walked over to Jordan and squeezed her fingertips. "You're a good kid," she said, "and you're welcome to come back next summer, too, if you'd like."

She gave Annie a sidelong glance, and nose in the air, marched into the kitchen.

CHAPTER NINETEEN

An hour and a half before her bus left for Corvallis, Jordan went home to pack up the clothes and other small items she left behind when she moved to the ranch for the summer. Her father and Dusty were both home when she opened the front door. Cooper, looking surprised, smiled quietly and patted the empty spot on the couch between him and Dusty.

"Hello, stranger," Dusty said, looking genuinely happy to see her. Cooper raised his eyebrows and patted the couch again.

Jordan glanced uneasily at the two of them and managed a thin, "Hi," before hurrying past them.

Dusty followed her to her room where he leaned against the door jam with his arms crossed. Sporting a tight shirt that drew attention to his biceps, and beaming at her with a cocksure smile, he looked equally capable of breaking hearts in the classroom and crunching bones on the football field.

"Know what?" he said, "we'll both be seniors this year."

"I guess we will. I hadn't thought about it that way." Jordan gave him a half hug. "Good for us, Dusty."

"I know you're in a hurry, but some day I'd like to talk to you about what it's like up there at Oregon State. If I have another good football season, I might have a chance for an athletic scholarship."

"That's good to hear. I hope you knock their socks off, if that's what it takes to get you into college." She looked him in the eye. "You need to work on your grades, though." She took a blouse off a hanger, folded it neatly and placed it in a paper grocery bag. "Wish you could convince Jude to finish high school ... at least get his GED."

"Jude isn't doing so good. Those guys he's living with are a bunch of losers. Don't say anything to Dad, but I think he's doing drugs."

"Right, like I'm going to be sharing secrets with our father." She placed a sweater into the bag on top of the blouse. "What makes you think Jude is doing drugs? How often do you see him?"

"Mostly when I happen to run into him. He barely speaks to me. What's wrong with our family, Jordan?"

Jordan shook her head as she folded and packed the few items left in her dresser.

"Dad's been pretty cool lately. He wants you to come back, you know. I think he'd let Jude come home, too, if we could find him."

"Please, Dusty. It's okay to talk to me about college, or Jude, or just about anything else, but not about Daddy. You don't have a clue when it comes to him."

"I know him better than you do. He came down on me pretty hard about going to practice and all. Now that I made first string, he don't seem so bad, and him and Perry come to every home game."

"Well, you're lucky. I played basketball all four years I was in high school, and Daddy didn't come to a single one of my games." Jordan looked around her nearly empty room. "I've got to scoot or I'll miss my bus. Let me know how you're doing, okay? I'll write after I get settled and send you some brochures."

• • •

When Jordan arrived at the Corvallis bus depot later that afternoon, Riley was there to pick her up. She was so happy to see him that she jumped into his arms and wrapped herself around him like a chimpanzee. She gave him a kiss and tasted liquor on his breath, which struck her as odd for a Thursday afternoon.

The minute they were inside his apartment, he grabbed her and kissed her hard, keeping his mouth on hers while he backed her into the kitchenette and up against the counter. The metal edge of the countertop dug into her back as he pressed against her, holding her head between his hands and bruised her lips with liquor tainted kisses.

His hands quickly reacquainted themselves with her body, squeezing and exploring, deftly peeling off her blouse and shorts in the process. She wrapped her arms around his neck, and when he dug his fingers into her butt cheeks to lift her off the floor, she turned to jelly, not strawberry or peach, but the hot pepper kind, and she screamed with pleasure as he forcefully made love to her in the corner of the kitchenette.

After taking a moment to catch his breath, he plucked her clothing off the floor and shoved it at her, saying, "Get dressed, munchkin. You look better with clothes on." Then he kissed her on the forehead, swatted her bare bottom and left the room.

Jordan scrambled into her shorts and blouse, and gently touched her fingertips to her sore lips. Thinking something wet might make them feel better, she made herself a vodka tonic and asked Riley if he wanted one, too. When he didn't answer, she checked and found him asleep in his recliner. She had many stories about her summer on the ranch to share with him, but he didn't like her to wake him, so she took her drink over to the window where she could sit and watch the evening traffic. She looked at the time. She had been in Riley's apartment for exactly eleven minutes.

In the weeks that followed, she longed for another eleven minutes like those as she watched their hot September reunion turn cool as spring rain. She couldn't figure out why a third summer of separation could make such a difference, however it was obvious the man filling her thoughts all summer had become distant and edgy. His smiles were few and forced. She felt tolerated rather than loved.

• • •

The first week in November, Jordan was surprised to receive a letter from Dusty.

Dear Jordan,

Thanks for the brosures. We didn't do too good this year. We beat North Medford though. The coach said he'd write me a letter to the coaches up there. I already applied for a scholarship. I made first team all conference which is good. Mom said she sent you the article out of the paper.

Did you know Dad broke his arm? He did it at one of my games when he fell in the bleachers. I didn't know about it until after the game was over. He can't work till he gets his cast off. He's getting unemployment, though, so everything's cool.

Are you coming home for Thanksgiving? Write me back when your not studying. ha ha

Dusty

Even though Dusty's poor spelling and grammar were irksome, Jordan was pleased to hear from him, and he was spot on when he joked about how much time she spent studying. In order to complete her pre-veterinary requirements by mid June, she needed to take physics, organic chemistry, and biochemistry. She was hitting the books all right.

Dusty's surprising news that their father broke his arm probably meant he was drinking again. Her heart went out to her mother and the emotional gyrations she went through every time Cooper jumped on or off the wagon. Cynical after her father's eighth return to the bottle, Jordan didn't get her hopes up anymore.

When Thanksgiving came around, she briefly considered going home, but opted to use the time to work on her relationship with Riley. If the way to a man's heart was through his stomach, she would try to get there by making him the best Thanksgiving dinner he ever ate.

The oven in his kitchenette was too small for a turkey, so she substituted Cornish game hens. She made sausage stuffing, potatoes and gravy, and baked a pumpkin pie from scratch.

Riley cracked a beer as soon as the first football game aired on TV. When dinner was ready, he devoured his meal, ate two pieces of pumpkin pie, and went back to watching football. Even before Jordan was finished with the dishes, he was asleep in his chair, so she switched off the TV, removed his shoes and helped him into bed.

She spooned her body around him and pressed her face into the back of his t-shirt, wondering if this was what it felt like to be married. She yawned and snuggled closer, content to be next to her man and pleased with the way her meal turned out.

. . .

Two months later, on an otherwise ordinary Sunday afternoon, Jordan told Riley she had to go back to the dorm so she and her study partner could prepare for an important exam. Riley grabbed her by the hair and pulled her nose to nose.

"So where does that leave me? Seems like you're always writing papers or going to labs, or studying for something or other."

"The classes I'm taking are hard," Jordan said, "harder than anything you ever took." She tried to pull away, but he was holding her hair so tightly she was helpless. His heavy lidded eyes, just inches away from hers, suddenly looked more menacing than sexy.

"You're hurting, me, Riley."

"I don't care—I'm sick of this. I figured you would have given up by now, or at least changed your major." He let go of her hair and gave her a shove. "I don't think I can deal with this for another four years."

After she went ahead with her study plans, he stopped calling her, and every time she called him, his line was either busy or he didn't pick up. He didn't open the door, when she rang the bell to his apartment. She looked for him in his favorite bar, and searched the OSU horse barns where he hung out occasionally, but found no sign of him. She spent two sleepless weeks, crying, phoning him at all hours and making herself physically ill.

For a month she was on autopilot—going to work, going to class, barely aware of her surroundings. By the beginning of spring term, having reluctantly accepted the fact the relationship was over, she completed her senior year like a racehorse pounding toward the finish line, rarely socializing, focused solely on making grades and graduating. Even receiving word in April that she had been accepted to veterinary school didn't brighten her spirits the way it should have.

. . .

With her mind on her studies, Jordan hadn't given much thought to the upcoming graduation ceremony. She was planning on having her diploma mailed to her until she got a letter from her mother saying they were coming to Corvallis for her graduation—they being her mother, father, Uncle Perry, and Dusty. Jordan wasn't really surprised when Jude wasn't coming, but she was astonished to learn that her father and Uncle Perry were making the trip.

It was warm and slightly overcast on graduation day. Jordan left the door to her dorm room ajar so her family would be sure to find her, and shortly before 10:00, they trooped in: her mother wearing a new dress, fresh hair cuts for the men, and the whole group shiny as show dogs.

In spite of her ho hum attitude toward the graduation ceremony, she came close to crying as she hugged them one by one. When she hugged her father, she could feel him trembling inside the thin, polyester shirt he was wearing.

Since there was time to kill before the graduates assembled, Jordan suggested a campus tour. She volunteered to drive, since she knew all the short cuts and one-way streets. Her mother sat up front, and the three men squeezed into the back of Cooper's '85 Chevy Nova.

"Is there a 7-Eleven around here?" Perry asked, before Jordan had driven halfway down the block. "We could use a little somethin' to drink."

Jordan drove a few blocks to the convenience store where Riley used to buy beer, and as soon as the men were inside, she turned to her mother and said, "It's great to see all of you, Mom, but I'll be glad when this day is over. If Daddy does anything to embarrass me today, I'll kill him."

Annie smiled weakly and heaved a sigh. "We are so proud of you, Jordan. Coop and I never even finished high school, and here you are graduating from college. Your father's been telling everybody he knows about you getting into veterinary college. I've heard Perry brag some, too."

"Does that explain the beer? Are they buying beer so they can celebrate *my* graduation?"

"Let it go, Jordan." Annie touched her daughter's arm. "I know you won't believe me when I tell you this, but your father very much wants to be here, so can we please get through this day without a fight?"

Jordan spoke few words as she drove her passengers down Washington Way, past the Lab Animal Resource Center and the Veterinary Research Lab, across Thirtieth Street so Dusty could have a look at the football stadium, and through an older section of campus where some of the lecture halls and administration buildings were located.

Annie took a particular interest in the rhododendron bushes, some of them taller than the house in Klamath Falls. Dusty ogled the Lycra clad coeds who were jogging through campus and asked about the seating capacity of Parker Stadium.

Having no interest in brick buildings and majestic deciduous trees, Cooper and Perry sat in the backseat drinking beer and eating Cheetos.

CHAPTER TWENTY

In the fall of 1991, as Jordan began her first year of veterinary training, McKenzie transferred her Southern Oregon University credits to Oregon State and changed her major to Forestry. Tired of living at home, discouraged by her microscopic paychecks, and unable to find the right guy in Klamath Falls, the unmarried Scott sister decided to go dear hunting in Corvallis.

The timing was perfect. Jordan's previous room and board scholarship was strictly an undergraduate arrangement, so she needed to round up some roommates to help with her rent, and McKenzie was her obvious first choice. Wendy, her freshman year roommate, moved into a sorority her sophomore year, and as Jordan learned later, got married and dropped out. Jordan wouldn't have picked her as a roommate anyway, even though the girl did treat her better by the end of the school year. Her next roommate would have fit in, but she graduated and got a job in Portland.

Jordan found Bailey, from Grants Pass and Catherine, from Prosser, Washington, on a list of students looking for roommates provided by Student Services. The four young women rented a two-bedroom furnished apartment on Jackson Street, with Jordan and McKenzie bunking in one room and Bailey and Catherine in the other.

The weekend they moved in was a zoo, as the four young women cleaned house, arranged and rearranged the furniture, unpacked their books and belongings, and acquainted one another with their pets. The blue clapboard, bungalow style house bulged at the beams with four women, all their gear, a pet rabbit, a large tank of tropical fish, and a venomless rattlesnake named Herb.

Bailey, a microbiology major, was relieved to find someone who would let her keep her rattlesnake, a high school biology project that had wormed its way into her heart. She kept Herb in a glass terrarium where it dined on live mice that Bailey skimmed from the research labs.

"Herb's the greatest pet ever," she told her roommates. "He only rattles if you pester him. He can't get loose, so you don't have to worry about him crawling somewhere he's not supposed to or pooping on the floor."

Catherine, who wore wire rimmed glasses because they made her look smart, and who was almost as quiet as Herb, was majoring in Spanish. When asked about rooming with a snake, she first declined, then decided it would be okay as long as Herb's terrarium stayed in the living room and not in the bedroom, where she planned to keep her tropical fish, and where, as it turned out, she kept herself most of the time.

Jordan's contribution to this newly assembled menagerie was a white rabbit with brown markings—a doe with almond shaped patches of brown around her eyes. Cleopatra was one of Cousin Athena's rabbits. During the second summer Jordan spent at the ranch she watched Cleo grow from a blind, naked kit into an active youngster that seemed to thrive on human interaction. Athena insisted Jordan take the two-year-old rabbit with her when she began her veterinary training, and showed her how to make cheap litter out of shredded newspaper.

McKenzie was the only roommate without a non human companion and seemed oblivious to the creatures in the apartment, even the two legged ones at times. She was high on her own renaissance, almost giddy to be living for the first time without adult supervision, and though she wasn't as serious a student as her three roommates, she was nonetheless highly skilled at doing her own kind of research.

"I don't think you can beat the male/female ratio in the School of Forestry," she told Jordan a few days after classes started. "Well, maybe in med school or law school you might. Do you know what the odds are in vet school?"

Jordan laughed. "Good grief, McKenzie, I never gave it a thought. I'd say it's about half and half based on the people taking the GRE exams when I did."

"Well I can tell you for sure there's mostly guys studying forestry, and I'm going to bag my own Paul Bunyan real soon—hopefully built like Paul Bunyan, too." She grinned. "Know what I mean, jelly bean?"

Jordan took out an obscenely large loan to cover her four years in vet school. Having roommates helped her pay the bills, but she was always on the lookout for ways to make a little extra money. Her tuition was frightening and her textbooks outrageously expensive. It just about made her ill when she had to pay two hundred dollars for a *Small Animal Anatomy* textbook because all of the used copies had been taken.

Midway through October, an opportunity to make a quick hundred dollars came up when her advisor, Dr. Frazier, asked her and another financially challenged student to transport a Black Angus bull to a farm near Rickreall. A registered breeder, the animal had been loaned to the college for a birth weight study, and satiated by the steady stream of blond, brunette and red-hided heifers brought to his pen during the six months he spent on campus, the bull had a decidedly mellow disposition. Jordan figured hauling that bull a mere twenty-five miles would be the easiest money she ever made.

"I'm sure you realize this is an extremely valuable animal," Dr. Frazier told Jordan and the student who was to accompany her. "I couldn't begin to put a price on this bull's head, however it's more than either of you can afford if anything goes wrong."

The other student selected to make the trip was Drew Murphy, a broad shouldered farm boy from the Hermiston area who was two years behind Jordan in the veterinary program. He was surprised when she told him her name. His best friend from high school, a state champion wrestler, was also named Jordan.

Jordan and Drew loaded the bull into a double horse trailer with the center partition removed. The Angus was an impressive beast, solid black with a broad chest and huge head. Drew estimated its weight at upwards of a ton, and although the bull had been dehorned and dehornied, its sheer size made him potentially dangerous. If he were to charge, it would be like being hit by a car going thirty miles an hour. Even if he accidentally stepped on one of their feet, he could do some damage.

After several minutes of prodding failed to get the bull into the horse trailer, Jordan fastened a harness around its head. Drew used the harness to pull the bull up the loading ramp, and as soon as the animal was inside, he shoved the ramp into the trailer and quickly closed the doors. Jordan secured the latch and within minutes the vets-to-be and their live cargo were heading north on Highway 99.

Jordan and Drew found plenty to talk about as they drove through the small towns and patches of green and gold farmland west of the Willamette River. Drew grew up on an onion farm in Echo, Oregon, about ten miles south of Hermiston. His parents raised a few head of cattle in addition to growing onions, so he wasn't entirely out of his element when it came to hauling bulls.

Jordan was impressed by the confident way Drew maneuvered the truck and trailer through traffic, how his strong hands gripped the wheel and shifted gears. Working in the Umatilla County sun had produced large brown patches of freckles on his face and arms, and Jordan decided he was good looking if she ignored the freckles. She had a feeling he was looking her over, too, so she used the truck's side mirror to do a quick makeup check. No lipstick on her teeth. Hair messy, but kind of sexy looking.

Suddenly a black blob appeared in the mirror next to her face. A black blob? She sucked in her breath when she realized the Black Angus bull was hanging halfway out the back of the horse trailer. In a split second, its knees were dragging along the asphalt, and the next thing Jordan knew, the prize bull was a large black ball in the middle of the road growing smaller by the second as she and Drew sped down the highway.

"The bull!" she screamed. "Ohmygod,ohmygod,ohmygod! The bull got out. Stop the truck, stop the truck!"

"Stop screaming," Drew cautioned, hoping to calm the young woman he'd been paired with. He peered anxiously in the rear view mirror and slowed to thirty-five miles an hour, dividing his attention between the spot of black fur behind them and the highway ahead.

"Holy cow," he sputtered, his deep voice suddenly higher. "How'd it get out?"

Jordan stuck her head out the window in hopes of getting a better look. Two cars swerved to miss the hapless creature and another one almost ran into the back of the now empty horse trailer. She watched in agony as more cars lined up behind them, blocking her view.

"Stop," she wailed when they rounded a curve. "We've got to go back."

"I can't stop in the middle of this traffic." Drew stepped on the gas. "Look for a place big enough for a truck and trailer to turn around in."

They drove several miles without encountering so much as a wide spot in the road. Jordan leaned forward, clutching the edge of her seat with both hands while she scanned the road ahead. Her heart was pounding and her mouth had gone dry.

"There," she cried out. "Take that driveway!"

Drew made a quick right hand turn onto a graveled driveway, driving faster than he normally would on an unpaved road. Dust and rocks flew in all directions as the truck and trailer bounced toward a ranch-style house about fifty yards off the highway. The driveway completely encircled the house, so within seconds, he and Jordan were flying back the same way they came in, gravel ricocheting off the truck's undercarriage like Rice Krispies spiked with gunpowder.

Neither one of them spoke as they sped south. Finally Jordan got her tongue around the question that was on both of their minds.

"Do you think … its dead?"

"Probably," Drew muttered. "Either dead or hurt so bad we'll have to put him down."

Jordan pinched her knees together.

"Just pray nobody ran into him," Drew added. "I've seen what can happen to a car when it hits a deer. That bull would destroy a car. He'd even put a hurt on an eighteen-wheeler."

"No shit. If he gets hit by a semi, we'll be responsible for the world's largest road kill."

Jordan nearly choked on a ripple of laughter. Almost immediately the laughter turned into sobs.

"I'm sorry, Jordan."

"Why are *you* sorry?" she blubbered. "The latch must have come undone, so it's my fault. Oh, man, I'm dead meat."

"It wasn't entirely your fault. Please don't cry."

They retraced the rest of their seemingly endless tracks without looking at one another or saying a word. Nothing along the highway seemed amiss—no traffic backed up, no rubberneckers, no flashing police lights or emergency vehicles, yet it felt as if they must be getting close to where they last saw the bull. They drove until they were certain they passed the spot where the bull fell out, then turned around and headed north again, and less than a mile from where they turned around, Jordan saw something big and black up ahead.

"Over there," she said, pointing toward the side of the road. "It's him! You're not going to believe this."

Drew switched on the trailer's hazard lights and pulled the truck and trailer onto the shoulder. Just ten feet off the highway stood two thousand pounds of shiny black bull with all four feet on the ground, calmly munching the roadside grass that tickled his belly.

"Amazing," Drew whispered, as if the sound of his voice might spook the contented, and more importantly, living, breathing bull. "I never would have guessed we'd see that big fellow alive again."

They checked the bull over, and with the exception of two skinned knees and a bruised shoulder, the animal wasn't badly hurt. Using its harness plus some of the roadside grass for bait, the two students loaded the bull for the second time. This time both Drew and Jordan checked to make sure the trailer door was locked.

When they arrived back on campus, Jordan threw her arms around Drew's thickset body and gave him a hug. The hug was an unexpressed, "Thank God the bull didn't get killed, thank God that's over and thank God I didn't lose a hundred bucks," all rolled into one spontaneous gesture. Thinking about it later, she hoped that was the message he got and not something else.

• • •

Over pizza and beer that same evening, Jordan told McKenzie the whole story. Her friend was less interested in what happened to the bull than she was in the man who was driving the truck.

"So you gave him a hug. No big deal. Do you like him?"

"Well, he seemed like a nice guy ... good looking ... not my type, though."

"What do you mean?"

Jordan shrugged her shoulders. "You know—somebody you might like to have as a friend, but not somebody you'd want to sleep with."

McKenzie grinned and bit the tip off a slice of pizza. "I don't have the vaguest idea what you're talking about."

"Come on, we all look for certain things in a guy. The other day you told me you were looking for a Paul Bunyan type. Does that mean you wouldn't go for a short guy?"

"No, short guys are fine. Remember Todd Crane, my locker partner? He was short, but that had nothing to do with the size of his …"

"Mack-en-zie!" Jordan shook her head. "Is that all you ever think about?"

"Hey—this isn't about me. I believe we were talking about why you didn't want to sleep with this new guy."

"Well, that wasn't it exactly."

"Yes it was. So, tell me. What's not to like? Good looking—you said so yourself. Great future. A lot in common. What's the problem?"

Jordan thought for a moment. "I wouldn't exactly call it a problem; it's more like a preference."

"Is this a guessing game? Is it his freckles?"

"No, freckles are okay, although he's got an awful lot of them."

"His age?"

"Well, I would prefer someone older."

"Right. Like that brute Riley who you can't seem to get over."

Jordan sighed. "Drew's just too nice, that's all. He made me uncomfortable he was so nice."

"You mean, he probably wouldn't make you his slave the way Riley did? You are a sicko, my friend."

Jordan swished a mouthful of beer around in her mouth before swallowing it. "I'm sorry, but I just can't imagine having sex with someone so sweet and polite. He'd probably do it with his clothes on."

McKenzie laughed until she snorted. This infected Jordan, and the two friends chuckled and joked about courteous sex until they were teary eyed.

"You're the best," McKenzie sighed after she stopped laughing. "You're a little out of touch sometimes, but you're the best."

Jordan blew her nose in a napkin. "It felt good to laugh like this again, McKenzie. I'm so glad you're back in my life."

CHAPTER TWENTY-ONE

One evening, when the apartment on Jackson Street was quiet and all four roommates were busy with their studies, the doorbell rang. Bailey opened the door and ushered Dusty inside. Struggling during his first term at OSU, Dusty dropped by occasionally to get help with algebra, so Jordan wasn't surprised to see him until she saw the look on his face.

"It's about Uncle Perry," he said quietly. "He tried to kill himself last night."

Jordan dropped the textbook she was reading. "Oh no, Dusty, not Uncle Perry. Is he going to be okay?"

"He's alive, but I guess he's in bad shape. We need to go home, Jordan. My girlfriend's letting me borrow her car."

During the seemingly endless drive home, Jordan and Dusty tried to figure out why their Uncle Perry would try to take his own life. He was an easy going guy who laughed at all of his friend's jokes, even the lame ones. He had a good job, and everyone liked him, even Annie. He didn't have a family, but he did have a cool golden retriever.

The following morning, they got the rest of the story. Two weeks before his suicide attempt, Perry was fired when his boss caught him pouring whisky into his thermos bottle. It seems the best body and fender man in Klamath County had been sipping spiked coffee all day every day for the twenty-odd years he was in the work force.

Jordan, Dusty, and Annie went to Merle West Hospital to visit him. Unfortunately, Perry was so heavily sedated he had no idea anyone was in the room. Cooper stayed home and drank himself into a stupor. He didn't go to the funeral, either, when Perry died three days later. Instead, he picked up the golden retriever his crazy friend had named Sonofabitch, and brought him home to become part of the Miller family.

With her primary benefactor gone, Jordan needed a part-time job. After looking for a month, and not being able to find something that she could work into her challenging schedule of labs and classes, she was about ready to apply for another loan when she ran across a help wanted ad in *The Daily Barometer*.

Fraternity cook. Experience a must. Plan menus, purchase supplies. Send resume, salary history to PO Box 28-B, 97339

Jordan landed the job, and before the week was up, she was back in the kitchen, this time responsible for the care and feeding of sixty-two young men—sixty-two hollow legged wildebeests, as she came to call them.

She was surprised to find out that Drew Murphy, her partner in the Angus bull incident, was the fraternity's House Manager. His position didn't put him in charge of discipline, which Jordan felt was sorely needed, but he did have responsibility for the budget, including the food budget, plus collecting dues and paying bills. For that he received free room and board. A pre-veterinary junior, Drew was impressed by the fact that Jordan was already in vet school.

"I wish you wouldn't tell people I'm practically a veterinarian," she protested.

He grinned. "Somebody needs to toot your horn!"

Since Jordan didn't have a car, Drew drove her to Safeway once a week to shop for groceries. They filled one shopping cart with eggs, cereal, bread, milk, peanut butter, lunchmeat, tuna fish, cheeses, chips, and so on for breakfasts and lunches. The frat boys, under the watchful eye of their House Manager, prepared those meals themselves.

Jordan cooked the evening meal, which usually included some combination of pasta, chicken, beans or hamburger, a big green salad, canned fruit, and the huge sheet cakes she learned to bake when she worked in the Snell Hall cafeteria. Drew and Jordan filled a second shopping cart with the dinner supplies. She was lucky a strong young man like Drew was willing to help her carry two carts full of food from the store to the car to the fraternity's pantry.

After Perry died, Dusty stopped by Jordan's apartment more frequently. He was a reserve linebacker on the football team, although he hadn't seen much action. He was still trying to decide on a major, but every one that sounded interesting had too many math requirements.

Jordan began looking forward to his visits. Her brother always had some wild experience to share with her or a new joke to tell.

"Hey, Jordan—did you know there's an official Oregon State lip balm?"

"No-o-o. What is it?"

"Cow shit. It's better than anything you can get in the store, because once you put it on, you stop licking your lips!"

By the beginning of spring term, Jordan had settled into a comfortable routine. She was enjoying her job at the fraternity, even though it sometimes interfered with her studies. The frat boys, who appreciated her tasty dinners, began calling her "Cookie." Drew found every possible excuse to talk to her and never seemed to run out of questions, even highly personal ones, which probably seemed innocent enough to him since he made his own life an open book. She was certain he had a crush on her. She thought he was naïve, too immature and way too willing to please to be taken seriously.

Near the end of April, Drew asked if she would help with the fraternity's spring house party where, "everyone gets blitzed, and things get a little wild. It's definitely the coolest party on campus."

The party menu she decided upon was simple: barbecued hamburgers, chili, garlic bread, chips and salsa, in ten times the normal quantities she would make for dinner. There were plenty of volunteers to man the barbecue, but they asked her to stick around while the food was being served just in case they ran out of something. From what she saw being unloading that morning, they certainly wouldn't run out of beer.

The afternoon of the Saturday night party, the frat boys moved the tables and chairs out of the dining room and flooded it with a good two inches of beer. Jordan stopped in the middle of making hamburger patties to see what the commotion was about and watched as five or six upperclassmen tested the waters. Shoeless and shirtless, most of them in shorts or cutoffs, they would run through the entry hall then slide feet first down the entire length of the slippery dining room floor. Whoever slid the farthest received the loudest cheer.

When Jordan looked in on them about a half hour later, the upperclassmen had been joined by the rest of the wildebeests, turning the beer slide into a free-for-all. Beer was being pumped nonstop out of a keg. Most of the guys drank only about half of what made it into their cups, threw the rest into the fray and filled up again. From time to time more beer was added to the floor to replenish what was soaked up by clothing or by the hardwood floor itself. Now she understood why the dining room always smelled like stale beer.

Drew saw her and waved. The patches of freckles sprinkling his broad chest and arms were a vivid contrast to his pale white torso, and like a neon rash, they glowed at her from across the room. He filled two cups with beer and hurried over to where Jordan was standing.

"Here you go," he said, shoving one of the dripping cups into her hand. Beer glistened on his bare skin, and his cargo shorts were plastered to his thighs.

Jordan pointed her cup at the near riot taking place in the dining room. "That beer thing is rather amazing. Is it legal?"

"You mean the beer slide? It's a tradition—sort of a celebration of spring. You aren't getting all serious over this, are you? Hey—are you through in the kitchen? I want to show you the rest of the party."

As Drew led her up the stairs to the second floor, Jordan heard loud music and shouts coming from one of the boy's rooms. Drew opened the door just as the people inside shouted, "fiddle!"

The small room was packed with young men and women in various stages of inebriation, each holding a cup, a can, or a bottle of some brand of beer. A country/western song was blaring out of four speakers mounted on the wall, and everyone in the room seemed to know the words. Jordan was surprised so many people at the party liked country music.

Drew read the confusion on her face. "Okay—here's how it works. It's all about the lyrics. You're supposed to take a drink of beer every time you hear the words, fiddle, devil, or bow. I think they're in the song twenty-seven times or something like that."

He grabbed two beers out of a cooler filled with ice. "They'll keep playing the song over and over all night."

The beer tasted pretty good to Jordan, and before she knew it, she was yelling the three magic words like a seasoned pro. She polished off two beers in no time.

Dinner was a mob scene with people pulling half cooked hamburger patties off the grill and stuffing them into their mouths while they were still hot. Bag after bag of chips disappeared, and more than one bean from the pork and beans went sailing through the air. The feeding frenzy ended when the band arrived, and the beery dining room planks turned into a dance floor.

Drew kept Jordan's cup filled all evening. He tried to get her to dance with him, but she told him dinner was over; it was time for her to go. She was also beginning to feel the effects of the beer, and figured she had better get going if she hoped to make it back to her apartment without getting lost.

Drew persisted. "You haven't tried the bong yet. You can't leave till you try the beer bong."

The bong turned out to be a clever device for the rapid consumption of beer. Crudely fashioned from a length of rubber tubing, a large funnel, and a metal clamp, and utilizing the principle of gravity feed, the odd looking mechanism made it possible to consume a lot of beer without even swallowing. The bong user would crimp one end of the tube with the metal clamp to close it off, and then pour at least one, usually two cans of beer into the funnel. Another person would hold the funnel high over the user's head until he indicated he was ready. When the clamp was released, the beer rushed nonstop out of the funnel, down the tube, and down the user's throat in mere seconds.

Jordan wasn't having any part of it. "It'll spill all over my face. Either that or I'll throw up."

As Drew egged her on, a small crowd gathered around her and began chanting her name. Embarrassed, Jordan started giggling. The longer she looked at the silly contraption, the harder she laughed. When she finally got her giggles under control, Drew handed her the bong and filled the funnel with beer.

"Cook-ie, Cook-ie, Cook-ie," the wildebeests chanted.

"Okay, okay," she said to her fans, "You'll be sorry."

She stood up, put the end of the tube in her mouth, closed her eyes, and released the clamp. To her surprise, the beer slid right down her throat. Before she had time to panic, let alone throw up, it was all in her stomach. This thing was amazing. Suddenly Jordan didn't want the party to end. That beer bong was way too much fun. She tried it twice more, then stopped when she began feeling woozy. She could barely walk a straight line when Drew steered her down the hall.

As soon as they were inside his brightly lit room, Drew kissed her on the lips, leading her by the hand to his unmade bed. He kept his lips on hers and his eyes closed while he fumbled with the buttons on her blouse.

Tempting warmth spread through Jordan's body when Drew started to undress her. It had been over a year since she had sex with Riley, and her body ached for a dose of those mind altering sensations, yet even through her drunken haze, a fragment of rationality told her that sex with Drew wasn't right. He was too good to her, too vulnerable, and she didn't want to complicate their friendship. Oh how she hated to stop him, though. Even if he was just a friend, he was still a man, and the weight of a man's body on hers felt good.

She moved her mouth from his lips to his ear. "No, Drew, I can't ... we can't do this."

"Yes we can," he said, breathing hard. He tried to kiss her again, and when she moved her head away, he mumbled something into the blankets.

"I mean it," she said, louder this time. "This isn't right. I ... you're my friend, Drew. You'll know what I mean in the morning."

"No I won't. You're the one, Cookie. Don't do this to me."

Jordan maneuvered the bottom half of her body out from under him, leaving Drew on his stomach with his face buried in the blankets. She sat up and sloppily buttoned her blouse. Her mouth tasted like a sewer. She tried, but couldn't think of anything comforting to say to him, so she patted the back of his close cropped head.

"Please," he begged, grabbing her hand. "Please don't go."

The following Monday she quit her job and applied for a second student loan.

CHAPTER TWENTY-TWO

Two weeks after the fraternity party, Jordan caught a glimpse of Drew in the campus bookstore, and hoping to avoid him, she slipped to the rear of the store. He caught up with her in the t-shirt section, and sporting a bashful grin, held out his hand and apologized. Too embarrassed to speak, she smiled and nodded as she grasped his hand between hers. There was a wariness in his eyes, like an animal that has been mistreated yet still longs to be loved. She wanted to give him a hug and an apology of her own. Instead, she thanked him quietly and watched with some remorse as his broad shoulders disappeared behind the stacks.

• • •

Spring is definitely in the air, Jordan decided, smiling to herself when Catherine burst into the apartment announcing a rattlesnake was one thing, but she refused to live any longer with a sex crazed rabbit. The Jackson Street roommates were supposed to keep their bedroom doors shut, however coming and going at different times of the day and night, they would sometimes forget, and Cleo would hop onto Catherine's bed and hump the daylights out of her stuffed animal collection.

This happened twice during winter term, and Jordan thought it was a hoot; in fact she and McKenzie laughed themselves silly over it one night. Lately, the rabbit's lustful behavior seemed to be occurring more frequently, and Catherine's moon face was shiny and pink when she threatened to move out if Jordan didn't get rid of her pet.

Jordan conceded, and after Catherine left for class, she picked up Cleopatra and cuddled her. "I know exactly how you feel," she whispered into the fur on top of the rabbit's head. Warm and contented, Cleo ground her back teeth together, making a purring sound.

Getting Cleopatra out of her bedroom was something of a moot effort on Catherine's part, because Jordan never planned on keeping her pet rabbit for longer than a year. It would be foolish to take a rabbit to Washington State where she would spend the next two years of her training, so she sent Cleo back to Klamath Falls.

Athena laughed out loud when she heard Cleo's story. "I won't sell your little friend," she promised. "You can visit her whenever you want."

• • •

Similar to what occurs in the medical profession, an important part of a veterinarian's training takes place in affiliated or college-sponsored animal hospitals. Veterinary students are assigned rotations at these round-the-clock hospitals that require them to put in long hours and work many days in succession, making T.G.I.F. meaningless, and vacations or holidays something the rest of the world experienced.

Since Jordan juggled part-time jobs and a heavy class load during most of her college years, she was better equipped than many of her fellow students to handle the demands of the hospital schedule; in fact she thrived on it. Although the basic curriculum afforded numerous opportunities to work with live animals, she considered the hospital experience, where she dealt with actual emergencies as opposed to planned exercises in the labs, to be truly practicing her profession.

Her preceptorships, which gave her a chance to work with established veterinarians, were similarly positive experiences, and her last three years of training flew by before she knew it, definitely before she was ready for the adventure to end.

The Veterinary School held its commencement ceremony separate from the rest of the Oregon State students. The dean of the OSU College of Veterinary Medicine spoke during the ceremony, and the president of the Oregon Veterinary Medicine Association administered the oath.

It was such a joy to see her name, *Jordan A Miller, Doctor of Veterinary Medicine,* in black and white script in the middle of her diploma. She tried to visualize it framed and hanging in her own office like the professionally framed diplomas she saw in the clinics where she worked during her preceptorships.

Nobody from Jordan's family was present for her vet school ceremony, which didn't surprise her. She figured Dusty was the one who had convinced her family to attend her undergraduate commencement, but he never made the football team and left OSU in the middle of his sophomore year. Uncle Perry was gone, Annie was working full time, Jude was living like a street urchin, and Cooper was still drinking himself into oblivion.

Jordan attended a fancy champagne dinner where she celebrated with the few graduates she became acquainted with during vet school. After that festive evening, she packed up her books and rode the big gray dog back to Klamath Falls for the last time.

She felt more of a letdown than the euphoria she expected when the long hours of study and the demanding exams were over. It was disconcerting to leave the sheltering arms of academia to face real world challenges such as getting a job, paying off her loans, and unfortunately—living at home again. With no money and no position, she had no other choice.

She hadn't been around her father much during her four years at veterinary school, and those visits were decidedly chilly, especially on her part. After Perry's suicide, Cooper waded ever deeper into the sauce. Sullen and belligerent, if he talked to Jordan at all it was to say something callous or brainless, and he constantly reeked of alcohol. Jordan wondered how her mother could stand to sleep in the same bed with him.

When he could no longer manage his addiction, Cooper lost his job. This happened about a year before Jordan received her license to practice, so he spent his days at the hiring hall, picking up whatever work be could get. In spite of his dependency, he was still a hard worker. The supervisors and foremen in town knew he would give them a full measure of work for a day's pay, though no one seemed willing to take him on full time.

While her father was working or waiting for work, Jordan could be found nearly every morning, sitting at the kitchen table, writing inquiry letters or assembling and mailing her papers. She was diligent in her research and correspondence, even though every day between 12:30 and 2:00 o'clock, the mailman brought her neatly folded pieces of hell in envelopes with her name on them.

After the mail came, and she revised her cover letter for the umpteenth time, she would walk to the county library to look through the Help Wanted section of *The Oregonian* or to use the copy machine. She stayed late, and then spent the rest of the night at home immersed in a book, almost any book. She read historical novels, thrillers, pot boilers, westerns, anything that could take her to another place and time.

Living at home again was made worse by the fact that none of her high school friends were around. Kimberly lived in Kirkland, Washington where Hunter worked for Costco. Morgan and her little family lived in Albuquerque, and McKenzie worked for the Forest Service. Stationed at Camp Sherman in Central Oregon, McKenzie was geographically the closest, but still not within walking distance the way she and her sister had been during high school.

Dusty, who worked at a plywood plant, bought himself a truck, and when he could, he drove his sister to where she needed to go. In spite of being their father's favorite, and in the opinion of his siblings, a spoiled brat when he was a child, Dusty had matured into a hard working young man with a big heart and a fondness for fun, and oh, did he love the ladies.

• • •

In May of 1996, The Colton family gathered to celebrate their fortieth annual reunion. It had been a year since Jordan received her veterinary license, so Douglas and Carson decided to give her a temporary job by putting her in charge of the branding. She accepted gladly, delighted to be back in her version of heaven—hair full of sunshine, nostrils full of dust, cowhide rubbing against her jeans, and in the company of men she could count on.

"We got us a good crop this year," Carson boasted, as he and Jordan rode behind the cows and winter-born calves they rounded up that day. "We've gone to using all Angus bulls …"

"Which produce smaller calves and a lower mortality rate," Jordan interjected.

Carson removed his hat and ran his fingers through bronze hair flecked with gray. "Can't tell you much anymore, can we?"

Jordan patted the neck of the chestnut mare she was riding. "I guess that sounded a bit smart-alecky, didn't it? I just want you and Uncle Doug to feel confident I will do a good job for you. I'm dying to prove myself and frustrated I haven't found a veterinarian who wants to hire me."

"Why not set up your own practice? Me and Doug would use you, and we could introduce you to some of the other ranchers around here."

"Oh, I couldn't do that, Uncle Carson. I'm not ready, not good enough. Plus the state requires me to work at least one year for an established veterinarian before I can even consider setting up my own practice." She sighed. "Then there's the money. It would take way more money than I have or will have for a long time to buy the equipment, lease space, hire an assistant or at least a receptionist, buy insurance, pay off my student loans, and so on and so on."

Jordan let Carson ride ahead of her. She didn't want her personal concerns to cast a shadow on such a glorious day at the ranch, so she slackened her reins and relaxed, taking pleasure in the warmth of the sun and the aroma of leather, horsehair, and crushed grass. She leaned across the saddle horn to rest her head on the horse's neck, then sat up and tightened the reins when her chestnut and the rest of the horses, sensing they were close to home, picked up the pace.

There was a good turnout for the fortieth reunion, so Jordan had plenty of willing volunteers for her branding crew. Jude came, partly because Dusty gave him a ride, but also, Jordan assumed, because he probably hadn't eaten a decent meal in weeks. Cooper didn't come, which was no surprise, since he hadn't been to a reunion in fifteen years.

Jordan and Annie were among the first to arrive that morning. Annie headed straight for the kitchen to add her secret ingredients to the pots bubbling on the stove, and Jordan made a mental note to add chopped jalapeno peppers and orange marmalade to baked beans the next time she made them.

Dusty helped the Colton men prepare the meat—a whole steer cut lengthwise into two halves. After digging a massive pit in the ground and building a fire in the bottom of it, the men carefully wrapped the two sides of beef in wet burlap. They lowered the beef onto the hot coals, then filled the hole with dirt and left the wrapped beef there for five or six hours until the meat was so moist and tender that the youngest child at the dinner table could cut it with a fork.

The elder Coltons, who were thicker in the middle than they used to be, spent the better part of the day whooping and hollering over poker or pinochle. Grandma Leona, the last of her generation, stayed at the poker table all day, refusing to give up her "lucky chair."

Athena and her family arrived late, diaper bags and portable playpen in tow. Jordan thought branding fifty-three calves that afternoon was a major accomplishment until she watched Athena juggling three children under the age of six.

"You'd think we'd have gotten the hang of it, raising rabbits and all," Athena chuckled, one child wrapped around her chubby knees, one asleep on her shoulder, and the baby nursing from a sagging breast.

Jordan looked down the V of her shirtfront at the slight curve between her own breasts—all she could round up when it came to cleavage—and thanked her lucky stars for two small blessings.

CHAPTER TWENTY-THREE

The sandy haired young woman behind the reception counter searched through some papers on her desk. "Dr. Warner had to stitch up a kid that was attacked by a coyote, um, it was a goat kid, of course." She smiled shyly as she nervously clicked her ballpoint pen. "You did say you were Jordan Miller, didn't you? 4:00 o'clock interview?"

"Yes. I'm a little early. Is there a problem?"

"Oh, no. Dr. Warner should be back any minute."

Jordan sat across from a man with a sheep dog the size of a small refrigerator and a woman with a part shepherd puppy. She felt she looked professional in the charcoal gray interview suit that had been hanging in her closet for over a year before she got this chance to wear it. She folded her hands in her lap and tried to relax, wondering if the two people across from her could hear how hard her heart was beating.

Jordan knew the town of Prineville was located somewhere in Central Oregon, because it was always lumped together with Bend and Redmond in weather reports; however she had never been to Prineville or anywhere else in Oregon's high desert country. On her way to the interview, she passed through miles of juniper trees interspersed with rocks, tumbleweeds, and sagebrush, so when she drove down a winding section of Highway 126, she was surprised to see a charming town nestled at the bottom of the hill, amply blessed with deciduous trees and older, well maintained neighborhoods. It appeared to be a smaller community than Klamath Falls, which was comforting.

The Davidson Park Veterinary Clinic was average in size with a dreary interior compared to clinics Jordan had visited in the past. Whereas most clinics were painted white or pastel and liberally decorated with pictures of animals, the walls of the Davidson Park clinic were a smoky gold color with dark walnut trim. There was a poster advertising a high protein dog food near the front door, a small aquarium against the back wall, and behind the reception-ist's desk, a cat calendar and a cuckoo clock. Except for the distinctive smell of wet dog hair, kibble, and disinfectants, someone wandering inside might not even realize it was a veterinary clinic.

A cuckoo bird sprang from its elaborately carved wooden house to an-nounce the 4:00 o'clock hour. Ten minutes later, a tall, dark haired man wear-ing blue jeans and a denim shirt strode into the room. Hands on hips, he scanned the waiting area, spending half a second looking at Jordan before turning to the receptionist.

"Is he late, Emily? Did he call?"

The receptionist gestured to the man Jordan assumed was Dr. Warner, and both of them disappeared into the back of the clinic. After a few minutes, the young woman returned and motioned for the woman with the puppy.

"Dr. Warner will be with you shortly," she said to the man with the sheep dog. She didn't say a word to Jordan about when her interview was to take place.

The cuckoo marked the half hour, then three quarters. The telephone rang and Jordan heard the receptionist make an appointment for the next morn-ing. Still no sign of Dr. Warner.

At five fifteen, the receptionist left her post and asked Jordan to follow her down a narrow hall. The sign on the door at the end of the hall read, *Kent Warner, DVM.* The office behind the sign was almost as dark as the reception area, its gloomy gold interior brightened somewhat by an unadorned window on the back wall. Several files were neatly stacked on a credenza under the window, and rows of books stood at attention in shelves along one wall.

The dark haired veterinarian in the neatly pressed denim shirt sat behind a desk too large for the room. His suntanned face showed traces of smile lines, but his eyes, blue as his shirt, were cold.

"Well," he said, thumbing through the folder on his desk, the folder Jor-dan sent in response to his ad, "it appears you are a girl." He raised his eyes and squinted at her as if checking to make sure.

The totally unexpected girl remark threw Jordan for a loop. "That's true," she said, instantly despising her insipid response.

"I thought your application was from a man. Jordan's usually a man's name." He propped his elbows on the desk and tented his fingers, tapping his two pinky fingers together like pincers while he stared at her.

Jordan shifted her weight from one foot to the other while she told him her story—how her father had a buddy named Jordan who was killed in Vietnam, and because he was certain she was going to be a boy, he gave her his buddy's name before she was even born. She went on to say that her mother and father used to talk to her when she was still in the womb. "Not that I remember, of course," she added quickly. They would ask how little Jordan was feeling, or if little Jordan liked spaghetti, or other silly things people say to their unborn children. She joked about the fact that mothers during the sixties often got carried away when it came to names, and she could have ended up with a name like Skye Blue, or Zodiac, or Moon Zappa, or something far worse than Jordan. She finished with a fragile laugh and made a mental note to stop talking so much.

"Never mind all the entertaining details. Your parents may have given you a man's name, but I need a real man for this job." He picked up her papers and organized them into a neat stack. "I'm in the middle of cattle and horses here; sheep, goats, sometimes llamas. This is not just a small-animal clinic, although I do that, too."

"But, I'm stronger than I look," Jordan argued in her own defense, realizing all of a sudden that her suit and pantyhose were a liability rather than a way to make a good first impression.

"I have my doubts," he countered.

He scrutinized the petite woman standing in front of him. He could see how off balance she was, and hoped he could get her out of his office before she started to cry.

"Where are the men, anyway? All I seem to be getting is applications from women."

Such blatant gender bias got Jordan's back up. "You know you are forbidden by law to discriminate on the basis of sex when it comes to hiring."

His expression hardened. "Don't give me that crap. I know what I need, and it's not some whiney little woman who'll call me in the middle of the night, asking me to help with some emergency she can't handle herself. I'm not looking for somebody to answer phones here. I'm looking for somebody who could become my partner someday. What does the law say about that? That you can't discriminate regarding the race, etc. etc. etc. of your business partner? I don't think so."

Jordan crawled back into herself, and tucked her hair behind her ears as she felt the hated redness creeping up her neck.

Dr. Warner put her papers back in the folder she chose so carefully when she mailed them. "I'm sorry you had to drive so far, Miss …" He looked inside the folder. "Miller."

He walked around his desk, smiling for the first time when he reached out to shake her hand. She gripped his hand as hard as she could. She *had* to get this job.

"Why don't you try me out?" she blurted. "Like you said, I drove a long way today, so why don't you let me demonstrate my capabilities?" Her heart was pounding, and she wasn't sure how much longer she could stand there wobbling in her pumps. "Give me some kind of a test. If I fail the test, I won't have anybody but myself to blame during the long ride home."

He scowled at his watch. "What kind of a test? I don't give tests."

"Let me treat a cow or a horse, so you can see how good I am with farm animals. I'm willing to do anything to show you how strong I am, and how experienced I am with commercial animals."

He arched his eyebrows. "Anything?" He weighed whether spending any more effort on this girl was worth his time. "Maybe you could … wait here while I make a call."

The call didn't take long, and when he returned he told Jordan to follow him to his truck. On their way out of town, he explained what her test was to be.

"Rocky Jamieson is a friend of mine. One of his cows is in estrus, and I promised to see it first thing tomorrow morning. Since you're asking for a test, we'll do it tonight instead. In fact, the timing would be better tonight."

He paused before glancing in Jordan's direction. "Think you can artificially inseminate Rocky's Hereford?"

Jordan nodded, a glazed expression in her eyes. She had studied the procedure and watched teaching assistants artificially inseminate cattle in animal husbandry labs. She assisted once, but had never done one solo. Her mind spun as words and diagrams leapt from the pages of her textbooks.

Artificial insemination is the deposition of spermatozoa in the female genitalia by artificial, as opposed to natural, means. It is most commonly practiced with dairy cows, and is often used by beef cattle ranchers who do not want to incur the expense of maintaining their own bulls. The procedure is somewhat more reliable than using a bull with unproven breeding efficiency and safer than breeding a heavy, mature bull to a young heifer.

She tugged at the hem of a skirt that barely covered her knees.

Rocky Jamieson, was a heavily built rancher with a florid face, who talked almost as rapidly as his stubby legs covered the short distance to the barn. He laughed and joked excitedly as he escorted the veteran veterinarian and the wannabe veterinarian out to the barn.

"Glad you could get here so soon, Kent. I noticed the heifer was in standing heat about noon. If you can make this happen tonight, we've got a real good chance it'll take."

He took a quick look at Jordan as they walked toward the barn and lowered his voice. "Who's the girl?"

"It's kind of hard to explain, Rocky. Let's call her … an intern for the time being. She's going to try to inseminate your heifer. Don't worry, I will finish the job if she isn't successful." He handed his "intern" a large bag containing the necessary equipment and said, "Okay, Miss Miller, let's see what you learned at vet school."

Inwardly, Jordan steamed over Dr. Warner's off-handed treatment of her, and vowed to impregnate that cow if it took her all night. She removed her suit jacket and laid it on a hay bale.

"I'll need something to stand on," she told Rocky, pleading with her eyes. "Not a ladder though." Rocky moved Jordan's jacket to a harness peg and dashed to the other end of the barn.

While he was gone, Jordan acquainted herself with the heifer. She ran her hand along the young Hereford's wiry, rust-colored hide and patted her rump. The heifer turned her head, then resumed munching the feed in front of her. Jordan lifted the heifer's tail to prep her, cleansing the rectum, vulva, and most of the tail while Dr. Warner stood outside the stall with his arms folded. Since she couldn't begin the insemination process until she had something to stand on, Jordan and Dr. Warner waited in silence until Rocky returned with an empty baling wire spool and a large, cast aluminum tub.

Jordan decided to use the spool. "It looks a little teetery, but the tub is too wide."

She set the spool on the floor behind the heifer, kicked off her pumps and used one panty-hosed foot to check its stability. It wasn't quite even, so she stepped down and removed the clump of manure that was making it wobble. She climbed up again, this time with both panty-hosed feet, and declared the spool stable.

Continuing the prep, Jordan scrubbed her hands and arms with disinfectant. That morning while dressing for the interview, she lamented not having a long sleeved blouse to wear with her new suit. As she rolled her short sleeve up as far as it would go, she realized anything longer would have been a real problem.

After everything had been disinfected, she transferred the thawed semen into one end of a disposable plastic insemination pipe and attached a syringe to the other end.

"How much is in here?" she asked Dr. Warner.

"Enough. I've got a spare unit if you need it."

"Over my dead body," she muttered to herself, and to better the odds for a successful pregnancy, she made sure every drop of the semen made it into the insemination pipe.

Dr. Warner hadn't brought a disposable glove for Jordan to use during the procedure, so she lubricated her right arm up to the armpit, then applied more lubricant to the inside of the heifer's vagina. Holding tight to the insemination pipe, she lifted the heifer's tail and carefully inserted the pipe followed by her entire arm.

Stay toward the spine. Find the cervix.

Unaccustomed to such an invasive procedure, the heifer swished her tail out of Jordan's left hand. Jordan grabbed the tail again and forced it to one side while she continued probing with her right hand. After locating the external opening of the cervix, she carefully manipulated the pipe through the cervical canal. To be successful, she had to deposit the sperm at the intersection of the cervix and the uterus, but she was running out of arm.

She pressed the right side of her face against the heifer's rump, gritted her teeth and stretched her arm and fingers another inch.

"I'm almost finished," she said out of the side of her mouth. With her face firmly pressed against the heifer's backside, she slowly expelled the contents of the insemination pipe, holding her breath until she was sure the pipe was empty.

"Not bad," Dr. Warner noted after Jordan withdrew her sticky arm.

"Think you got it?" Rocky asked.

"I'm positive," Jordan said, with far more confidence than she felt.

She knew it would be 50 to 60 days before the heifer came into heat again if she hadn't done it right. Hopefully, by that time, she would have made herself indispensible to the Davidson Park Veterinary Clinic.

"Where can I wash up?" she asked Rocky. She turned to Dr. Warner. "And when would you like me to start?"

"Not so fast," he protested. "I'm still not sure you're the person I need."

"But you promised ..."

"I didn't promise a thing. How do I know the insemination took, and besides, the test was your idea, not mine."

"Let's stop by the house," Rocky said, smiling affably. "You can clean up there." He took Jordan's jacket off the harness peg and draped it over his arm. "Would you like a drink? Kent and I usually have a scotch whenever he gets out this way. You like scotch?"

To say she could use a drink at this point was an understatement, even though she wasn't sure what scotch tasted like.

"I'll have whatever you're having."

As she followed the two men toward the rambling ranch house, Jordan struggled with exhaustion, feelings of hostility, and the sickening thought she might have wasted her entire education. She wanted more than anything to end this strong woman performance and climb into a hot bath with a good book. The bath would have to wait, though, because the job interview from hell wasn't over. She would show Dr. Warner that not only could she do a man's job, she could drink like a man, too. She wasn't about to leave Prineville empty handed.

CHAPTER TWENTY-FOUR

The small fishing boat Dusty borrowed for the day putted along the west end of Klamath Lake. It was close to freezing that early October morning, colder than the tepid water lapping against the sides of the boat. The disparity in temperature created a cool mist that hovered over the lake's shallow edges and clung to the three men in the boat like a wet shroud.

Inside a stand of dried up tules, a flock of mud swallows scolded their early morning intruders. Awakened by the sound of the boat's motor, the chattering birds fluttered about in consternation, their quick bursts of flight rustling the dry bull rushes and cattails and disrupting an otherwise peaceful arrival of dawn.

The boat was full to overflowing with three passengers, one dog, fishing gear, bait, lunch, and a cooler full of beer. Dusty wasn't fully awake, but neither was his father or Jude. Only Sonofabitch seemed unfazed by the early hour as he leaned his chest into the bow of the boat and sniffed the cool air.

Jude sat on one of the benches, hugging his knees and making like a turtle with the collar of his windbreaker. His cap nearly covered his ears, and the only time he moved was to drag the sleeve of his jacket across his runny nose.

Dusty congratulated himself for the masterful job he did getting his father and brother together for the day. "Free beer and a stringer of eighteen-inch rainbows," he told Jude. "Can't beat that combination. You can eat for three days off what you'll catch, so you're nuts if you don't come."

Cooper, who hadn't been fishing since Perry died, jumped at the chance to be with his boys. "You bring the lunch," he told his youngest child, "and I'll buy the beer."

Dusty remembered thinking his father hadn't looked good the last time he saw him. This morning, sitting with his shoulders hunched against the cold and sporting a two-day stubble, he looked like an old man. Maybe he had a hangover, or maybe he was just tired, but he was quieter than usual when he took his customary place at the rear of the boat, and just before he pulled the cord on the outboard motor, he'd popped a handful of pills into his mouth.

As they headed toward deeper water, and the fog began to lift, Dusty stopped worrying. The drone of the motor and the sound of water swishing against the side of the boat were making his heart sing. He had been thinking about a fishing trip all summer, and though it was late in the season, his timing might turn out to be perfect. Even the oldest and wisest trout became less cautious when winter was approaching and the supply of insects began to wane.

As the morning sun began making its daily climb over the surrounding hills, a tern swooped overhead, folded its wings, and dived into the water without making a splash. It emerged after several seconds with a small fish in its beak.

"Good omen," Dusty hollered to the others.

Jude looked up, then buried his neck in his collar again. Cooper yawned and stretched and told a joke about a fishing contest between Saint Peter and a kingfisher. His joke fell short, so he sat his cigarettes on the seat beside him and told Jude to help himself. Jude grabbed one and smoked it greedily.

By the time they reached their favorite fishing spot, the fog had burned off and a light breeze chopped the water, so Cooper turned off the Evinrude and lowered the anchor. When Dusty asked if it was Miller time, his father gave him a thumbs up. He handed each son a can of beer, then cracked one for himself. The three of them sucked on their beers while they rigged and baited their lines.

Jude crimped an extra sinker onto his line. "What do you hear from Jordan?" he asked his brother.

"She got a job. In Prineville. Couple weeks ago." Dusty searched through the carton of night crawlers for the feistiest squirmer and threaded it onto his hook.

Jude blew on his hands to warm them, then took another swipe at his runny nose. "Wonder how much she makes. Maybe she'd spot me fifty bucks or so."

Dusty shrugged.

The three men decided to try still fishing first. If they didn't catch any fish that way, they would change tackle and head for another part of the lake to troll for a while.

Sonofabitch turned restless as soon as they stopped, so Dusty made him lie down in the bottom of the boat. The golden retriever gave his best abused dog look, and then fell asleep with his muzzle on his forepaws.

During the first hour, they had two nibbles, but no fish. Jude pulled a sandwich out of the lunch bag, and started to eat it.

"Hey, jerk wad," Dusty snipped. "It's too early for lunch."

"Tough tittie," Jude said between bites. "There wasn't time for no breakfast. Besides, I need something to soak up this beer."

"When was that ever a problem? Just hang it over the side—the way we used to when we was kids." Dusty chuckled as he stood up, unzipped his fly, and proudly arched a stream of urine into the water.

"Can't do that anymore," Jude said with his mouth full.

"Sure you can. Remember how Dad used to hold those pissing contests? Man, you'd pee so hard your face would turn red."

"Yeah, but that's when we was kids. I don't feel like waving my dick around in broad daylight."

"Afraid a fish might think it's a worm?"

"Ga-a-a-a!" Jude took a swipe at his brother but missed. Dusty clamped his lips together to keep from busting out laughing, and batted Jude's cap into the lake. He leaned over the side of the boat to grab the cap before it sank, and handed it back to his brother soaking wet.

"I'm sorry, bro. You know I love ya."

"Yeah, and you're full of baloney, too. Maybe that explains why you have to pee all the time. Baloney's mostly water, you know."

Jude slapped his brother on the back and laughed out loud. Dusty laughed, too, and Cooper chuckled and wheezed until he was out of breath.

Jude grinned and put his cap back on, ignoring the water that trickled down his cheeks.

Dusty couldn't have been more pleased with how well the day was going, fish or no fish. He and his dad and brother celebrated blue skies and Sundays with another round of beers while they changed tackle. Jude traded places with his father and eased the boat into trolling speed.

Cooper's pole arched and the tip began to jerk. "Fish on!" he yelled as he braced himself for the pull of the fish as it fought the sting of the hook. "Feel's like a big one!"

"I've got one on, too," Dusty shouted, quickly reeling in his line to keep it from going slack. "I hope we're not tangled, Dad. Those strikes came awful close together."

"Shit!" Jude groused. "I knew this was gonna happen."

"It's still early, Son, so stop your belly-achin'. Cut the engine 'til we get these fish in the boat."

Dusty and Cooper both landed their fish, and over the next half hour pulled in four more nice trout ranging from sixteen to twenty inches in length. After Dusty slipped his third fish on the stringer, he took over motor duty to give Jude a chance to focus on fishing.

"Son-of-a-bitch!" Jude cursed, when another half hour passed without so much as a nibble.

Sonofabitch raised his head, looked around expectantly and thumped his tail a few times. When nobody paid any attention to him, he laid his muzzle back down on his paws.

"Don't worry, Jude," Dusty said, patting his brother on the shoulder. "We'll split the catch."

Jude flipped him the bird.

Two hours later, when it appeared the fish had stopped biting in that part of the lake, Cooper suggested they try Rocky Point. With a buzz and a whirr, the three fishermen began reeling in their lines.

"I must've hooked some weeds," Jude said, feeling a slight tug on his line as he reeled it in. "Wonder how long I been draggin' them things around?" When his line reached the boat, there weren't any weeds on the hook, just a trout, six or seven inches long. Jude lifted the lifeless fish out of the water without the aid of a net, and the three men watched it swing back and forth on the end of the line.

"Too small. Can't keep it."

Jude frowned at his brother. "I know that, butthead!" He squinted at the fish on his line. "Don't matter, anyways. He's a goner."

"Let me take a look," Cooper said.

He stumbled across two bench seats and accidentally kicked Sonofabitch when he sat down next to Jude. He twice grabbed for and missed the dangling fish, then caught and held the line.

"The hook barely caught its lip," he said, pointing at the fish's mouth. He gently removed the hook, and lowered the fish into the water where he cradled it within his cupped hands. He rocked the small trout back and forth a few times to pass water through its gills, and after less than a minute, the fish began to wiggle. When Cooper separated his hands, the fish rolled over, exposing its pale underbelly, then worked its fins to right itself.

"See, it's okay."

The fish swam erratically for a few seconds, then flipped its tail and swam under the boat. When its black-spotted back emerged on the other side, it looked as if the fish was going to make it.

Suddenly a shadow darkened the boat, and the three fishermen watched in amazement as an American white pelican swooped down and plucked the ill-fated fish out of the water. The huge bird, with a wingspan of eight feet or more, barely rippled the surface as it scooped up the trout with its pouch-like beak.

"Holy shit!" Dusty exclaimed.

Jude's face was white with astonishment. "I could have touched that thing it was so close."

"Too bad they taste like mud," Cooper remarked.

The pelican prepared for flight by tucking its head back into its shoulders and resting its large beak on its chest, beating the air slowly, but powerfully, to gain altitude. There being no wind to speak of, the only sound was the flapping of the bird's wings, as the graceful giant flew off with its prize. The three fishermen gazed at the pelican until it became a white speck against the distant humpback hills.

Nobody felt much like fishing after that, but there was still half a cooler of beer left, and they couldn't let that go to waste, so they let the boat drift as they joked and hooted and lied about the size of their fish and the size of their peckers. It was a wonder they were able to coordinate their efforts well enough to load the boat onto the trailer when the day's adventure came to a close.

Dusty was grinning like a jack-o-lantern when he drove his fishing buddies back to town. He had just spent a whole day on the water with his dad and his brother, caught the biggest and the most fish, put away the most beer, and here he was, tooling down the highway in his own truck, towing his own boat … well, nobody would know the boat didn't belong to him.

He lowered his window to breathe in the crisp evening air. The air always smelled sweet after he'd had a few beers. He toyed with the idea of going to McDonald's after he took the others home; pull his boat through the drive thru and watch the girls' eyes bug out.

Suddenly a deer darted across the road. It stopped on the shoulder, temporarily mesmerized by the headlights, and then ran directly into the path of the pickup. Dusty cranked the steering wheel hard to the left and missed the deer, but the extra weight of the boat and trailer caused his light truck to fishtail back and forth across the highway. When he slammed on his brakes, the truck and the boat skidded for a hundred feet before flipping upside down in the ditch.

Dusty, who wasn't wearing a seat belt, was thrown from the truck and crushed by the boat when it landed on top of him. His father, brother, and Sonofabitch escaped with minor injuries. The coroner's report listed Dusty's blood alcohol level as .11.

CHAPTER TWENTY-FIVE

Pale and twitchy, Jude joined the rest of the pallbearers sitting in the front row. Jordan placed a spray of yellow roses on the foot of Dusty's coffin before sitting next to her mother.

Dusty looked painfully lifelike in his unadorned coffin—better in death than the rest of the family looked in life that afternoon. Annie's swollen eyes were hidden behind sun glasses. Cooper, wearing an ill fitting tweed sport coat, was unshaven and thinner than the last time Jordan saw him. Slumped in his chair, staring at his hands, his jawbone was moving back and forth just below the temple. Even though Annie sat between them, Jordan could still smell the stink of alcohol on him.

Not being churchgoers, the Miller family entrusted the final arrangements for their son and brother to a funeral director they met for the first time the day before the funeral. For Dusty's farewell, the effusive gentleman with thinning hair pulled a few sugary words out of a can and gave a wooden recitation of the Twenty-Third Psalm. There was no spirit or hope expressed in Dusty's eulogy, no references to his personality or character, just the most basic details of his short life read off the back of an envelope by a person who didn't even know him.

After the funeral, Dora, who moved into subsidized housing after her husband skipped town, invited everyone over to her tiny apartment. Her sons, Joseph and Angel, who never lost touch with Dusty, were two of the pallbearers. Joseph lived with his mother and worked at a pizza parlor on Washburn Way. Angel was an apprentice bricklayer in Chico, California.

All three of Jordan's high school friends gathered at Dora's apartment after the funeral. McKenzie had driven down the night before from Camp Sherman. Kimberly flew Horizon Air from Seattle and Morgan happened to be in Klamath Falls visiting her parents when the accident occurred. She was the one who told her sister and Kimberly about Dusty's accident.

"What a shitty reason to get together," Jordan said when Kimberly called to tell her she was coming. "Do you realize I haven't seen you since your wedding? Does it take something like this to bring us back together?"

The first few minutes after the funeral were tough, when she hugged each one and choked out a "thanks for coming," and the four friends stood around making small talk. When they met up again at Dora's place, the tension eased in the sociability provided by food and chatter and the relief that sets in when a funeral is over. Finding it impossible to hear over the babble inside the crowded apartment, the four young women pulled their chairs into the hallway.

"Much better," Morgan said as she reached inside her purse and pulled out a fistful of baby pictures. "There was barely room to breathe in there."

Kimberly took a sip of punch out of a paper cup. "I wish we were here for a baby shower or a wedding."

"Yeah, like mine," McKenzie said. She took a bite of brownie. "So, tell us about your new job, Jordan. It took you long enough."

"You don't know the half of it. It took me a year to even get an interview, and then, well, you won't believe what I had to do to get the job."

McKenzie leaned closer. "I didn't know there was a casting couch in veterinary land. Did you have to screw somebody?"

Kimberly shrieked, and Morgan covered her face with her hands, knocking her glasses askew.

Jordan blushed and bit back a smile. "Sh-h-h! They'll hear us in there."

Kimberly fanned herself with a paper plate. "You never change, do you, McKenzie. You might even be getting worse."

"If that's possible," Morgan added.

McKenzie grinned and leaned back in her chair.

"Listen, my friends, screwing my new boss wouldn't have been all that bad. He's drop dead gorgeous."

McKenzie's eyes brightened. "Aha, the plot thickens."

Jordan shook her head. "It's nothing you'll ever find in any romance novel. Let me finish."

"Please do," Kimberly said, mouthing "shut up" to McKenzie.

"I had to artificially inseminate a cow!"

Jordan's three friends looked at her with blank expressions on their faces.

"Isn't that what veterinarians are supposed to do?" Kimberly asked.

"Well, yes, but you guys don't understand the whole picture, and how badly I wanted that job, and how I was wearing a brand new suit and heels, for Pete sake. Plus, it was my first artificial insemination. To do one of those, you have to shove your arm into the cow's vagina all the way up to the uterus. Besides that, the man interviewing me, who's my boss now, didn't really want to give me the job in the first place, because I was a woman and too small, so he was using the insemination to see if I could handle farm animals. He didn't believe I could do it. I did, though, and I think he still wishes he hadn't let me talk him into it."

Morgan touched Jordan's arm. "How did it feel in there?"

"Warm and goopy—all the way up to my armpit."

Morgan looked at her sister and made a face.

"How long have you been working for this guy?" asked Kimberly.

"Six weeks."

McKenzie gave her friend and ex-roommate a disapproving look. "And he's still giving you a hard time?"

Jordan nodded.

"Like, how?" Morgan asked.

"Well, he's keeping me guessing, that's for sure. One day he sends me halfway across the county to deal with one of his crankiest clients, then he'll change tactics for a few days and assign me brainless jobs like giving distemper shots, or doing paperwork, or cleaning up around the clinic. And he's such a perfectionist. I can't do anything without him correcting me on the smallest detail. I think he's trying to break my spirit, and some days it works."

McKenzie stood up and began massaging Jordan's shoulders. "So, when are you going to get your poop in a group, farm girl?"

"I ... Where do you come up with this stuff, McKenzie?" Jordan asked, somewhat annoyed. "Well, I'm not quitting, if that's what you're intimating. At this point, I'm not even sure if I want to work for that man, but I can't let him win, either. It took me too long to get hired."

"Be careful," Kimberly cautioned. "If you don't win, he could give you a rotten recommendation."

Jordan lowered her head and let McKenzie's kneading fingers do their magic. "Yeah, I've already considered that."

The door to Dora's apartment opened suddenly and Jordan's parents stepped into the hallway. Cooper nodded to the four young women, and head lowered, walked toward the stairs leading to the ground floor.

Annie hugged her daughter's friends, graciously accepting their condolences, and a lump formed in Jordan's throat as she listened to her their kind words. When Annie left, the hallway became uncomfortably quiet except for the squeaking of the steps as she and Cooper walked down to the main level.

"I'm not surprised they left early," Jordan said as soon as she felt certain her parents were gone. "It was probably Daddy's idea, since Dora didn't have any booze." Her friends exchanged knowing looks. "I guess it would be in bad taste, though, to serve liquor after a funeral like this one."

In spite of her own somber observation, talking about liquor all of a sudden made Jordan want something stronger than punch. The folding chairs were uncomfortable, and the people inside the apartment would have to walk around their little group on the way out, so Jordan suggested they find a place where they could have a drink and some privacy. Her friends jumped at the suggestion and the four of them spent the rest of the evening at a table in the Wi-ne-ma Hotel. Morgan passed around pictures of her two children. Kimberly complained about the rain and the horrific traffic jams in Seattle, and McKenzie shared some of her crazy experiences as a rookie forest ranger—adventures wild as wild fire when McKenzie was the one doing the telling.

Jordan drank scotch and soda, then Bailey's on the rocks, nodding from time to time as she tried to follow the drift of the conversation. She kept thinking about the cemetery and Dusty's coffin waiting to be lowered into a hole in the ground. Inwardly she raged over her father's dispassionate response to the death of his youngest child. He was responsible for it, wasn't he? He furnished the beer that day, and a lot of it, according to Jude.

At a quarter past midnight, Jordan got up to leave. "I'm wiped," she told her friends. "You guys can close the place down if you want, but I need some sleep."

"Are you okay to drive?" asked Kimberly.

"I'm fine. I'm fine."

Her eyes burned and she tripped over a crack in the sidewalk while walking to her Jeep. She needed a good night's sleep if she was going to drive back to Prineville the next day.

For once she was glad the porch light was still on, because without it she wouldn't have been able to find the key hole. She opened the door quietly, a wasted effort, since her father was still up, smoking a cigarette and watching TV in his t-shirt and boxers.

His eternal presence in that same spot on the couch all of a sudden infuriated her. Just once couldn't he be in bed when she got home? Just once couldn't he be sitting in the green chair reading a magazine or a book or cleaning his nails or doing anything besides waiting for her to come home and watching TV? Couldn't he say something pleasant instead of leering at her with that smirk on his face?

"Stop looking at me that way," she mumbled as she closed the door. "I hate it when you look at me that way. My conscience is clear, which is more than you can say."

Cooper started to protest, but springing like a released coil, Jordan came undone.

"You are such a rotten excuse for a father. You have no right to pass judgment on me or anybody for anything. You killed Dusty, last Sunday. You killed him, and you don't even act like you're sorry."

Jordan felt her mouth go dry, and though she was crying on the inside, she felt energized by her own spiteful words.

Cooper's face reddened and his dark eyes narrowed into slits. He lunged at her with his hands clenched as if to choke her. She knocked his legs out from under him with a move she learned handling frisky calves. His legs were a lot longer than a calf's, so she was surprised he fell so easily.

She looked around for something to throw at him before he got up, and when she couldn't find anything, she kicked him in the ribs. He grabbed her by the ankle, but she managed to escape, screeching and crying at the same time.

Sonofabitch started barking. Thinking this must be some sort of a game, he ran across the room and grabbed the hem of Jordan's skirt in his mouth. When Jordan yanked her skirt away, the dog jumped on Cooper, nudging him with his snout and nipping the sleeve of his t-shirt.

"Git!" Cooper snapped, pushing the dog away.

He rubbed his ribs where Jordan kicked him and slowly rose to his knees. Jordan took a boxer's stance and shook her fisted hands at him, bouncing like a fighter in a ring, daring him to stand up and resume the fight.

Just try me, and I'll smack you so hard.

The barking and yelling woke Annie, who hurried into the living room clutching her robe to her chest. She watched in bewilderment, as her daughter bounced around her husband, who was still on his knees.

"What in the world is going on?" she cried. "Have you two forgotten what day this is? Are you both so drunk you can't show Dusty some respect?"

She began swinging her robe at both combatants, whacking them over and over as if trying to smother a fire.

Sonofabitch didn't like this new game, so he tucked his tail between his legs and retreated to a corner where he laid his muzzle on his forepaws and looked up through bottomless eyes at the crazy humans who were waving things around and yelling at each other.

"Tell your daughter to go back where she came from," Cooper growled, pointing at Jordan and stabbing the air with his finger. "She's turned into some kind of a hell cat, I'm tellin' you."

He struggled to his feet, rubbing the spot where Jordan kicked him. "The sooner she's gone, the better I'm gonna feel." He picked up Annie's robe and draped it over his knees while he slowly sat down on the couch. He coughed once and smoothed his hair before reaching for his cigarettes.

"That's fine with me," Jordan said, suddenly drained of energy. "For your information, I'm leaving in the morning and never coming back."

As she left the room and headed for bed, she stumbled over her own feet. When she turned to her mother for a good night hug, Annie brushed her aside.

"Go to bed," Annie said. "You're no saint."

CHAPTER TWENTY-SIX

Six months after vowing she would never come back, Jordan drove from Prineville to Klamath Falls in what *The Herald and News* called "the worst blizzard to hit central and southern Oregon since the 40's and the worst ever in March." She hadn't been home more than ten minutes, just beginning to warm up, when Annie hit her with the double whammy—Cooper had terminal cancer and wanted her to euthanize him.

Weary from the long drive, and stunned by the news, Jordan experienced a surge of conflicting emotions that night when she looked into her father's sleeping face. The next morning, however, when she tried to convince him euthanasia was wrong and assisted suicide was a better option, their first conversation since Dusty's funeral turned into a nasty verbal sparring match.

The day after the storm, while Jordan drove north, fuming over her father's treatment of her and seriously thinking about honoring his shocking request, she ran into less snow when she approached Bend and even less in Prineville. Reaching her apartment late in the afternoon, she went to bed and slept for thirteen hours.

When she arrived at work the following Monday, Harry, the clinic's permanent resident, bumped against her legs and nagged at her with his squeaky tenor meow until she picked him up. He was always hungry for affection after spending the weekend alone, so she ruffled the cat's long black hair and nuzzled his head under her chin before putting him down.

"How's it going?" Emily asked as she followed Jordan into the storage room where the coffee pot was located.

"Could be better. I found out my father has terminal bone cancer. I may seem a little out of it today, so please bear with me."

Emily's eyes widened. She started to say something and stopped when Dr.

CHAPTER TWENTY-SIX

Warner walked in.

Always distant first thing in the morning, the veterinarian nodded at the two women and poured himself a cup of coffee. He spilled a few drops and immediately wiped them up. Impressed by the fact he didn't leave the spill for her or Emily to take care of, Jordan wondered if he did his own ironing. The legs of his jeans had perfect creases down the front.

"Stick around," he said to her. "There's an elkhound on the way with a face full of porcupine quills. If you need my help, I'll be here about half an hour before I head for Jamieson's."

Jordan pulled her lab coat off its hook. "I'm sure I can manage."

Within minutes, the quiet morning was interrupted by a staccato of yelps and the sound of frantic toenails scraping on tile. Hurrying out front, she saw a highly agitated Norwegian elkhound, pawing at the huge beard of quills embedded in his muzzle and down the front of his chest. He had rubbed his hair off in several places, and several quills were stuck through his tongue, causing him to drool profusely.

The dog needed to be tranquilized right away. The more it struggled, the more the surrounding muscles would contract around the quills, embedding their hook-like barbs deeper into the animal's flesh. If untreated, the quills in his chest could eventually work their way into the dog's internal organs.

Juno weighed close to seventy pounds, and Jordan was having trouble keeping him on the examination table, so she reluctantly asked her boss to hold the dog down while she administered the tranquilizer. After Juno was subdued, she went to retrieve her forceps and bumped into Dr. Warner as he was leaving the examination room.

She crossed her arms over her chest to give him room to pass, and told him she was sorry. Cupping her by the elbows, he lifted her off the floor and out of his way.

"No problem," he said, an amused expression on his face when he put her down. "You don't weigh much more than that dog."

After thanking Dr. Warner for his help and closing the examination room door, she rested her forehead against the cool doorframe for a second. Had her boss just flirted with her, or was he simply making some kind of a statement about her size?

One by one, Jordan clipped and extracted the hundreds of quills buried in Juno's face and thickly furred chest. When finished, she applied antiseptic to the puncture wounds, then wrapped the quills in a paper towel. Clients usually asked for the quills so they could show them to their friends.

After a subdued Juno left the clinic, Jordan checked the day's schedule. She was pleased to see a full slate of appointments and relieved Dr. Warner wouldn't be there looking over her shoulder, although he was a better mentor than she originally thought he would be.

At 9:00 she treated a litter of seven Sheltie puppies, a squirming mass of brown and white fluff needing their 6-week vaccinations.

Her next appointment was with Mrs. Taylor's Russian blue. The gray cat with green eyes had to be immunized against bordatella, more commonly referred to as kennel cough, so The Kitty Korner would allow it to board there while Mrs. Taylor went on vacation.

She anaesthetized another cat, a Maine coon, in order to clean its teeth. The cat's human companion thought the procedure was to prevent tooth decay and was surprised when Jordan told him the plaque on a cat's teeth harbors a potent strain of bacteria that could eventually lead to kidney failure if not removed.

After the two cats, she treated a German shepherd with diarrhea, a beagle with an infected toenail, a mutt with lumps in its groin that Jordan feared was lymphoma, and so it went throughout the day.

At 4:30, she had a walk-in. Two young brothers had ridden their bikes to the clinic with their sixteen-month-old hamster. The older brother, who looked to be about ten, explained how their pet hadn't been eating lately, that it slept most of the time and didn't use its wheel anymore.

The hamster was in a shoebox with a dozen or more holes punched in the lid. Unfortunately, after Jordan removed the lid, she discovered the hamster was dead, still slightly warm, but no heartbeat. When she told the boys there was no sign of life, their eyes grew round and their faces puckered up as they looked first at the motionless hamster, then at one another. When the younger boy saw a tear roll down the older boy's cheek, he grabbed onto his brother's arm and wailed.

Jordan did her best to console the youngsters, telling them it was just a co-incidence that their hamster died on the way to the clinic. She complimented the boys on the good job they did making a carry box, and explained how lucky they were their pet lived to be a ripe old age in hamster years.

They listened intently while she talked about rodents as pets, telling them the average lifespan for a hamster was usually ten to twelve months. When she asked them what they wanted her to do with their pet's carcass, they had a short conference and decided to take it back home with them.

"We'll make him a new box," the older brother said, "A nicer box, one without holes in it. Then we'll bury him in the back yard. That's where Dad buried our cat."

It was after 6:00 when Jordan treated the last animal, a nanny goat she examined outside in the parking lot in the back of a pickup. A piece of cheat-grass was lodged in one of the goat's eyes. After carefully removing the spiky barb, Jordan squeezed some Terramycin into the animal's eye, and sent the rest of the tube home with the goat's owner.

Finished for the day, she checked the animals in sick bay before locking up for the night. When she walked by Dr. Warner's office, she saw he had returned and was sitting at his desk reading a newspaper. She turned to leave just as he looked up and saw her.

"How did the afternoon go?" he asked. "Whose goat was that?"

Jordan stood in the doorway, hoping he didn't think she'd been snoop-ing.

"It was Mrs. Vaughn. She said you used to take care of her sheep before she sold them and started raising goats. Evidently she likes to bring her animals into town when they need a vet. She says it saves you the trip."

"I remember her. Mousy little woman."

"How did things go for you at Rocky's? How's my new heifer?" Jordan's artificially inseminated heifer recently gave birth to her own heifer calf.

"I didn't see her. I'm sure she's fine. Rocky didn't have time for a scotch, though, so I came back here." He looked up from his paper. "Feel like a drink?"

Jordan nodded, wondering if he was getting ready to fire her or just being social.

The doctor spread his copy of *The Central Oregonian* across his desk and took a bottle of scotch and some paper cups out of a drawer. He filled both cups half full. "Sorry, no ice."

He pointed to the only empty chair in the room and told Jordan to have a seat. Jordan hesitated, then picked up the cup sitting on his desk and drank from it. The mellow liquid warmed her throat all the way down to her stomach where it landed with a thud.

"Cat got your tongue?" He smirked and leaned back in his chair. The smile lines marking the outside edges of his eyes, crinkled across his temples and disappeared into his hairline.

Jordan sighed. "I'm just tired. It's been a long day, and I didn't have time for lunch. You wouldn't have any crackers around, would you?"

"I've got something better."

He tossed a Costco-sized bag of unshelled peanuts on his desk and told her to help herself. The two of them started cracking and eating peanuts until a pile of shells covered the newspaper.

"What's in the news?" Jordan asked, trying to make conversation.

"Another article on those dogs they impounded for chasing livestock. Have you been reading about that situation down in Bend? A beagle and a golden retriever pup got picked up for chasing sheep. According to state law, they have to be destroyed."

"I haven't read about it. As you know, I come from a ranching family, so I see it as a tough call. The rancher's sheep or cattle could panic and run into a fence or over a cliff, or even die of fright. The state can't allow that to happen to a person's livelihood."

"These dogs weren't hardened sheep chasers." He poked his finger at a picture of two dogs huddled together in a cage, their noses pressed against the wire. "They were just out for a lark. It was their first offense, according to *The Bulletin*."

Jordan giggled. "First offense sounds so silly, as if sheep chasers are handcuffed and taken down to the station to be fingerprinted … make that pawprinted."

They both laughed. Their fingers accidentally touched while reaching for the same peanut, and Jordan jerked her hand back. She let her boss have the peanut in contention and selected another one.

"The county has given them a stay of execution, you know," Dr. Warner continued. "I guess technically that puts them on death row. Do you realize how many letters and phone calls Deschutes County has received since this news hit the papers?"

"Quite a few, I suppose."

"Over 500—far more than most murderers who get the death sentence. I guess humans behind bars aren't as appealing as two small dogs in a cage."

"I still say we can't afford to let our emotions rule, Dr. Warner. You know the press will take the side of the underdog, so to speak." She giggled and reached for another peanut.

"It appears we're on opposite sides of this issue, Jordan. Would you like to bet on what happens to those two little criminals?"

Jordan didn't think the doctor was serious, so she discretely declined the wager. The mood seemed to have changed all of a sudden, making her feel small again, so she drank the rest of her scotch and stood up to leave.

"I really should go, Dr. Warner. Thanks for the drink. Peanuts, too."

He got out of his chair. "I wish you'd drop the Dr. Warner, Jordan." He wrapped the newspaper around the peanut shells. "Just call me Kent from now on. Emily calls me Kent if you haven't noticed."

"Okay," she said, trying not to smile too broadly. "I can do that. Starting tomorrow."

As she backed out of the office, she felt an overwhelming urge to curtsey, and though she planned to make a graceful exit, she backed into the door jam.

"Oops—gotta go!" she chirped, and dashed down the hall before he could see her reddening face.

As she climbed into her Jeep, she realized she hadn't thought about her father all day, in fact the argument they'd had two days before seemed like ancient history. She still had to decide what to do or not do for him, but there definitely were more pleasant things to think about. It had been a crazy, thoroughly delightful Monday—a day of porcupine quills, peanuts, cats in crisis, dogs on death row—and she couldn't wait to get back to her own apartment where she could practice saying "Kent" until it sounded halfway natural.

CHAPTER TWENTY-SEVEN

Winter in eastern Oregon seems to hang on forever, spoiling plans to go camping or freezing the lilacs. In the western half of the state, spring arrives in an explosion of pastels; whereas east of the Cascades, crusty splats of leftover snow and moisture-blackened patches of dirt still cover the countryside like a black and white Holstein cowhide.

Coop won't miss these long winters, Annie told herself, as she walked into the living room to check on him.

It was too early to turn on a lamp, but the light from a lamp would chase away the dusk that veiled the scuffs and stains on her well worn furniture and slowly transformed her shabby little house into a sanctuary of shadows. This was her quiet time, when most of her work was done and she could sit for a few minutes.

Today was her day off, so she had shopped for food, bought ten dollars worth of gas, which had to last till the end of the month, picked up a prescription, paid the electric bill, and with a new skill she learned over the last few months, changed the sheets on her husband's bed without waking him. Dinner was in the oven and the laundry was done—folded, ironed and put away.

Her husband of twenty-six years was sleeping a few feet away, breathing heavily but breathing on his own. This had been one of his good days, not so much coughing and none of those terror filled moments when he woke up wide eyed and fighting for air, barely able to muster the breath to call out her name.

She tiptoed to the side of his bed and stood there watching him sleep. He seemed to sense her presence, smiling the same shy smile that seduced her at seventeen. She pushed his gray-streaked hair back from his forehead and searched his face for some indication as to how he felt.

The fading light softened his facial features, masked the angularity and dark hollows and made his skin look almost feminine, thin and delicate as chiffon. She slid the back of her hand along his cheek to check for stubble. She shaved him every other day and looked forward to the silky feel of his freshly shaven skin and the gratitude she saw in his eyes.

She remembered when this twig of a man was whole and hard bodied, so handsome she couldn't look him in the eyes without blushing. His hair was jet black when they first met, his skin tanned and healthy with the hot blood of a teenager pulsing just below the surface. He was a forceful young man with way too much attitude, but at some point early in their relationship, he cast a spell on her she was never able to break, not even during the worst of his drinking bouts or a lifetime of scrimping to pay the bills.

During these quiet afternoons, questions that have nagged her for years came out of their hiding places, unanswered questions that pestered her thoughts like head lice.

Why did the man I married give so much of himself to his job and his friends, and so little to the kids and me? Why did it take something like this to make him love me again?

Until Cooper realized how sick he was, he didn't seem to care what Annie did, or even whether she was home. The only time she could remember the two of them really connecting was during the first few years they were married, when the kids were little and they talked about owning their own home someday and saving up for a pickup truck. As the years passed, and the kids got older, he spent more and more time with his booze and his buddies, always quick to criticize when he finally staggered home, and never handy with praise or sympathy.

He hasn't said I love you in years, but I know he does. He gets tears in his eyes when I wash his hair. He tells me it's because his hair hurts, but I don't think that's the reason.

Annie tucked the bedding under the foot of the mattress where it had pulled loose, and patted the neat corner she made. Having no idea how to address a dying man's fears, she concentrated instead on being a good nurse-maid.

"Try to make him comfortable," the doctor said to me. Such puny words—barely a Band-Aid for the kind of pain Coop is dealing with. Some days I wish he would just go to sleep and never wake up.

Not today, though. Not tomorrow. Not for a while.

Like a spent toy, she collapsed into a chair. It was too soon for her husband to die, much sooner than either of them imagined, although they never really talked about death until after they got the news. Every day she bathed him, changed his clothes, helped him to the bathroom, practically spoon fed him, all the while listening for any changes in his breathing. She filled his prescriptions, took him to the doctor, sometimes to the emergency room, and whenever she had a spare minute, she poured over the endless medical bills and state insurance forms.

She rested her head on the back of the chair and stretched her legs. Closing her eyes, she pictured herself living in a tidy house or small apartment with time to do whatever she wanted. A feather of anticipation tickled her breast when she allowed herself the luxury of imagining what life would be like when it was all over, when she would be free to come and go as she pleased. She could go shopping—just to look, of course, not to buy. She might invite Jude, maybe even one or two of his friends, over for dinner. She could drive up to Prineville to see Jordan, or maybe go to the movies with her friend, Dora, or visit Aunt Sandy and her family in Pendleton.

Such thoughts made her feel almost human until she imagined herself at the funeral with everyone hugging her, telling her how sorry they were, saying nice things about him, and then guilt kicked her reverie out the window.

When Cooper moaned and cursed his tight bedding, Annie moved to the side of his bed to loosen the thin cotton sheets encircling his legs.

"I must have washed these sheets a thousand times," she whispered, a lump rising in her throat. She clasped her hands and said a little prayer, not to be in this room when they used one of those sheets to cover his face.

She looked out the window at the cool lavender shadows creeping across the patches of snow that clung to the weeds in the front yard. She picked up one of her husband's hands and held it to her breast, savoring memories of strong, rough hands caressing her skin. Once the calloused badge of a working man, his hands were soft as a chamois cloth.

Dinner wouldn't be ready for another half hour, so she pulled back the bedcovers and slipped between the sheets to lie next to him. Without making a sound, she draped an arm across his chest and rested her head in the hollow of his shoulder.

CHAPTER TWENTY-EIGHT

Jordan turned east on Highway 26 and drove alongside the Ochoco Reservoir for ten miles. She took another look at the directions Emily scribbled on the back of a phone message slip: "Large black mailbox. Williamson in silver letters. Twenty-two miles past the Walton Lake cutoff."

Heading north toward Mitchell, she swerved to miss the over spray from a big gun sprinkler irrigating the pasture on her right. Steaming when it hit the pavement, the water smelled like raindrops on hot asphalt during a thunderstorm. In the pasture on her right, a couple dozen baldies, crossbred from Hereford and Black Angus stock, were munching grass or relaxing in the sun, their black hides a stunning contrast to the vivid green field they grazed in.

She reflected on how good it felt to be away from the clinic for a change. After working for Dr. Warner for ten months, she was now responsible for the small-animal portion of his business, which meant being at the clinic from 8:00 o'clock in the morning to 5:00 or 6:00 o'clock on weekdays and until noon on Saturdays. She was pleased he showed so much confidence in her, however revenue-producing farm animals were still the heart of the profession and the heart of her heritage, and she hadn't realized how much she missed doctoring livestock until she stepped into her mucking boots that morning.

And what a day to pull duty in the country! The sky was flawless, and the resulting sunshine was playing hide and seek with the utility poles lining her route. A faint breeze stirred the sagebrush and wildflowers growing on every inch of land that hadn't been plowed or cleared for pasture. Clover, lupine, yellow wyethia, columbine, and Indian paintbrush were all in bloom. Jordan lowered her window to breathe in the subtle blend of June fragrances. Even the sun-warmed dust smelled good.

When she reached the Williamson ranch, she discovered the driveway was a good quarter of a mile long and desperately in need of gravel. The truck

Kent asked her to take, the clinic's backup truck, was a tinny old Toyota that bucked and rattled all the way down the rutted road. Jordan rolled her window back up, but the dust filtered inside anyway.

Manhandling the pickup, she scanned the thirsty pastures on both sides of the driveway for the horses she was there to vaccinate. Kent would have made the trip if he hadn't driven to Crooked River Ranch that morning to see what he could do for a pair of llamas that had suddenly gone lame. For a chance to gain more llama experience, Jordan would gladly have traded places with him, but at least she was comforted by the fact her boss believed she was capable of vaccinating a few horses.

As she drove down the rutted road, she noticed how rundown the ranch was. A sagging barbed wire fence lined both sides of the road, and sunbleached tumbleweeds, blown from parts unknown, were stacked against the fence three and four deep in some places. What looked like several decades worth of cast off farm equipment littered a field next to the barn.

Nearing the end of the road, she saw a weathered shingle farmhouse surrounded by overgrown bushes and waist high weeds. Three people were standing on the front porch—an attractive, suntanned woman wearing an oversized plaid shirt and two men, one hatless, one wearing a black western hat. There was something familiar about that hat. And Jordan nearly drove into a fence post staring at it.

"Can't be," she gasped. *There must be a million hats like that in Oregon.*

As she came closer, she realized the hat she was looking at was one in a million, because it was the black hat tattooed on her heart and the man who broke it.

She swallowed hard and pulled behind a Ford pickup that was parked in front of the house. The Ford's red paint had oxidized over time into a ruddy pink. There was dried cow shit all over the tailgate and a bumper sticker that read, "Save a horse. Ride a cowboy." Jordan stared at the sticker while she waited for the dust to settle and her heart to slow down.

"Well I'll be damned," she heard Riley say as he and the other two people walked over to her truck.

"Who are you?" the woman asked, when Jordan rolled down her window. The woman's shirtsleeves were rolled above the elbow, and she wore no makeup. She wasn't heavy, but she looked like she could hold her own in a bar fight.

"We thought you were the vet," she said. "This looks like his rig."

"I *am* the vet."

Jordan stepped out of the truck and grinned through her teeth. She hoped no one could see was shaking, but it was hard to hide knocking knees in slim legged jeans.

The hatless man was skinny as a sapling and his nearly bald head was sunburned. "Where's the fellow that usually comes?" he asked, his hands on his hips. "Our horses aren't just everday horses, they're Kiger mustangs. We paid a pretty penny for those horses."

Jordan pulled her medical bag out of the Toyota. "I'll take good care of them," she said with as much confidence as she could muster. "Dr. Warner had to take care of an emergency in Crooked River Ranch. He wouldn't have sent me all the way up here if he didn't think I could handle your horses."

The thin man didn't appear to be convinced.

"Besides," she added, "Kiger mustangs are noted for their gentleness, so they should respond well to a woman's touch."

"The stud doesn't need a gentle touch," the woman snipped. "It needs a kick in the rear once we get it vaccinated." She smoothed back a lock of hair that had fallen across her forehead, while she checked out Jordan's tight jeans.

"Make a decision, Dallas. This girl doesn't look big enough to take a turkey out of an oven, let alone keep those horses under control. The mosquitoes are bad this year, so we need to vaccinate right away." She peered down the road as if hoping to see the regular guy coming to the rescue.

"I know her from college," Riley said, poking the underside of his hat to move it higher on his forehead. "She might not look like it, but she really is a vet." He patted the woman on the shoulder. "Don't worry, honey, she'll do a good job for us."

Honey? Jordan wanted to disappear into a hole.

"Well, go ahead little lady," the thin man said, "but I'm calling to complain, just so you know."

"This way," Riley said, pointing toward the barn.

Jordan purposely walked a few steps behind the two men to give herself a moment to gain some composure. Half way to the barn, Riley stopped and turned around.

"Oh, by the way, this is Dallas. He's managed my wife's ranch for years."

Wife? Jordan's first instinct was to run back to the Toyota and get the hell away from that place, but running off without completing her assignment would lessen the respect she had thus far managed to gain with her boss. Besides, she couldn't let on to Riley that she still had feelings for him.

"My name's Jordan," she said, extending her hand to the thin man. Dallas clasped the tips of her fingers and gave her a wimpy handshake. She upped his grip and gave him the squeeze and pump of a used car salesman. Dallas gave Riley a questioning look, then wiped his hand on the front of his shirt as if ridding himself of something sticky.

Jordan and the two men walked in silence through the huge expanse of weeds and wild grass that grew between the house and the barn. Dallas broke the ice by asking Jordan where she was from.

"Klamath Falls," she replied, "well, more Henley than Klamath Falls. My family ranches in the Henley district."

"I lived in Beatty when I was a kid," Dallas said. "We used to play Henley in basketball once in a while. Always lost to them, though."

When they reached the pasture next to the barn, Jordan got her first glimpse of the six Kiger Mustangs she was there to vaccinate. The five brood mares were dun colored. The stallion, in a pasture of his own, was a red dun. All six horses bore the characteristic black dorsal stripe down their backs and hooked, black tipped ears, unusual and eye-catching markings on horses with tan hides. She was awestruck by their wild equine beauty and surprised to find such gorgeous horses on such a dilapidated ranch.

Dallas harnessed the mares one at a time and led them over to Jordan and her carefully arranged serums and syringes. He stroked the sides of the horses' necks and spoke gently to them while Jordan first checked their teeth, then their hooves before vaccinating them for West Nile virus, rabies, tetanus, and encephalomyelitis.

Ignoring Riley, Jordan spoke directly to Dallas. "Their hooves are in amazingly good shape."

"It's characteristic of the breed," Riley commented. "The walls of their hooves are real thick. They almost never go lame."

Jordan nodded in agreement. Finished with the mares, she put the used vials and syringes in a disposal bag and walked over to the pasture where the stallion was watching the proceedings with a protective interest. The stallion wasn't as subdued as the mares, so Dallas had to rope him first, then ride him bareback for two or three turns around the pasture before he settled down.

"They'll probably be a bit lethargic for a day or two," Jordan told Dallas after finishing with the stallion. "Call me if you notice any other changes such as decreased appetite or more than a mild fever."

She gave the foreman an approving look. "By the way, I saw how you handled that stallion. You wouldn't be a professional cowboy, would you?"

A grin wide as the Columbia River rippled across his face. "Well, I did a little rodeoin' before Mr. Williamson hired me. Nothing big. Never did Sisters or Pendleton."

Jordan smiled at him. "Bet you could still bust a few broncs."

Dallas straightened his shoulders and dug his hands into the frayed pockets of his Wranglers. "Maybe so," he said, obviously pleased. "I've got to check on something in the barn." Long legs slicing through tall grass, he was gone in a flash.

Stinging from a lack of attention, Riley shot daggers at Jordan the way he used to when she did something against his will. "I have my own horse," he told her, "part quarter horse. I can ride just as well as Dallas, and my wife could ride the pants off you."

"Good for her." Jordan closed her medical bag and secured the clasp. "Look, I don't know how you ended up here, Riley, but you always said you wanted to be a cowboy. I'm happy for you. You got what you wished for."

"And you got what you wanted, if all you want out of life is a career." He looked her full in the face. "Don't you ever get lonely, munchkin?"

CHAPTER TWENTY-EIGHT

"That's none of your business."

Jordan headed for her truck. Riley walked alongside, matching her stride for stride and trying to get her to listen to him.

"Hey, miss know-it-all, we just bought us a new bull. As long as you're here, why don't you take a look at him?"

"What's wrong with him?"

"Nothing's wrong. I'd just like you to check him out. We paid two thousand dollars for him at a bull sale over in Powell Butte, so he'd better be able to do get the job done." He winked and grabbed her by the elbow.

Jordan jerked her arm away. "So, what do you want me to do—get a sperm sample?"

"Oh Jeez," he gulped. "Not that. Just tell me what you think … you know … in general. He's over there, on the other side of the barn."

Riley was quiet during the short walk to the barn, so Jordan took advantage of a few minutes of tranquility to savor the sweet smelling clover, the warmth of the sun on her shoulders, and the sound of cheatgrass slapping against the fronts of her boots.

Dallas was closing the barn's double doors when they passed by, so Jordan spoke loudly enough for him to hear.

"I'll be glad to give you fellows an evaluation of your new bull, but please keep in mind I look at animals as a veterinarian, not a cattleman. I don't claim to be an expert in the cattle business."

She picked up the pace as she walked past the barn. The two men followed, and she could hear them talking, not so quietly, behind her back.

"Why is she checking out our bull? I've been buying bulls for fifteen years, for Chris' sake."

"She might see something we missed. Besides she's got a nice ass, doncha think? See it wink at us when she walks? Wink, wink, wink, wink." He made a kissing sound. "Don't you just love tight jeans, Dallas?"

Wishing she was on her way back to Prineville, Jordan berated herself for not saying no to looking at Riley's bull. When she reached the corral, however, she was pleased she took a few extra minutes to observe the impressive animal he was so proud of. The massive, reddish brown creature commanded instant respect as it lumbered around its enclosure, chest out, head erect, eyes alert, ready to challenge anything that got past the gate. Jordan thought the bull's broad white forehead and wide-set eyes made him look intelligent, too, although he didn't need a Phi Beta Kappa key to do the job he'd been bred for.

"He's a beauty!" Jordan shouted to the two men as they approached the corral. "My Uncle Doug says his best Hereford bulls are the ones with strong shoulders and lean hindquarters. Your bull fits that description perfectly, plus he's got good thickness across the back."

"I knew he was a good bull," Dallas huffed, glaring at Riley, "or I wouldn't have bought 'im." He started for the ranch house, then stopped and turned around.

"Glad to meet you, miss," he said, his face softening. "Come back any time."

Riley waited until Dallas was out of earshot before moving closer. Squinting into the sun was making Jordan's eyes water, but she could tell Riley was looking her over as if she was his latest livestock acquisition.

"Our bull's got a healthy looking toolbox, don't you think?"

"Toolbox? I haven't heard it called that before. If you are trying to embarrass me, Riley Palmer, save your breath."

Riley grinned sheepishly and continued to stare at her.

"Speaking of boxes …" Jordan shaded her eyes with her hand, "what's the deal with your mailbox? It says Williamson, not Palmer."

"Williamson was my wife's name. Her father left her this spread when he died, and we haven't gotten around to changing the mailbox. We've been married for five years and moved out here six months ago."

Jordan felt a sting of jealousy, and made an effort to sound nonchalant when she posed the question she was dying to ask. "So, where did you meet her?"

Riley looked surprised. "In Molalla, at the Buckeroo Rodeo. It all happened pretty quick."

Jordan started walking back to the clinic truck. Riley caught up with her and draped an arm over her shoulders.

"I still think about you sometimes, munchkin. You can always call me, you know. We could meet somewhere."

Jordan ducked under his arm. "That will never happen." She tucked her medical bag under one arm and started jogging away from him.

Riley ran after her. "Don't be so sure. I think you still have the hots for me. You used to do anything I wanted."

"Not anymore."

When she reached the Toyota, she stopped to catch her breath before sliding onto the front seat. Riley glanced at the ranch house, then walked over, planted a boot on the running board, and leaned inside the truck's open window, so close Jordan could smell his aftershave. She looked into the sleepy blue eyes of the pseudo cowboy who had wrapped her around his little finger for three years and said, "You should ask for the regular guy the next time you need a vet out here."

She turned her key in the ignition and rolled up the window. Relieved she hadn't succumbed to Riley's advances, she wheeled a semicircle of dust around the biggest mistake of her life.

CHAPTER TWENTY-NINE

"How well do you know the Williamsons?" Jordan asked her boss when she returned to the clinic. Kent was in the sick bay checking a Jack Russell terrier he had been treating for a stubborn infection.

"I've only been out there twice. Well enough, I guess."

"What do you think of them?"

He palpated the terriere's throat and checked inside its mouth. "They're okay. A bit lazy, maybe. Why do you ask?"

"Well, they treated me like I was some bimbo impersonating a veterinarian, and one of them sort of … made a pass at me."

"Really." Kent turned his head to look at her.

"Did you know they were going to give me a bad time?" Jordan asked, somewhat defensively.

Kent raised an eyebrow. "Are you questioning my decision to send you there?" He wrote something in the terrier's file and closed the door to the cage.

Jordan felt a tingle in her armpits. "No, but I don't think you realize what goes on with some of those turkeys."

"Don't be so naïve. You're an attractive woman, and I knew when I first saw you, that is, interviewed you, that there could be trouble down the road. You'd better suck it up if you're going to get along in this business, especially in this neck of the woods."

Jordan felt her face flush. *Did he really say I was attractive?* She grabbed her lab coat and quickly poked her arms into the sleeves. She could never find a coat that was small enough, but at that moment she was relieved to slip into the generous folds of a garment that covered her tight jeans.

She sat down at her desk to catch up on paperwork, and was just finishing her notes on the Kiger mustangs when, Emily returned from lunch.

"You've got people waiting out front. I'll send you the woman first. She seems to be in the biggest hurry."

"Anyone we know?"

"I don't remember seeing her before. I think she has a cat that needs to be put down."

Jordan put on her clinic face, washed her hands and smoothed the front of her lab coat. Dr. Warner scoffed at her lab coat, saying it was pretentious, but she was convinced it made her look more professional.

"Put her in the second room, Emily. I'll be right there."

When Jordan entered the examination room, a tall brunette with an expensive looking cat carrier was waiting for her. The woman, wearing a silk blouse and suede pants, didn't look like a typical Central Oregonian.

"Mrs. McDermitt is it? I understand you have a sick cat."

So thin it looked like month old road kill, the brown tabby hissed at Jordan when she reached inside the carrier to retrieve it.

"What's the cat's name?" Jordan asked. She was alarmed at how underweight the cat felt when she picked it up and placed it on the stainless steel examination table.

"Carmelo," the woman replied. "You know—he's sort of that color."

Jordan nodded, as she palpated the kidneys and felt for tumors. The trembling cat shed wisps of hair onto the slick steel platform and growled when Jordan inserted a thermometer into its rectum. "Your cat has a slight fever, and I noticed some swelling in its lymph nodes. Has he been vaccinated for feline leukemia?"

The woman looked annoyed. "Of course. We had a wonderful veterinarian in Santa Clara." She made a face as she brushed the cat hair off her pants. "Carmelo won't eat a thing. I even tried ground up steak, and he barely licked it. I'm sure we're going to have to … I hate to say, "put him to sleep," because he sleeps all the time. That's what we're going to have to do, though."

Jordan fell silent. "Let me draw some blood first. He may have picked up some kind of a parasite. A blood scan will also show us if there are other problems, or rule them out."

"No need to go to all that trouble. He is a sick, sick cat, in fact he's dying." She bent down and picked up her carrier. "And after you put him to sleep, I'd like him to be cremated. If you'll just take care of this for me, I'll pay for everything today."

When Jordan ran her hand along the cat's back she found virtually no flesh on either side of the backbone. As she continued stroking him, the cat's trembling changed to a rumbling purr.

"How old is Carmelo?"

"I don't know. About four, I guess." She waved her manicured hands in exasperation. "Why are you asking me all these questions? Can't we just get this over with? My husband's waiting for me in the car."

"I'm trying to make sure we do the right thing, Mrs. McDermitt. I have no history on this cat. Euthanasia should be our last resort."

"You look awfully young to be a veterinarian. Maybe you haven't seen enough sick cats to know when it's a hopeless case. This is my cat, and he's sick, and I want you to put him out of his misery."

She closed the door to her empty carrier and pounded out of the examination room on stiletto heels. Jordan heard the woman tell Emily she was having her cat put to sleep and cremated.

"Do you take American Express?"

Unaware of its sentence, the cat looked up at Jordan with yellow-gold eyes that were disproportionately large for such a thin face. Since the reception area was almost full, and Dr. Warner was going to be gone the rest of the afternoon, Jordan decided to wait until the end of the day to destroy the woman's cat.

At 5:30, after treating Arnold Boyd's chocolate Lab for worms, it was time to check on the doomed tabby that was curled up on a towel, fast asleep. Jordan started to collect the serums she needed to complete the arrangement she had with the woman from California, but decided instead to do the blood draw she wanted to do in the first place. Her gut, as well as everything she learned in vet school, told her it wasn't right to euthanize an animal without at least trying to determine what was wrong with it. The state wouldn't execute a criminal, would it, before gathering all possible evidence?

It took only a few seconds under the microscope for Jordan to determine the cat's problem: a bacteria-like blood parasite commonly carried by ticks. She could save this cat by giving it intravenous fluids and antibiotics. Within a week, Carmelo gained a pound and a half and no longer slept twenty-four hours a day. Emily let him out of his cage one morning, not entirely by mistake, and the cautious tabby, still painfully thin, decided to explore the room out front. When Harry, the big black clinic cat saw Carmelo, he quickly chased him back into his cage.

"I think I'm going to take Carmelo home with me," Jordan told Emily a month later, when the cat weighed a healthy seven pounds.

Emily's eyes grew round. "What about the money?"

"What money?"

"The money that woman paid to have him put down. And cremated, too."

"We need to issue her a credit. Then will you please send her a release form authorizing the adoption?" Jordan thought for a moment. "I will bet you a latte that Mrs. McDermitt signs the form and never returns. In the meantime, that cat is *dead*, okay?"

Emily smiled and nodded.

Jordan put the cat into a cardboard carrier. "Come on, dead cat. Let's see how you like your new home."

In the weeks that followed, Jordan found herself referring to the tabby more and more as dead cat, and by the time the adoption was official, she had shortened its name to just plain Dead.

Dead followed his new human companion everywhere she went, and even rode in the car with her when she went shopping or ran errands. Plump and princely, sleeping at the foot of her bed every night, the rescued cat purred every time she so much as touched a whisker, and disregarding everything she knew about animal psychology, Jordan believed Dead was truly grateful.

. . .

After five months of calling Dr. Warner "Kent," his name still stuck in Jordan's throat to say nothing of the fact she froze whenever he came within three feet of her, so she decided to call McKenzie, who never seemed flustered by members of the opposite sex. Maybe McKenzie could give her some pointers.

"Is that you, farm girl? I thought you dropped off the face of the earth."

"Well, I've been working my butt off, McKenzie. Same as you, I suppose."

"Yeah, most of the time. It's cool, though, don't you think? How do you like Prineville? What's the word on your father?"

Jordan cringed. Surely McKenzie was simply inquiring after her father's health. Surely the awful family secret that plagued her night and day was locked up tight in the little house in Klamath Falls.

"Still in a lot of pain. He's not going to get any better, you know." Jordan felt it was best to keep details to a minimum around McKenzie, who could be relentless when hunting for information.

It hardly seemed possible it had been nearly a year since Dusty's funeral. The two friends called one another occasionally, but as winter came and went and they got more deeply involved in their new jobs, they were either too busy, too tired, or the roads were too bad to visit one another. This time, desperate to talk to someone about her growing feelings for her boss, Jordan asked McKenzie to meet her for dinner.

The US Forest Service station at Camp Sherman is only about forty miles from Prineville as the crow flies, but to drive from one place to the other is a hike, so Jordan and McKenzie decided to split the distance and meet in Bend. McKenzie had been to Bend several times since moving to Central Oregon and suggested they have dinner at Ernesto's, in the basement where the businessmen hung out, and where they could order off the bar menu.

It was still warm that night when Jordan drove into Bend to find the city's normally clear air tinged with the smoke from a distant forest fire that cloaked the trees, buildings, and distant hills in a powder blue haze. The setting sun was a huge, red-orange ball that hung over Mt. Bachelor like a gaudy Chinese lantern, and its orange reflection combined with the smoky haze had turned the sky into a swirling mixture of the creamiest shades of apricot, blue-gray and almost rose. She was a half-hour early, so Jordan stopped her Jeep on the side of the road to gaze at the eerily beautiful landscape.

The basement at Ernesto's was crowded with people in all manner of dress, from shorts and running shoes to business attire, so she felt comfortable in her long denim skirt, t-shirt, and sandals when she walked to the back of the room to claim a table.

When McKenzie entered the restaurant ten minutes later, she waved to Jordan from across the room before stopping to chat with a man wearing a spotless western hat who was sitting at a table with three other men wearing shirts and ties. McKenzie said something that made them laugh, and the four men ogled the curvy brunette while she wound her way through the tables in her painted on, stone washed jeans.

The two friends whooped and hugged and spent the first hour totally oblivious to the restaurant crowd as they talked nonstop about whatever popped into their heads. They polished off several tall frosty glasses of beer and a plateful of pizza squares while they picked apart Kimberly's husband, who had recently become her ex-husband, and compared what they purchased out of Morgan's Pampered Chef catalog. They talked about the forest fire, now nearly contained, that had been burning around Little Lava Lake for a week, and McKenzie bragged about a black bear she helped capture.

"He got busted for raiding campgrounds, and did he ever stink! We turned him over to the Department of Fish and Wildlife, and they released him in some remote area past the Santiam Junction. Our coworkers wanted to euthanize him, but me and my partner won out. Even though that bear smelled like poop, he was an awesome fellow. I like to think he's alive and well, eating huckleberries and making bear cubs, not rotting in a hole somewhere. How do you deal with that, anyway?"

"Deal with what?"

"With giving animals the kiss of death or whatever you call it."

Jordan eyed her friend thoughtfully. "It's the least favorite part of my job, and I only do it when the animal is terribly sick or injured. Your bear may have been a nuisance, but it was healthy. It makes me furious when I read that a bear or some other animal is killed just because it gets into someone's garbage. We're the intruders around here, not them."

McKenzie nodded in agreement.

"So, who's the nifty guy in the hat?"

McKenzie rolled her eyes. "He's a total jerk. All hat and no cattle, as they say. One of the guys at work figured we would hit it off."

"Any Paul Bunyans at Camp Sherman?"

McKenzie used the menu to fan herself, "I've come to the conclusion that Paul Bunyan is a myth. Most men just want to drink and get laid—that goes for the Forest Service or whatever." She leaned across the table. "Please tell me there's more to life than hot sex and cold beer."

Jordan laughed and doodled a lopsided heart in the condensation clinging to her beer glass. "You're way ahead of me in the sex department, McKenzie. In case you don't know, I haven't had sex with anyone since Riley. Can you imagine?"

McKenzie shook her head.

"Of course you can't imagine something like that, you …you little rabbit."

McKenzie grinned. "You mean to tell me there isn't one eligible man in Prineville? Not even a cowboy?"

Jordan looked over at the table where McKenzie's drugstore cowboy sat with his buddies. "Don't get me started on cowboys."

She took a sip of beer and lowered her voice. "Listen, McKenzie, I've been waiting all night, all week, to talk to you about this. There *is* somebody I'm sort of becoming interested in. You're not going to believe this, but I think I may be falling for the veterinarian who owns the clinic. You know—my boss."

McKenzie leaned closer. "The Nazi? I thought you hated him. I thought you said he treated you like dirt."

"Well, he's eased up some. I think he appreciates how good I am with our clients, better than he is most of the time. He has more or less turned the small-animal part of his practice over to me, and we had a drink together one night after work. He asked me to start calling him by his first name."

"Which is …"

"Kent."

"Hm-m-m." McKenzie tried to think of a clever word that rhymed with Kent: *spent, bent, tent, dent,* and was about to declare Kent's name a loser when she remembered something else. "Clark Kent was Superman's real name, wasn't it?"

"I think so."

"I like it—Paul Bunyan for me and Superman for you."

Jordan smiled at the crazy way her friend's mind worked.

McKenzie motioned for the waitress. "How old is he?"

"Thirty-nine. I saw his date of birth on a form on Emily's desk."

"Kind of up there. Married?"

"Divorced. His ex-wife came by the clinic once to get some papers signed. They barely spoke."

"What does the ex look like?"

"Nice."

"Nice, schmice. Is she attractive? Does she keep herself up? Is she fat?"

"Well, she's not fat. I think she's pretty, in an outdoorsy sort of way. She's taller than I am, light brown hair, frosted. Is that enough?"

"Not great, but better. Any kids?"

"No. At least I don't think so. He hasn't mentioned kids. He doesn't have any pictures on his desk."

"You don't know whether he has any kids? I would have found that out a long time ago."

Jordan swirled what beer was left in the bottom of her glass. "We're professionals. Professionals don't discuss personal shit at work."

"Come on, Jordan, that's a copout, and you know it. I can't believe you and your boss just talk shop all the time."

Jordan took a quick look at the menu. "Well, we're unbelievably busy. There's no time to sit around and talk."

McKenzie rolled her eyes. "You know, Jordan, for a smart person, you are really obtuse. You've got a safe, professional atmosphere there, don't you, you and the vet, talking about shots for Spot or Mittens' kittens. What do you suppose he would think if he found out you were a living, breathing person, someone who eats peanut butter by the gallon, someone who's crazy about old fashioned folk music, someone whose favorite word is shit."

"It is not my favorite word. Listen, McKenzie, please get serious for a minute, will you? I've been doing everything I can think of to prove to him that I'm competent. I've been fighting gender bias since the day I interviewed with him. Small talk isn't going to cut it with this guy." She gave her empty glass to the waitress. "Plus, this is not a man to be toyed with. When he gets mad—well, I don't even want to go there. He seems to be loosening up with me, but I try not to argue with him if I can help it."

McKenzie shook her head. "That sounds an awful lot like Riley, my friend. I think you need to find out more about this guy before you get too serious."

She grabbed Jordan by the forearm. "Damn. Here comes the cool dude."

Jordan watched the man in the white hat wind his way toward their table. From the pearl snap buttons on his shirt to his silver-tipped Justin boots, he was a perfect parody of the western hero in a black and white movie.

"Whatever you do," McKenzie said, "don't encourage him." She rolled her eyes. "Oops. For a minute there I forgot who was sitting at my table."

• • •

McKenzie's advice nagged Jordan like a bad itch, yet every time she tried to make casual conversation with Kent, she panicked. He was often moody, so she chose her words carefully when they worked together or avoided him by keeping busy. At the end of the day, after she kicked off her shoes and poured herself a drink, she chided herself over missed opportunities.

She had established a comfortable routine for herself in her cozy apartment. After reading the mail and eating a low cal dinner, she fixed herself another scotch to sip on while she took a long, hot bubble bath, and while languishing in the tub, her thoughts often turned to Kent, who also lived alone. She wondered what he did after work, and pictured him in a red plaid Pendleton shirt, sitting in a black leather recliner with a glass of scotch in his hand, reading the evening paper. His Irish setter would be lying at his feet on a rag rug in front of a gray stone fireplace. She had seen the Irish setter, however the rest of her imaginings were straight out of an Eddie Bauer catalog.

Dead, who seemed to think Jordan's bubble bath was for his own personal entertainment, followed her and her drink into the bathroom every night. He jumped onto the edge of the bathtub to watch the water pour out of the spigot and kept his eyes on the bubbles rising closer and closer to his perch. He followed Jordan's every move when she washed herself or dipped under the water to rinse off, and stared at the water swirling down the drain when the bath was over.

One night, while she was shaving her legs, Dead reached out with his paw and took a swipe at her disposable razor. She stopped mid stroke and mildly scolded him, but he reached for the razor again when she took the next stroke.

Jordan giggled. "You think this is odd, don't you, Dead? Not only does your human companion use soap and water to wash herself, she scrapes off some of her hair. That's because we humans associate hair with animals, and since we want to distinguish ourselves from the lesser mammals, no offence, of course, we remove it when it grows in certain places. Females worry about hairiness more than males do because, God forbid we should look like men, most of whom are animals, anyway." She laughed out loud.

Dead sat still as a cougar stalking its prey, his eyes trained on the razor.

"Not funny, huh? Well I've been meaning to ask you something, Dead. Do you think we could let a couple of other animals into our lives?" A delicious shiver ran through her body at the thought of it. "Things are pretty quiet around here, you must admit."

She set her plastic razor down, and watched Dead carefully negotiate the edge of the bathtub to investigate it. He took a sniff, and then batted the razor with his paw until he knocked it onto the floor.

"Hey you little rascal, now look what you've done."

Hearing disapproval, the cat bolted from the bathroom and sat in the hallway to watch her through the open door. Jordan picked up the razor and placed it on the opposite side of the tub and called for him to come back. Dead flicked his tail a couple of times and stood his ground.

Jordan took another sip of scotch before resting her head on the back of the tub. She scooped a handful of bubbles out of the water, and used them to cover her breasts in a frothy bra. She wondered what she should wear the first time she invited Kent to her apartment, and decided it was time to replace her buckshot underwear with something new and provocative. She languished in the thought of their first kiss, relaxing as the water warmed her shoulder blades and played across her belly.

CHAPTER THIRTY

As the fire danger signs along Highway 97 dropped from severe to high to moderate, Jordan's feelings for Kent were heading in the opposite direction. She was amazed at how effortlessly he went about treating the animals placed in his care. His veterinary knowledge was almost encyclopedic, and there was a wild, hard edge to him she found extremely attractive.

She finally decided McKenzie was right about getting to know him better, so she began bringing up topics other than work—a question here, a joke there, gradually revealing some of the more human details of his life. Once she got started, it wasn't nearly as difficult as she imagined. No, he didn't have any children, but he might like one or two. He had a Red Cross five gallon pin. He didn't own a black leather recliner, but he did have one in beige naugahyde. He was an avid Trailblazer fan, and when she told him she played on the girls' basketball team in high school, she sensed a new level of respect.

After discovering there was a soft underbelly inside the veterinarian's spotless shirts, she found herself daydreaming about trading places with the animals he examined, wondering how it would feel to be touched by his strong, gentle hands. At times, it became almost painful to work alongside him, so at night, when she was settled in her apartment, she eased her frustration with one or two cocktails and a glass of wine with dinner. A few drinks also helped her sleep through the night, instead of lying for hours, wrestling with her conscience over what to do about her father.

One night in October, Jordan woke to the sound of someone pounding on her door to her apartment. Confused, she stumbled into the living room and groped for the light switch next to the front door. Looking through the peephole, she found herself staring at Kent, his stern face magnified by the peephole glass. She fumbled with the deadbolt before opening the door a crack, and not waiting for her to ask him in, Kent shoved the door open and stormed inside.

"What's the matter with you? Why didn't you answer the phone? Didn't you hear the doorbell?" His words bounced off her forehead like chips from a buzz saw.

"The rendering plant is on fire," he barked, pointing to a distant glow lighting the night sky. "They saved the horses, but some of them are injured and we need to get down there—now!"

Hands on hips, he stood in the open doorway, glaring at her. He hadn't looked at her with such disdain since the day he discovered the person applying for his position was a woman, and Jordan feared the inroads she recently made into his psyche had suddenly been blocked.

Remotely conscious of the cold air streaming through the door, and totally caught off guard, Jordan felt a chill that was partly physical and part sheer panic. Hugging herself for warmth, she staggered into the bedroom, pulled a pair of baggy jeans over her pajama bottoms and threw a sweatshirt over the top. She nearly fell off the edge of the bed when she leaned over to put her boots on.

After grabbing a jacket, she sheepishly followed Kent down two flights of steps to the parking lot. He didn't say a word to her as he backed up the clinic truck and gunned it in the direction of the orange sky.

The deserted streets of Prineville seemed to yawn and stretch to greet them as the clinic truck barreled through the dark—past the historical county courthouse, past Pioneer Park and through every intersection between second and twelfth. Jordan had forgotten to bring gloves, so she clamped her freezing hands between her knees.

When they reached the outskirts of town, the one road leading to the rendering plant was jammed with people hoping to get a look at the biggest fire in Prineville's history. Dozens of onlookers, wearing hooded parkas or sheepskin jackets, were milling about the property like free range livestock. Drivers honked their horns trying to get others to move, and volunteer firemen bellowed instructions to one another as the town's emergency fire whistle screamed into the night.

Kent rolled down his window and hollered at a group of people standing in the middle of the road. "I'm a veterinarian. We're here to check on the horses!"

As they slowly maneuvered through the crowd, Jordan looked down at the upturned faces, faces made alien by the fire's glow, leering faces with yellow teeth and darkly shadowed eyes. She wanted to get to the horses as quickly as possible, but wanted even more to separate herself from that milling crowd.

Whipped into a fury by a gusty southerly wind, the roar of the fire sounded like a fast moving freight train. Huge vats of rendered fat fueled flames shooting hundreds of feet into the air. The fire was so intense, the heat from it could be felt inside the truck which was at least thirty yards from the blaze.

An eight-foot hurricane fence surrounded the property on which the several large brick and frame buildings of the rendering plant were situated. A maze of chutes and holding pens, as well as everything else made of wood, was on fire. Flames licked the legs of an old water tower, the tallest structure in the compound, and Jordan watched in awe as the tower tumbled onto the buildings below like a crispy marshmallow falling off the end of a stick.

"Too bad they weren't still using that thing to hold water," Kent commented.

A fireman, wearing a helmet but no protective clothing over his parka and jeans, appeared to recognize either Kent or his truck as the two veterinarians approached the gate.

"The horses are up there," the fireman yelled, pointing toward a dimly lit enclosure about a hundred yards from the conflagration. "They think the fire was started by some crazy animal rights group that set it after they let the horses loose. We got all the horses back in the corral. Some of them got hurt, though, when they tried to jump the fence."

"Can I get my truck up there?"

"The frontage road's full of equipment, but I think you can still make it. Some fire, isn't it? Every firefighting machine we could round up is here, and we're getting a second water tender from Redmond. The big building in the center is the problem. It's hotter'n hell in there."

Kent put the clinic truck in four wheel drive, and winding through the fire trucks and police vehicles, he created his own path up the rocky slope, never taking his foot off the gas until the truck's headlights flashed on horseflesh moving in a blur of colors.

Seeing the horses, Jordan's anxiety over Kent's cool behavior was replaced by a concern for the animals' well being. Trying hard to maintain a professional demeanor, her voice sounded thin and girlish, like the playback on a voice recorder, when she asked him what he brought in the way of medications.

"Everything we could possibly need was already on the truck. I also brought along a pistol." He looked at her for the first time since they left her apartment. "You can carry the lantern."

Jordan counted twenty horses inside the aluminum fenced corral. Eyes white with terror and nostrils flared, they ran helter-skelter, first in one direction, then the other, nearly colliding with one another as they searched for an escape. Some kicked their fellow prisoners. Others reared up on their hind legs and pawed the air, their whinnies sounding like shrieks. Never had Jordan heard horses whinny like that.

"The wind is adding to their restlessness," she said to Kent, her teeth chattering. "Even if there wasn't a fire, horses would be skittish on a night like this because the wind interferes with their sense of smell. They're totally lost without it."

Kent ignored her attempt to impress him with her equine knowledge as he silently unlatched the gate and entered the corral. Jordan followed, and watching their step, she and Kent isolated the three horses with the most serious injuries. Once the injured horses were separated from the main group and in the familiar company of humans, they calmed to some extent.

The most agitated of the three animals was an aged black gelding with a deep cut high on its left shoulder. The sweat-stained horse had to be maneuvered into a chute before the two veterinarians could get near him and Kent could suture its wound. Jordan held the lantern, and when she moved it up to the gelding's eyes, she saw he was blind.

"No wonder he's frantic," she said, patting the horse's neck. "All of his senses are failing him tonight."

The other two injured horses were both mares. The swaybacked chestnut had a bad limp, and the pinto was lying on its side, barely able to lift its head. Kent told Jordan to check the pinto while he saw to the chestnut. It was beginning to get light enough to see, so he told her she could extinguish the lantern.

Lying with its head on the ground, the pinto stared at Jordan with one wild eye when she knelt down beside it. She checked the mare's spine for fractures, a tumor, an abscess or bone spurs, manually flexed the joints on all four of its legs, and checked its hooves for damage. Nothing appeared to be wrong with the animal other than old age and exhaustion.

"I think she's fine," she told Kent. "Just old and tired. How's the chestnut?"

"Badly herniated. Must have injured itself when it tried to jump the fence. Let me have a look at the pinto."

She held her disappointment in check when Kent reexamined the pinto, and was relieved he didn't find something she missed. He patted the pinto on its spotted flank. "This one and the gelding will make it, but we'll have to destroy the chestnut." He stood up and walked toward the gate. "I'll be right back."

Jordan wandered over to the chestnut. A large bulge, the probable cause of the mare's limp, protruded from its right groin. Surgery would have been the course of treatment for a younger horse, but not for that one.

Though still restless, the rest of the horses were less frantic now that day was dawning and the wind was dying down. All at least twenty-five years old, they were a pitiful looking lot, shaggy-haired with lackluster hides stretched over protruding bones, droopy lower lips, and balding manes or forelocks. Though they had escaped the fire, it was doubtful any of the horses would find new homes. Ultimately they would end up as dog food, candles or glue.

Hearing the crunch of Kent's boots on the frozen ground, she turned to see the glint of a pistol in his hand. "You'll frighten the horses," she cried, when he walked over to the ailing chestnut and pointed the pistol at her. "Don't you think we should inject her?"

"This is your fault, Jordan. If you hadn't been drunk on your butt when I called, we would have been here sooner, and this horse wouldn't have injured itself trying to escape. You could have prevented this."

Jordan held up her hands in protest, watching helplessly as Kent aimed the pistol at the mare's head. Even though she knew it was coming, she yelped when the pistol went off, and then bit her lip to keep from crying or saying something she would later regret. The roar of the pistol sent the black gelding into a frenzy. The pinto raised its head, and the rest of the horses fled to the opposite end of the corral.

Kent put the pistol in his medical bag, locked it and headed back to his truck. Jordan pacified the gelding and coaxed it and the pinto to the far side of the corral where the rest of the horses were milling about—restless, but no longer in a state of panic.

When she returned to the truck, the man she hoped might one day take her in his arms was leaning against it with his arms folded across his chest and a look on his face confirming what she feared in her heart.

You've got a problem, young lady. When I first met you, I worried that being a woman, you might not want to get up in the middle of the night if we had an emergency. I never dreamed you might not get up because you were drunk."

Jordan sucked in her breath. "I wasn't drunk."

"You were snockered. As it turns out, those horses were spared by the bleeding liberal animal lovers that freed them. We had no way of knowing that, though, and we should have been here."

Jordan pressed her hands against her temples and looked down at her feet. Her heart, or her stomach, or both were doing flip flops, and she was shivering like a scolded pup. The front of Kent's jacket was open, so she moved closer and placed the palm of her hand flat against his chest. It was a bold move, but it felt good to be close enough for him to wrap his jacket around her … if he accepted her apology … if he cared about her at all.

She could feel the heat of his skin through his shirt when she looked up at him and said, "I'm sorry, Kent. I'm truly, truly sorry. I swear it will never happen again."

Encircling her wrist with his fingers, he lifted her hand off his chest and moved to one side. Jordan jammed her hands in her pockets, and looked down at the veil of frost whitening the dry grass. When she raised her eyes, Kent was still looking at her.

"I can't tell you how disappointed I am in you, Jordan. You're intelligent.

You're honest. You do what you're told." He hesitated. "I thought you might be the perfect partner for me."

The impact of his words surged through her brain, fragmenting her thoughts into alphabet soup. Not *were* she wanted to scream at him, *are! am!*

"I *am* the perfect partner," she said, hiding her desperation. "I still did my job tonight, didn't I? I didn't make any mistakes."

"Not this time, Jordan, but what about the next?"

"There won't ever be a next time, I promise you."

"I wish I could believe that, but I've seen this happen to veterinarians before—some new, some who've been practicing for years. Dealing with unpleasant, sometimes distraught clients, the highs and lows of the profession are huge. Many find it hard to strike a balance, and they end up drinking."

"You drink," Jordan said, choking back tears.

He frowned at her. "I like to have a drink now and then. Have you ever seen me take more than one?" He zipped his jacket closed. "Some people can stop at one. Some can't."

He motioned for her to get into the truck, and as she buckled her seatbelt, Jordan looked over at Kent's black leather medical bag. It had been behind the seat when he picked her up. Now it was perched between them like somebody's pet poodle.

"I'd like you to take a few days off," he said, after starting up the truck, "so you can give some serious thought to whether you can handle this job."

Jordan swallowed the *no* on her lips.

Kent leaned across the seat. "And you need to understand that I'm going to be thinking about it, too."

She pressed her lips together and silently begged her tear ducts to freeze. She didn't dare reply or her voice would betray her. If she cried, she would look pathetic, too weak for the pressures of the profession, too weak to say no to that second drink.

When they reached the edge of the compound, Kent slowed for a final look at the fire. The firefighting equipment had been moved closer to the conflagration, and two hoses were streaming broad arcs of water on the main section of the plant. There was more smoke pouring from the burning buildings than flames; however it was obvious the rendering plant was a total loss. In a few hours, when the smoke cleared and the firemen and their equipment were gone, nothing would be left but charred ruins.

CHAPTER THIRTY-ONE

Cooper half opened his eyes, experiencing for a fraction of a minute the sublime pleasure of that magical pit stop between sleep and consciousness. When his eyes fluttered closed again, his eyeballs settled into the deepest hollows of their sockets where they preferred to remain, shielded from the tiniest spark of light and requiring no effort to assemble half or whole bits of information into something tangible.

He languished in this semi conscious state until another part of his mind woke up pleading for another smile, another meal, another day. At that point his eyes snapped open, straining the darkness for a scrap of light or any other indication he was still in the world of his birth. His eardrums hunted for something familiar—water dripping in the kitchen sink, a car driving by, a dog barking, his wife's gentle breathing. He couldn't detect a distinguishable sound.

A thick fog closed around him, high as his ear lobes. It wasn't a wet or smothering fog. It was feathery and dry like the goose down comforter his mother used to tuck him in with when he was sick at home with the flu.

Am I in Heaven? I don't see any faces.

He struggled to bring his hazy reminiscences and disjointed sensations into focus. Using the thumb and forefinger of his right hand he slowly formed an O. He dug the fingernail of his forefinger into the fleshy part of his thumb and felt pressure, but no pain. When he moved his left foot, his toes curled under the weight of the blankets, too tight as usual, at the bottom of his bed. He lacked the strength to kick the blankets loose and give his legs more room, and that frustrated him. It was just plain wrong for a man to be tucked into bed like ground pork in a sausage casing.

As he reluctantly emerged from sleep, Cooper braced himself for the first wave of pain that screamed through the marrow of his bones from his toes to his tightly clenched jaw. The prescription drugs he was taking blunted the pain's sharper edges, thickened it into a throbbing ache, however pain was his constant bedmate, an insatiable whore whose only talent was letting him know he was still alive.

Isn't it time for my pills? Who put axle grease in my eyes?

He would go mad without painkillers, yet hated how they played games with his brain. Even during his waking hours, the drugs fuzzied his senses, made him feel as if an ogre was pushing a pillow against his face. His arms and legs, fingers, and especially his tongue felt thick and heavy. Even something as simple as drinking a glass of water was an effort.

I hate that damned water, Annie—can't you sweeten it a little for me?

After the cancer in his bones moved into his lungs, his heart began beating harder, but slower. The mattress he was lying on shuddered slightly with each beat of his enlarged heart as the vital organ heaved and sloshed in the center of his chest, making him feel, as well as hear, his own heartbeat. The resulting languid circulation caused swelling in his legs and feet and formed pools of fluid in his lungs. With tumors crowding his lung space, and fluid building around his heart, breathing was an effort. He developed a morbid fear of drowning and wouldn't let Annie shave him anymore or put a wet cloth on his face.

Although oxygen was being pumped into him day and night, his brain was still starved for the precious gas, a deficiency that caused him to alternate between delusions and paranoia. Most of the time he couldn't tell the difference between the fragments of his tortured dreams and the dull, repetitious activities that made up his wakeful hours.

Once in a while, the perfect woman would climb into bed with him, his fantasy woman, an exotic mixture of races with silky, caramel-colored skin and doe eyes. Her shiny black hair was waist length and dead straight. Her voice was softly soothing, and when she spoke, her lips curved slightly at the edges. Sometimes she spoke with her mouth up to his ear. More often she murmured into the skin of his neck making him tremble with pleasure and anticipation. He longed to stroke her silky hair, feel the hardness of her dark nipples pressing against his chest. If she gave him half a chance, he would show her how it felt to have sex with a real man, but she was a tease, a fickle bitch, who broke into a million pieces every time he reached for her.

A free floating dose of apprehension sat just below the surface of the dying man's consciousness, nagging at him, causing undue stress as he tried to figure out what was wrong. Did he forget to tighten the bolts when he changed that tire? Was he supposed to pick up something from the store on his way home? Did he lose his wallet? Where were the kids?

Time no longer had meaning for him. It stretched endlessly from dark to semi-dark to barely light and revealed no sign of what day it was, nor the month, not even the season. Had his birthday come and gone? Was the heat he had been feeling lately a fever, or a summer heat wave?

He slipped his hand under the elastic of his pajama bottoms and slowly felt along his right side, past his lean waist toward his thigh, pausing as he always did when he took this physical inventory to tuck his fingers under the curve of his protruding pelvis bone. From there he slid his hand down his abdomen to feel for his genitals. He cupped them for a moment, comforted by their warmth and the knowledge they were still there.

His pajamas fit him perfectly less than two months ago. He felt silly in pajamas, and only agreed to wear them because they hid the strange, emaciated body that had so quickly turned on him, a shriveled mockery of the athletic frame that used to be his. Never again would he have the strength to lift a rifle, let alone experience the rush of seeing a buck in his sites or the tug of a fish on his line.

He tried not to think about the inevitable, even though he knew his condition was going to get worse before he kicked the bucket. How much worse could it get? He barely had enough strength to turn on his side let alone walk to the john without help. Soon he would have to use a bedpan. Would he be in diapers before it was all over?

Why is Jordan being such a hard ass? Please ... Jordan ... anybody. Get me out of this stinkin' body!

CHAPTER THIRTY-TWO

As she lay in bed avoiding the day, Jordan glanced at the clock on her nightstand, imagining what she would be doing if she was at the clinic—8:00 o'clock: Emily's making coffee. 9:30: the Science Diet salesman would have called by now, expecting his monthly order. 11:00 o'clock: Beulah Trask's eight-week-old Border collie puppy should be there for its vaccinations and spaying. Would Kent handle the appointment, or had he rescheduled it?

She felt the brief touch of Dead's cool nose on hers, the only part of her that wasn't under the covers. The eight-pound tabby always walked up and down Jordan's back when it was time for her to get up. This gloomy morning he was also meowing to be fed.

At noon, she uncurled from her cutworm position and got out of bed. While she opened a can of Friskies Turkey and Liver in Gravy, Dead nipped at the calf of her leg to hurry her along. Hungrier than usual, the cat stood on his back legs to greet the food dish when she lowered it to the floor.

She stroked his broad back. "I'm sorry I forgot about you, Dead. I seem to be saying I'm sorry a lot lately."

Jordan fed her cat the previous night before making her own dinner: a small salad, two pork chops, leftover rice, and a glass of burgundy. She decided it must have been the two or three scotches after dinner that caused her to sleep so soundly she didn't hear the phone ring.

She pushed the button on the coffee maker. She filled it every night before going to bed, and if she hadn't screwed things up, starting the coffee maker would have been a simple part of her morning routine. Now it was a reminder that her life was still normal when she readied that pot, when she took her bath, when she ate dinner at the counter, when she fed Dead, when she left the clinic at 6:00 o'clock the night before.

Hunched over the counter like a tavern crony with no place to go at clos-ing time, mentally creating a to-do list for the rest of the day, all that came to mind was wash bathroom towels and pick up dry cleaning. She noticed there were four unanswered messages on her answering machine. She stared at the machine with its monotonous blinking light that seemed to be beckoning to her like a firefly inviting its prey. Halfway through her first cup of coffee, she gave in, pushed the new messages button, and listened to the tape.

Ping: "Pick up, Jordan. This is an emergency. Call me." Ping: "I know you're there, Jordan. Pick up the God damned phone." She buried her head in her hands. Ping: "Okay, I'm coming over. I don't know if you've unplugged your phone or what, but you're supposed to be on call!"

One message remained. "Shit, how many times did he call?" Ping: a new voice, female, still agitated, much weaker. "It's me. Your father's really bad off. I hate to bother you, but will you please call me before you go to work?"

Jordan rested her forehead on the countertop. "Not now, Mom. I can't deal with this right now."

She dragged herself into the living room. Still in her pajamas, she picked up the remote control and turned on the TV, looking for something to pass the time. After fifteen minutes of clicking through infomercials and soaps, she turned the TV off and walked over to the windows overlooking the park-ing lot. Her Jeep was in its assigned space, bright and shiny in the noonday sun, frost still clinging to the slim shadow it cast on the pavement.

Crying inside herself, she looked around her small apartment filled with plants and sunshine. She remembered how exciting it was to have her own place as well as the money to decorate it. Even before she got her first pay-check, she spent several Saturdays choosing a matching black and white checked sofa and love seat, oak tables, and a shaker style bedroom set. She continued the black and white color scheme in her bathroom and kitchen and bought a zebra striped comforter for her bed.

Heading for her second cup of coffee, she heard Dead making heaving noises in the kitchen. She waited until he was finished, then used a paper towel to pick up the wad of hair and Friskies he threw up. She flushed it down the toilet and gave her cat a reassuring pat on the head.

"Having a bad hair day? Me, too, Dead, me, too."

She listened to her messages again, hoping she might have missed some positive detail or a clue as to how she could make amends. Revisiting Kent's angry messages only worsened their sting, so she erased everything except the message from her mother. Listening to her mother's sweet voice again, Jordan decided there might be something worthwhile she could do after all, even if it was only to hold her mother's hand for a few days.

She threw a few clothes into a bag, changed the litter box, and put out enough water and kibble to last Dead at least three days. She wished she could take him with her; however Cooper would have a cow if she brought a cat into the house, and Sonofabitch might have a heart attack. Emily still talked about the dead cat she helped rescue and would look after him if need be, so Jordan was confident her new best friend, who slept sixteen to eighteen hours a day anyway, would be fine on his own for a couple of days.

On her way out, she took a last look around the apartment, and seeing her medical bag on the love seat, she decided to take it with her.

· · ·

Coming home should be a joyous occasion—a mother and father with arms outstretched, a brother or sister or two waiting for a hug, a dog leaping in excitement. There's a roast in the oven, lemon meringue pie for dessert, and nonstop chatter that starts in the driveway, floats through the front door and fills the house like the aroma of fresh baked bread. But that would be John Boy Walton's homecoming or one of Marmee's girls returning home after a grand adventure, not the rock that formed in the pit of Jordan's stomach the minute she parked her Jeep in front of her parent's house.

When Annie opened the door and saw her daughter standing there, her face turned into a puddle of tears. Jordan held her close and whispered, "I'm here, Mom, everything's going to be okay now," it felt so good to be back in her mother's arms, that she wasn't sure who was comforting whom.

As soon as Jordan stepped into the living room, Annie took her by the hand and walked her over to Cooper's bed. He was delirious, eyes half closed, moaning and rolling his head from side to side. The head rolling had created a crescent-shaped depression in his pillow.

"His pain must be a lot worse Mom."

"It's horrific."

A spit pan rested on her father's chest. Dark hollows nearly swallowed his eyes, and his face looked like a skull with fake eyebrows and a beard glued onto it. A beard? Jordan couldn't remember ever seeing her father with a beard. He looked so dreadful, it was hard to believe this was the same person who had cussed at her when she talked to him about assisted suicide a few months back.

His eyes flickered open without appearing to see anything. He closed them again, tighter this time, before resuming the awful head rolling and moaning.

"Oh, Mom."

The two women stood for a moment in bewildered silence. Annie went around to the other side of the bed to straighten the bedding, and used a corner of his top sheet to dab at her tears.

"How long has this been going on?"

"A week, off and on."

Jordan looked from the tormented face on the pillow to the one on the other side of the bed. "What are they giving him for the pain?"

"Percocet. Two tablets very six hours."

"That's what he was taking the last time I was here. Who's his doctor? His doctor should have upped his meds by now."

Annie shook her head. "I've asked Dr. Sitkum a hundred times for something better. He always says the same thing—that he can't prescribe anything stronger, that there's a law against it or something. I would have tried another doctor, but he's the only oncologist in town."

"The law in Oregon is whatever you've got the balls to make it," Jordan snipped. "Even ordering the drugs for assisted suicide takes some guts despite the fact we voted for it twice."

Annie's eyes widened with concern. "Oh, he doesn't want that. He told me he doesn't want to go that route."

"I know, Mom. I'm just venting."

Shocked by her father's rapidly deteriorating appearance, Jordan thought about the condemned horses at the rendering plant—bony, broken down animals, a day or two away from being slaughtered, yet somebody burned down the rendering plant to save them.

She ran outside to her Jeep and returned with her medical bag. Her hands shook slightly as she pulled out an ampule of liquid and a syringe and laid them on the kitchen table.

Annie tugged at the sleeve of Jordan's sweatshirt. "What are you doing? You wouldn't do anything without telling me, would you?"

"Don't worry, Mom, I won't do anything drastic. Not till you're ready. Not till he's ready. Most of all, not till *I'm* ready, and I'm not ready."

Jordan washed her hands under the kitchen faucet, and then filled the syringe while her mother stood by, watching intently.

"This is morphine, Mom."

Annie nodded and searched her daughter's face for a reassuring sign.

"He needs this. He should have been getting something like this for months."

Her mother nodded again.

"But too much of it will kill him."

Annie pressed her lips together into a thin line. "How much is too much?"

"Let's not get into that right now. I didn't bring enough with me, if that's what you're wondering."

Jordan evacuated the air out of the syringe, and felt a tingling sensation when she considered the fact that the injection she was about to give might be a dress rehearsal for something deadly. Holding the syringe upright, she returned to her father's bedside. When she couldn't find a vein large enough to administer the morphine, she applied a tourniquet, and after an adequate vein surfaced, she slowly injected the drug into his bloodstream.

Cooper opened his eyes when she applied the tourniquet, and this time he recognized her. His eyes registered sheer terror when she stuck the needle in, though he didn't resist. Within seconds, his shoulders relaxed, and the expression on his face mellowed.

Annie put an arm around Jordan's waist and leaned against her. Jordan did the same, and the two women hung onto one another for support as they swayed back and forth alongside the man now resting quietly on his pillow.

"Have you considered calling Hospice, Mom? They provide many wonderful services and would be a big help to you."

"I did," Annie sighed. Two lovely, lovely women stopped by the next day. Your father called them every name in the book and told them to leave. I was mortified."

Jordan gave her mother a little squeeze. "Why don't you try to get some rest, Mom? Daddy should sleep for several hours."

"How long can you stay?" Annie's eyes begged for more time than her daughter's short visit during the March snow storm.

"Two or three days. I needed some time off anyway." She closed her medical bag and set it on top of the refrigerator. "Why don't you lie down for a while? Don't worry about fixing supper. I cooked my way through college, remember?"

Annie nodded wearily and walked down the short hall to her bedroom.

Jordan placed the used syringe in an empty fruit jar, and looked in the refrigerator for something to scrabble together for dinner. Sonofabitch, roused by the sound of someone opening the refrigerator door, leaned against her knee, smiling like a political candidate. She patted him on the head and gave him a piece of cheese.

Since there wasn't much food in the refrigerator, Jordan checked the cupboard where the canned goods were stored, and took out a can of corn. When she reached for the knob on the next cupboard, the one her mother used for spices and a few miscellaneous items, her hand froze mid air. The next cupboard was the one with the squeaky hinge.

She hesitated before peeking inside, and when she didn't see a tall bottle wrapped in a brown paper bag, she took the sugar bowl out and placed it on the countertop followed by the salt box, a bottle of vinegar, a box of crackers, and several spice cans. In less than a minute, Jordan had emptied the entire cupboard.

She put everything back, making sure each item was in its original spot, and after another halfhearted look in the refrigerator, she decided a quick trip to Safeway was in store. At Safeway she could purchase some meat and vegetables to build a couple of meals around, and as long as she was making the trip, she might as well pick up a bottle of wine. Maybe two bottles. No doubt her mother could use a drink.

"Let's go for a ride, Sonny. I'll get you a treat, too."

CHAPTER THIRTY-THREE

During her second morning of what might soon become official unemployment, Jordan debated whether to call Kent and apologize. Would he think it was too soon, or was it already too late? She dialed the clinic twice and hung up before it rang through. She dialed a third time, held her breath and waited for Emily to pick up the phone.

"He's not here," Emily said, rapidly clicking her ball point pen.

"Where is he?"

"He's … um … at a ranch on the other side of Post."

"Why are you whispering, Emily?"

"I don't know—well, yes I do—he told me not to talk to you. He said he'd fire me if he caught me talking to you. You know how he gets sometimes."

"Has he told you why I wasn't there yesterday or today?"

"No. He's been real grouchy, so I'm guessing something serious must have happened. The radio said you guys helped save those horses from the fire. I thought maybe you just needed to get caught up on your sleep. Then you didn't come in again today, so I figured something was wrong."

"Something *is* wrong, Emily, but I can't talk about it until I sort a few things in my mind."

"Was he … did he get a little too friendly the other night?"

"Of course not. Good God, what made you say that?"

"I just wondered. I've seen the way he looks at you sometimes, but, hey—no big deal—I'm not even supposed to be talking to you."

After their conversation ended, Jordan couldn't stop thinking about what

Emily said, especially the "way he looks at you" part. Even if Emily was imagining things, Jordan was sure Kent missed her, if not her personally, then her work ethic and the smooth way the clinic operated under her supervision.

She wondered whether, if he did decide to fire her, it would go on her permanent record. She desperately needed to talk to somebody, to come clean about what happened the night of the fire and get some advice. Her mother would understand, but she wouldn't be home from work for hours.

Jordan called Dr. Sitkum's office and got a call back at noon. The doctor sounded rushed and defended himself when she asked him about the drugs Cooper was taking. He did, however, agree to meet with her on Monday.

The hands on the kitchen clock seemed to be stretching every second into a minute, so Jordan decided to kill some time by taking Sonofabitch for a walk. It was a sunny October day, typical fall weather for Klamath Falls, as she and the dog walked toward the north end of the street where a windbreak of half naked poplars cast tall shadows on the quiet neighborhood.

The fourteen-year-old golden retriever maintained a slow, steady pace at first, stopping every few feet to sniff the yellow leaves covering the road. Gradually, he spent more time investigating than walking until he was trailing behind, and when Jordan whistled for him to catch up, he ignored her.

While she waded through the ankle deep leaves, breathing their musty aroma, two young men drove by in a midsize pickup mounted atop oversized tires. The truck's monstrous tires swirled the leaves into small riots that sent Sonny to the side of the road, where he sat looking tired and miserable. Jordan tried to get him to move, but he stiffened his forelegs in canine resolve until she gave up and headed for home.

At 5:00 o'clock, Jordan filled two juice glasses with the burgundy she purchased the day before. She set one glass on the table in front of her mother's chair, took a sip out of the other, and stuffed the empty wine bottle into the garbage bag under the kitchen sink.

She hated to burden her mother with her troubles. On the other hand, she decided it might not be such a bad thing if listening to her woes took Annie's mind off her own worries for a while. She debated with herself all afternoon over how much she should disclose about what took place the night of the fire, the fire from two days ago that felt like a year.

Annie arrived shortly after 5:00, her cheeks pink from the brisk walk home. After getting a good night's sleep, ten years seemed to have disappeared from her face and five pounds off her shoulders. The pleasant expression she walked into the house with turned into a scowl, however, when she saw the glass of wine sitting on the table in front of her chair.

"What's this? Is this supposed to be for me?"

"I figured we might have a little glass of wine, Mom. It's Friday night. You know--TGIF? Besides, there's something I was hoping to talk to you about."

"So, what happened to yours?"

Jordan looked at the empty glass in her hand. "Whoa, what happened to it? I guess I finished it while I was waiting for you to come home. It's a small glass. I'll open the other bottle."

"No."

"No?"

"You can have mine, if you want. I know being here is stressful, Jordan, but drinking won't improve your father's health or make your issues with him go away. If it could, I'd be drunk all the time."

Annie slid the glass part way across the table. "Here. You take this, and I'll have a glass of water. We can talk while we eat. What did you make for dinner? It smells wonderful."

Jordan gazed at the six ounces of red wine sitting in the middle of the table. She wanted to grab it and gulp it down, feel the warmth spread through her stomach, let the fruity aroma tickle her nose. After all, her mother would probably think she was being wasteful if she dumped the wine down the drain. Annie never wasted a thing. She even froze the liquid from canned vegetables, so she could add it to homemade soup.

But how could she drink that glass of wine and then tell her mother what happened with Kent and the horses? Holding the glass of wine in front of her like a bomb about to explode, Jordan carried it to the kitchen sink. She tossed the contents down the drain before Annie could say anything, and before she lost her own resolve. She returned to the table with two glasses of water.

"You didn't have to go and do that," Annie said, slightly embarrassed. She held her glass up to the light. "The water's good here, don't you think?"

Jordan nodded woodenly.

Annie lit a cigarette and sat back in her chair. "So, what did you want to talk to me about? I'm sure you would have called me if there had been some sort of an emergency."

Her mother's refusal to drink even a small glass of wine put a different slant on things, and Jordan needed a moment to rework what she was going to say to her. While she took a slow drink of water, her eyes wandered to the gold and brown world outside the kitchen window and the perfect spider web that had been woven into one corner of the screen. There wasn't a spider in the web, no captured prey wrapped and stored for a future meal, just a single yellow leaf quivering in the wind.

"Well maybe we should talk about when you're going to quit smoking, Mom."

"I'll quit when I'm ready," Annie huffed. She saw the disbelief in her daughter's eyes. "I will. I'll quit after Coop's … after there's not so much stress in my life."

"Isn't the smoking hard on Daddy's breathing? And his clothes and bedding must be saturated with oxygen."

"I don't smoke that much, and I never smoke in the living room. Listen, sweetie, you didn't pour that wine to talk to me about the evils of smoking."

Jordan took a drink of water. "No … I wanted to ask you … about Jude. How's Jude? I'd like to see him."

Eyes downcast, Annie shook her head. "He could be doing a lot better. He's living in Merrill over a garage with three guys he went to high school with. I don't think any of them finished."

"Have you been there?"

"No, I don't even know where it is. He told me they have a toilet, a sink, and a hotplate, and they all sleep on the floor. It sounds pretty grim."

"Is he working?"

"Here and there." Annie looked at the tips of her chewed fingertips. "I think he just works as much as it takes to support his habit."

Jordan patted the back of her mother's hand. "I guessed as much. Do they have a phone?"

"No phone. We leave messages for each other on the bulletin board at the Salvation Army. The last time he was here, which was about two months ago, your father called him a pothead, and Jude said he'd never set foot in this house again. Sound familiar?"

Lost in thought, she finished her cigarette. "I suppose he'll come back eventually. Surely he'll come back after … the funeral."

Hearing the creak of bedsprings, Annie stopped to listen. The springs creaked again followed by a garbled, "Damn you, Jordan."

Jordan and Annie exchanged guilty looks and hurried into the living room. Cooper's legs were tangled in his sheets, and while Annie straightened the bedcovers, he closed his eyes and drifted back to sleep. When his eyes opened a few seconds later, they locked on Jordan, and though they were the eyes of a terminally ill man, they smoldered with indignation.

"You were talking about me," he said, his voice cracking.

Jordan avoided his eyes. "Don't you feel a lot better now, Daddy?"

"My back," he rolled onto his side, "is killing me." He pawed at the oxygen tubes dangling from his nose. "Still hooked up to these damn things? Can't you do anything right!"

Jordan moved away from the bed. "I don't know how you put up with him, Mom."

Annie shot her a look of disapproval. She made her husband take a drink of water, while Jordan left to prepare another injection. He started to say something, which made him cough, so Annie pounded him between the shoulder blades until he hacked a dark blob of sputum into the spit pan. After he stopped coughing, his shoulders rose nearly to his ear lobes when he tried to breathe without being hooked up to the oxygen.

Jordan returned with another dose of morphine. She knew how to give painless injections, but she could also hurt a guy, if she wanted to. She gave his inner arm a few light slaps in search of a good vein, and when she tightened the tourniquet, she saw disdain on his face, not fear.

Cooper complained of a headache, and said he felt hot. He raised his head to get a better look at what she was doing. "How much … is in that thing? Gimme enough this time, okay?"

Annie peeked over Jordan's shoulder. "Can't he stay awake for a while?"

Jordan didn't answer either question. She couldn't get past the disparity of her father lying in a comfortable bed with all of his physical needs being met, demanding an end to his life; whereas the rest of God's creatures use every ounce of their being to survive, even if it means chewing off one of their limbs if they're caught in a trap.

When Jordan injected him, Cooper's lower lip began to quiver and his eyes filled with tears. She had never seen him cry, didn't even think he was capable of it. Embarrassed and unnerved by the unexpected display of emotion, she walked out of the room as soon as she was finished.

She took a seat in the same hard chair she had been sitting in most of the day, pressed her fingers over her eyes, and tried to come to terms with the chaos in her life. Unsure if she even had a job, she still worried whether the clinic was functioning properly without her. She was concerned about her mother's emotional health, and tormented over what to do with her father. She felt a moral obligation to help him whether he appreciated it or not, but she felt a more urgent need to get back to Prineville, check on Dead, make amends with Kent—save her career for God's sake!

She wondered if she could open the second bottle of wine stashed behind the cracker box without her mother knowing about it. Maybe after she went to bed? A little wine would soothe her frazzled nerves. One glass would do it.

Annie walked by her daughter without saying a word. She took two unmatched plates out of the cupboard and set them on the table. Appearing drained by the simple act of setting the table, she sat down heavily and stared into space. The pink cheeks she came home with were gone, and there was pain and disappointment in her eyes.

"I know this isn't the best time to discuss it, Mom, and of course you wouldn't leave him now, but why have you stayed with Daddy all these years?"

Annie looked up at the ceiling. "Here we go again. Why does everybody have to ask me that question?"

Jordan pulled a casserole out of the oven and set it on the table. "So, what do you say to them?"

"First off, I'd like you to know that I'm getting tired having to defend myself all the time. Secondly, it's not that easy to explain. Part of the reason I stayed was because I couldn't make enough to support you kids."

She pointed at the glasses of water they were drinking when Cooper woke up. "What do you want to drink?"

"Water's fine," Jordan said, her tone as bland as the water itself.

"What most people don't understand," Annie continued, "is that your father doesn't care much for himself. It took me a long time to realize that. And if a person doesn't love himself, I don't think he's capable of loving anybody else. It's sort of like breathing. You breathe in, you breathe out. You take love in, you give love out. If you can't take a breath, there's nothing to exhale."

Jordan listened politely, skeptical but curious.

"I haven't always felt this way," Annie went on. "When Coop and I got married, I didn't have a very high opinion of myself when I didn't finish high school. It improved as you kids came along. My self esteem really changed for the better when I got a job. It's kind of a dumb job, but the people I work with respect me, and I bring home a paycheck. My job made me feel good about myself, worthy of being loved. It also made me realize that your father was in worse shape than I was, because he didn't feel good about himself even though he had a decent job."

"But the drinking. How have you been able to deal with that? And what about the way he treated us kids when he was drunk?"

"That's my worst nightmare. I should have stepped in sooner, stopped your father from passing his own self doubts on to you kids. Coop always made you, even Dusty when he got cut from the Oregon State football squad, feel like you didn't measure up, and if you didn't measure up, you weren't worthy of his love which he wasn't comfortable giving anyway. That may seem a bit convoluted to you, but I truly believe that's the way his mind works."

Jordan shrugged her shoulders. "Maybe that's why he set his standards so high."

"What do you mean?"

"If he rewarded us for something, it might look like he loved us, but if he set his standards so high we couldn't possibly succeed, he wouldn't have to reward us. It's pretty sick, when you think about it."

Annie set her fork down and looked her daughter in the eye. "Don't you have anything good to say about him?"

Jordan stared at the food growing cold on her plate. She was offended by the way her father was rejecting her attempt to lessen his pain. He must not have a clue how far out on a limb she was going when she gave him those injections. Then there were those tears she had just seen in his eyes. Could they have been some indication of genuine feeling, even love?

She recalled their old dog Max's final days, and how Cooper practically spoon fed his little buddy, wouldn't have him destroyed even after Max developed chronic diarrhea and he had to clean up after him. She remembered how he fussed over Peaches and how gentle he was when he milked her. After he brought Sonofabitch home, he quickly became the adopted dog's favorite member of the family, so he certainly seemed capable of loving animals and being loved in return.

Then there were the times she caught him pinching her mother on the butt, when he thought nobody was looking. That always made Jordan giggle and feel cozy inside.

She hadn't thought about it for years, but one of her favorite memories was how he used to blow smoke rings after dinner. He did it mostly for Dusty and Jude, who would try to out jump each other and wipe out as many rings as they could before they floated out of reach. Once in a while, though, he would say to her brothers, "This one's for your sister," and he would blow a ring that was low and slow. She would pretend it was a bracelet, and try to put her hand inside without breaking the circle. She always felt a little sad when the bracelet melted away.

A lump formed in Jordan's throat. "I probably have a few good memories."

"Well, you'd better hang onto them. Although you and your father haven't seen eye to eye for years, you may need a few good memories of him someday."

CHAPTER THIRTY-FOUR

The tiny wooden door snapped open, and a brightly colored cuckoo bird popped out to announce the hour. It chirped eight times, each "cuckoo" an exact replica of the first. Its brief performance over, the bird scooted inside before the door shut on its hand carved yellow beak.

Kent and Emily were looking for a missing receipt when the cuckoo sang the 8:00 o'clock song that turned out to be its swan song.

"Stupid clock," Kent grumbled as he walked behind the counter, pulled the clock off the wall and threw it on the floor.

The cuckoo bird bounced twice before landing on its side amidst a scattering of springs and splintered wood. Emily bent down and picked up a small piece of the clock that ended up next to her foot. Shocked into silence, she placed her hand across her breast and backed away.

Kent slid a wastebasket across the floor in her direction. "Clean this up before we open the doors. Then find that receipt."

The owner of the Davidson Park Veterinary Clinic walked back to his office. He propped his elbows on the desktop and tented his fingers under his chin while mentally preparing himself for the daily onslaught. When he allowed himself the time to think about it, Jordan Miller's presence was everywhere. It was her idea to paint the clinic's drab walls and woodwork a pale blue, and he had to admit, the place looked cleaner and brighter. She also brought him kicking and screaming into the world of computers by getting him to use a software program that tracked appointments and simplified the clinic's bookkeeping. She followed instructions, she was smart, and she was damn good at saving money. His small-animal business ran without a hitch when Jordan was around, which allowed him to spend more time in the field—caring for livestock, not pandering to whiney dog and cat lovers. She wasn't hard to look at either, but this drinking thing. If he had known about that, he wouldn't have hired her, even if she'd been a man.

Although the clinic usually closed at noon on Saturdays, he was so far behind he would be lucky to finish by 5:00 o'clock. Wondering if Jordan left any unfinished business, Kent left his office and walked into the back room where she did her paperwork at a small desk. Her lab coat hung in its usual spot near the door. Checking the pockets, he found a small set of keys, some sugarless gum, a paper clip, and a grocery receipt. Her familiar scent lingered in the coat's soft blue fabric, a scent so sweet it might cloud his reason if he let it.

He liked Jordan. He liked her a lot, and he could sure use her help right now. Everybody and their dog seemed to have found some reason to come into the clinic during the three days since the fire, and Emily was turning into a blithering idiot. He had been planning for some time to give his young receptionist the boot, but couldn't fire her until he knew whether Jordan was coming back or he hired her replacement.

He turned his thoughts to the interview scheduled for Monday. He had been impressed with the young man's papers when he received them several months back. Since things were going so well with Jordan at the time, he mailed the young man a polite decline and put his papers in the credenza.

The guy comes from a small town like Prineville, so he should fit in well here. And he's a man, for Christ sake. I feel better already.

• • •

Traffic was light on Highway 39 when Jordan drove to Merrill, passing by her old grade school and the road to the Colton ranch. She would have stopped for coffee, but didn't want Grandma Leona and the rest of her family to know she was in town.

The modest farms lining each side of the highway were separated from the road by sheep fence or barbed wire strung on green tipped metal poles. In some places, isolated split rail posts marked fences long gone. When she drove under the old aqueduct that transported irrigation water during the summer months, she recognized the ramshackle building on her left, a barn with swaybacked wooden doors that wouldn't keep out a kitten.

A thin layer of frost covered the dun-colored fields that were green the month before. Clumps of willow brush sucked up the last of the water in the irrigation ditches, and like giant tinker toys, huge metal sprinkler wheels, retired for the season, were parked here and there in the stubble fields adjacent to the ditches. The few cattle and horses that could be seen from the road were huddled together with their backs to the wind. Soon they would be eating the alfalfa that had been watered all summer by the sprinkler lines.

Smoke rose from a smoldering mound of dead potato vines in a field off to her right. Jordan could smell the smoke even before she drove past the controlled burn. Whipped by the wind, wisps of smoke danced over the remains of the pile like demon sprites celebrating the end of harvest.

The smoldering pile reminded Jordan of the fire at the rendering plant, and her heartbeat quickened when she recalled the heat, the noise, the fear in the eyes of the horses and the disappointed expression on Kent's face in that terrible morning's first light. She cautioned herself against dwelling on something she couldn't change, something that could send her to the loony bin if she wasn't careful.

She didn't think it would be all that difficult to find Jude. Merrill was barely a fly speck on a map, one of those towns where everybody knows everybody else's business. Surely someone would remember seeing a Chevy pickup with a crumpled right front fender and a flat black paint job straight out of a spray can.

She decided to stop at the Polar Bear drive-in for a cup of coffee. Her mother used to bring her and her brothers there as a special treat when they still lived on the farm. Jordan recognized the old "Drink Coca-Cola" decal that was sun baked onto the drive-in's front window.

A gray-haired man wearing a John Deere baseball cap took her order.

"I'm looking for my brother," she told him. "He's a skinny kid with a mop of reddish brown hair. Last time I saw him, he was wearing it in sort of a pony tail."

"I think I know who you're talking about." The man's teeth revealed a glint of gold when he spoke. "He's usually with a couple other guys. I don't know where he lives, though."

Sipping her Polar Bear coffee, Jordan took her time driving through the network of blocks between First and Third streets. Most of the houses were fairly small, and like the Polar Bear drive-in, appeared to have been built in the nineteen forties or fifties. Many of them were in need ot new roofs and paint and reminded her of her old neighborhood, now her parents' neighborhood, recently her new neighborhood again.

Just when she was about to give up, she saw Jude's truck in a jumble of assorted beaters parked outside a two story house. The hinged double doors on the garage weren't locked, so Jordan pushed one of the doors open and slipped inside.

The interior of the garage was stacked to the rafters with old furniture, boxes of clothes, castoff toys, magazines, kitchen implements, tools, tires, and plastic garbage bags bulging with beer cans. There was a motorcycle in one corner, nearly hidden behind more boxes and stacks of newspaper. Near the motorcycle sat an old wringer washer. Everything in the garage was covered in dust.

Jordan made her way through a corridor that sliced through the mess and led to a stairway. She tapped on the door at the top of the stairs and got no answer. She knocked louder and heard groans and the shuffling of feet.

"Who's that?" said someone who sounded like Jude. "What time is it, anyways?"

"How the hell should I know?" The second voice was lower than the first.

"Who's out there?" the first person demanded.

"It's Jordan. Jordan Miller. I'm Jude's sister. I don't need to come inside."

Jordan heard arguing and low, guttural noises.

"Can't you come back later? It's too freakin' early!"

"Jude, can you please come see me for a minute. It's important or I wouldn't have driven all the way out here."

"Okay, I hear you. Gimme a minute."

Jordan zipped up the front of her jacket and put her hands in her pockets. There was no railing protecting the stairway and its eight naked steps. The unpainted door was covered with dents and scrapes, and there were grimy finger and handprints around the doorknob and along the casing. While she waited, she scanned the assorted items stacked in the garage and didn't see anything belonging to her brother.

At least five minutes went by before the door opened and Jude walked out, unshaven with dirty hair clinging to the stubble on his face. The t-shirt he was wearing had yellow stains under the armpits, and there was a raveling hole in one knee of his baggy sweatpants.

He sat down on the top step with his knees hugged to his chest. Jordan sat down next to him and put an arm around his shoulders.

"Man, it's good to see you," she told him.

"How'd you find me?"

"I found your pickup. If you really want to hide from the world, you'll have to get rid of that thing."

"Nobody'd ever buy that piece of junk. I'll be drivin' it till the wheels fall off."

"Got any gas in it?"

Jude leaned out from under her arm. "Yeah, right, like I got someplace to go. What's it to you anyways?"

"You need to come home, Jude. Just for a visit. I don't think Daddy's going to be around much longer, and Mom …"

"Put a cork in it, Jordan. I been hearing that for months, and he's still kicking. What makes you think there's been a change?"

"Believe me, I know it will be soon. A day or two at the most."

"How can you be so sure, when even the doctor doesn't know?"

"I'm a trained professional, you know."

"Not for people."

"No, but there are other circumstances that you're not aware of. Let me put it this way—I have something to say about Daddy's situation now. I'm calling the shots."

Jude shrugged and covered one bare foot with the other to keep it warm.

"Besides, little brother, you stink. If nothing else, it would do you good to come home and take a bath. If you do, I'll see if I can rustle you up a steak."

Jude swallowed and moistened his lips. "Steak would be nice."

Jordan asked for his car keys, cranked up his truck and drove on fumes to the nearest service station where she filled the tank rather than giving him the cash.

"Don't think about this too hard," she told her brother when she returned his keys. He had gone back inside, and through a narrow opening in the door, all she could see of him was one bloodshot eye and the scraggly whiskers on part of his cheek. "Please come home, though."

Jude nodded before closing the door.

On the short trip home, Jordan noted the dappled clouds on the horizon, a quiet reminder that winter was just around the corner. When she got to her parents' house, she called the pharmaceutical supplier she used on a regular basis and told him she was working temporarily in Klamath Falls and needed some supplies shipped to her, FedEx, overnight delivery. A straight order of morphine would look suspicious, so she also ordered two bottles of antiseptic, some DMSO, amoxicillin, a box of syringes, and a few other items to round out a veterinarian's routine purchase. She paid with her own credit card, and then called the Prineville clinic for the third day in a row.

"Can I ask a favor, Emily? Will you please check on Dead after you get off work today? There's a spare key to my apartment on the key ring in my lab coat. Please put out more food in his dish and change his litter box. Pick him up and hold him for a few minutes—okay?"

"I'd love to! I miss that dead cat." There was a brief silence. "When are you coming back, Jordan? We're swamped."

"Do you think I'd be welcome?"

"Yes, yes, yes! We need you."

Jordan felt a sudden surge of hope. "Emily, my father is nearing the end. I came down here to try to make him comfortable and can't leave until I get him some stronger pain medication."

"I'm sorry. You never said much other than he had cancer."

"I know. I didn't know the whole story myself. Besides, I don't like to talk about stuff like that. Has Kent said anything more about me?"

"No, but I think I'd better tell you—he did ask me to black out an hour on Monday for some guy he wants to interview."

"He's already set up an interview? Is it somebody we know? Have you met him? What's the guy's name?"

"Um … Drew something or other."

Jordan stiffened. "Do you know where he went to vet school?"

"No. All Kent did was hand me a slip of paper with the guy's name on it. I wrote it in the appointment book. Hold on a minute; I'll check the schedule."

Jordan tightened her grip on the telephone receiver as she listened for Emily's return. She could hear Emily's voice in the background, other voices as well, and the sound of the clinic door opening and closing. Looking up a stupid name in an appointment book shouldn't take forever.

"Sorry, Jordan," Emily said, when she returned to the phone. "Like I said, we're swamped. Okay, I checked, and the guy's name is Drew Murphy."

Jordan nearly dropped the phone.

"Jordan? Are you still there? I didn't forget to push the hold button again, did I?"

"I'm still here, Emily."

"You don't know him, do you?"

"I have a funny feeling I do. Why is Kent interviewing somebody else so soon?"

"Well, things have been crazy around here with you gone. It's only been three days, but it seems a lot longer, especially when we have to work all day on a Saturday."

Emily lowered her voice. "I've got to find a different job, Jordan. Kent yells at me all the time, even in front of the clients. He makes me so nervous I fumble around and make mistakes, and then he yells even more. He broke the clock this morning. On purpose."

"The cuckoo clock?"

"Grabbed it and threw it on the floor. It's totally broken."

Jordan tried not to sound concerned. "I'm sorry you're having such a rough go of it, Emily. Please tell Kent I called. Tell him I need to talk to him right away. Tell him I'll try to reach him on Monday, and that I will be back as soon as I take care of a few details for my father."

"Okay," Emily sighed. "If you ask me, though, things don't look good for either one of us right now."

CHAPTER THIRTY-FIVE

The headline on the front page of the *Herald and News* read, "Senate to Vote on Hyde Bill." Jordan read through the article, hoping to find something to show Dr. Sitkum that would change his mind about the pain mediation he prescribed for her father. *"As an alternative to assisted suicide,"* the article stated midway through, *"the bill allows physicians to prescribe controlled substances for the treatment of pain."* Perfect! She made a copy of the article, and thanked the librarian for her help.

After settling into one of the few empty chairs in Dr. Sitkum's crowded waiting room, Jordan studied the other people waiting to see the town's only oncologist. Just inside the door, a dark eyed girl about four years old, with a large red bow tied on one side of her bald head, sat on her mother's lap. A diminutive gray-haired couple, arms linked, occupied a settee in front of the window. Every patient appeared to be accompanied by a friend or family member, except a heavyset man in oil stained coveralls. Head down, forearms resting on the tops of his thighs, he sat staring at the floor, clasping and un-clasping his swollen hands.

Jordan thumbed through an old copy of *People*, glancing occasionally at the patients coming and going. She had expected to find a somber atmo-sphere in the oncologist's waiting room, and was surprised at the number of smiles and jokes that were being exchanged.

Dr. Sitkum, whose pinched face looked as if he just got a whiff of some foul odor, was not among the smilers when she entered his office.

"Before you start," he said, adjusting his bow tie, "I want you to know that I am only doing this out of respect for your mother. I have a full waiting room, as I am sure you noticed." He pointed to the chair he wanted Jordan to sit in.

"Your mother tells me you have become a veterinarian. Do you get this kind of meddling from *your* patients?"

Jordan laughed half heartedly.

He leveled a cold stare. "You must admit, Miss Miller, treating an animal's pain is more straightforward than treating that of a human. Fewer nuances, so to speak."

"I don't totally agree, Doctor Sitkum. Animals may appear to be more stoic than humans, but I believe they experience greater pain than they outwardly reveal, so I've learned to be liberal when it comes to dispensing analgesics. I find it results in a quicker recovery."

"So that makes you an expert on treating pain in humans?"

Jordan looked down at her clasped hands. "No." She raised her eyes. "My father may not possess a raft of desirable characteristics, Dr. Sitkum, but he's not looking for pity. His pain is real."

"Have you given any thought to the legal issues involved? They are totally different for my patients than they are for yours."

"That's true. Humans can overdose, either intentionally or accidentally; whereas animals depend on their caregivers to determine how much medication they get. But, Doctor, my father is going to die no matter what you give him. What are you afraid of?"

Dr. Sitkum cleared his throat. "I was sued once. I won, and learned that even well intentioned pain relief is subject to criminal investigation should a patient die of an overdose. And now that we have legalized assisted suicide, the whole world is watching us, keeping track of how often we prescribe the approved drugs and counting the number of patients who end up taking them, physician-by-physician. This is a small town, Miss Miller. I do not want there to be doubt in anyone's mind that for my patients, it was the disease that killed them, not the treatment."

Jordan took the copy of the Hyde article out of her handbag and tossed it onto Dr. Sitkum's desk. "Here, Dr. Sitkum. You might find this interesting."

He unfolded the sheet of paper and studied it briefly before putting it aside. He walked around his desk and leaned so close she could see the enlarged pores on his nose.

"I am sorry to disappoint you," he said without a trace of warmth, "but I do not intend to change your father's prescription, nor increase the dosage. I cannot spend any more of my time discussing this with you, Miss Miller. Please give my best to your mother."

• • •

After meeting with Dr. Sitkum, Jordan arrived back at her parents' house before noon, and was surprised to see Jude's truck parked in the driveway. She hurried inside to find him washing his hair under the faucet in the kitchen sink. Seeing he was helpless for the moment, she hugged him from behind, ignoring his wet protestations.

When Annie came home for lunch, she squealed and nearly tackled Jude, who let her hug him for ten seconds before wriggling out of her arms.

Sonofabitch limped over to investigate the commotion and prod Jude with his nose. When the dog discovered Jordan was grilling cheese sandwiches, he sat on one of her feet and leaned against her shin bone until he got a handout.

"Stay for dinner, Jude, and I'll run to the store and buy you that steak I promised."

"Okay," Jude mumbled as he dunked a corner of his sandwich into his soup. He looked at his mother. "I'm not staying all night, though. Just because I came over here doesn't mean I'm moving back."

"I don't expect you to, Jude."

Annie got up from the table and ladled the last of the soup into a small bowl. She picked up the towel she used as a bib when she fed her patient and walked into the living room. Jordan exchanged glances with Jude, and they followed behind her.

Supported by pillows, Cooper sat nearly upright. Annie gave him a few private words of encouragement meant to relax him enough he could swallow the soup without choking. When he recognized Jude, a thin smile sneaked across his face.

"Well, look who's here," he said in a raspy voice.

Jude stood at the foot of his father's bed, gripping the foot rail so hard his knuckles were white.

"Yeah, it's me. Hi, Dad."

Two tears rolled down Cooper's cheeks and disappeared into his beard. When he motioned for a spoonful of soup, Jordan nudged Jude closer.

"How you feelin'?" Jude asked.

"Okay, I guess," Cooper said, clearing his throat. "I'll feel even better after … another shot."

Jordan had been gradually adjusting the amount of morphine she was giving her father, dispensing enough to curb the pain without making him sleep twenty-four hours a day. She was hesitant to do this, since sleeping was generally his most polite activity, but it was the right thing to do, and it extended her supply. He made it through the transition better than she expected and could be awake now without cursing at her for keeping him alive.

"It's too soon, Daddy."

Cooper's bony fingers curled around the Y of his oxygen tube. "So now you hooked me, you gonna dole it out like candy?" He shifted his shiny brown eyes to his son. "I bet … Jude's got something."

Jude fidgeted with his damp hair. "Don't look at me. I don't know nothing about that stuff."

"Worthless piece of shit," Cooper mumbled, turning his head away.

Jordan grabbed her brother by the arm and walked him into the kitchen. "Look," he said to her through clenched teeth. "I know he's sick, but he makes me so mad I could spit."

"There's not much time left, Jude. Humor him. Try to make peace."

"Right. Like that's ever going to happen." He raised his eyebrows. "Have you kissed and made up?"

Jordan shook her head. She was afraid bringing up the past would turn into some sort of screaming match, and easing his pain was turning into a huge burden. It could be weeks before the cancer took its toll. Meanwhile, she desperately needed to talk to Kent, meet with him face to face and convince him she was still his best choice for a partner. She would be ecstatic at this point, if he just made her his business partner. Her whole career was at stake, yet here she was coddling this sad wreak of a human being who would scarcely be missed.

"Can you come back tomorrow?"

Jude looked down, shaking his head. "Oh, man, I can't believe you're asking me to come back again."

He started for the front door. Jordan got there before he did, blocking his exit. A tenseness mushroomed between them until Jude muttered, "Jeez, Jordan, what do you want from me?" His sister's serious expression remained unchanged. "And what about my steak?"

Jordan smiled and put her hands on his shoulders. "If you come back tomorrow, I'll make you that steak dinner I promised, but Jude ..."

"Yeah?"

"You need to be prepared to say something nice to Daddy, even if you have to make it up. Do that and you can tell him goodbye and be done with it. Is that a deal?"

Jude fidgeted with his keys. "I guess so. This is the last time, though, okay?"

"Absolutely."

CHAPTER THIRTY-SIX

It was calm in the rest of the house, while Jordan lay in bed with her eyes open and her mind stuck in overdrive. She was almost out of morphine sulfate and couldn't keep ordering additional supplies of a controlled substance without raising a red flag with the pharmaceutical supplier. She couldn't keep her father in la-la land indefinitely, and wondered if she was emotionally stable enough to give him the final dose. If she didn't fall apart before, would she fall apart afterward? Could her flaky brother be trusted with such a dangerous secret?

Adding fuel to her insomnia was an urgent need to return to the clinic. If she didn't show up, apologize to Kent and hopefully salvage her job, he was going to hire someone else. It took her a year to get that job. How long would it take to find another one, especially with a dismissal on her record?

She rolled over, switching sides for the tenth time that night.

A good night's sleep was essential if she expected to think rationally the next day. To pull this off, she'd have to be mentally sharp, sympathetic to everyone around her, and tough as a badger.

To complicate matters, her father seemed to be feeling better. The last couple of days he had stayed awake for several hours at a time. Yesterday he even said a few words to her without ranting. He was definitely feeling less pain than when she arrived.

She tried lying on her back.

Should she tell him ahead of time? It would be more merciful to let him think he was receiving a regular dose—going to sleep for a few hours instead of … forever. God, how terrible that sounded! As promised, she would tell her mother, Jude as well, so they could try to make Cooper's last hours as pleasant as possible. Hopefully they wouldn't get too sentimental, though, or he would figure out what was going to happen.

At ten after five the next morning, Jordan slipped out of bed feeling like a train wreck. Hoping exercise would relieve some of her stress, she pulled on a gray sweat suit, laced up her cross trainers and tiptoed through the living room. In the near darkness of that early hour it was hard to tell whether her father was awake or not since he slept sitting up. He didn't say anything, so she sneaked by his bed and walked on cushioned soles through the kitchen to the back door.

Sensing the possibility of some fun, Sonofabitch followed, toenails clicking on the kitchen floor. Jordan ruffled the dog's reddish gold coat and motioned for him to stay. With a grunt and a groan, he laid by the back door.

Jordan started running the minute she left the house. She deliberately wore no jacket so she could feel the bite of morning on her breast. Within seconds, her nipples puckered into knots and her cold shoes whacked the frozen ground as if they were made out of wood.

Churn legs, churn. Kick up some dirt and gravel. Don't stop till your calf muscles scream and your thighs are hot to the touch.

After an exhausting run and a cup of coffee, Jordan dialed the clinic in Prineville. It was so early Emily would have barely had a chance to take off her coat, but Jordan was beyond worrying about proprieties.

"I wasn't at the interview," Emily said, sounding annoyed, "so I don't know how it went, and, no, he didn't hire that Drew guy, as far as I know. I finally told Kent you wanted to talk to him. I thought he might yell at me for talking to you, but he didn't."

"Tell him I'm the one who's doing the calling, not you, and tell him I'll be back soon—maybe even tomorrow."

Jordan's spirits improved after learning there was still a chance she could keep her job, then quickly fell when she realized that if she expected to meet with Kent the following day, she would have to administer a fatal dose of morphine that night. The seriousness and finality of doing what she'd only thought about doing up till now was terrifying, but she couldn't put it off any longer.

Annie teared up and asked for some time alone when Jordan told her.

She sat at the kitchen table by herself, smoking and staring out the kitchen window until it was time for her husband's meds. Jordan left the room when Annie called her employer to say she wouldn't be coming in to work that day. She took a shower while her mother ironed Cooper's pajamas.

The two women went through a pot and a half of coffee that day, and Annie smoked close to a pack of cigarettes. She jumped every time Jordan spoke and wrung the marrow out of every word she uttered.

After washing the breakfast dishes, Jordan organized the cluttered kitchen counter and mopped the floor. In between chores, she checked and rechecked the supplies she would need for that evening's procedure.

Just before lunch, her father asked for a "cocktail," and though he appeared to be jovial, there was an air of fear and vulnerability about him when she gave him the injection. A mute restraint filled the space between them like a huge balloon. Neither said what might have been on their minds for fear of popping the balloon and releasing the consequences, whatever those consequences might be.

Trying to make herself feel as if this was just another day, she busied herself with nursemaid tasks. She fed Cooper his lunch. She checked his pulse and blood pressure. She cleaned his oxygen plugs. He nodded approvingly when she loosened his blankets.

As the afternoon dragged on, she felt a need to get out of the house again, so at 3:00 o'clock, she told her mother she was going outside to look for something in the garage.

The Miller family's single car garage was twenty-odd feet from the house. The floor was part gravel, part dirt, and there was a large plank at the front end marking where the car should stop. Dust-covered Mason jars and limp cardboard boxes were stacked to the rafters on sagging wooden shelves. An old horse collar hung on one wall next to her father's long forgotten hunting jacket. For some reason the jacket caught her eye, and when she slipped her hand into its pocket, she found a crumpled cigarette pack with one cigarette in it and a lottery ticket from 1989. She picked up a sleeve and used it to wipe away a rogue tear that had rolled down her cheek.

• • •

Later that afternoon, while scrubbing potatoes for dinner, Jordan looked out the window and saw Jude sitting in his beat up pickup. It was only 4:30, however the ashen sky made it seem later than the hour. Her heart began to pound when she watched her brother get out of his truck and amble across the weedy front yard. The longest day of her life was suddenly coming to an end.

She calculated the timing. Potatoes would bake for an hour. Dinner at 5:30. Give Jude some one-on-one time with their father after dinner. Prepare the equipment. After the injections, breathing would slow, then stop. It could all be over by 7:00 o'clock.

Her heart was beating so fast that deep breathing couldn't calm it down. Feeling strangely detached from her own hands, she watched one of them open the oven door while the other one put three potatoes inside. After closing the oven, she held her hands out to inspect them and thought they looked foreign, almost as if they belonged to someone else.

She leaned against the kitchen counter while she trimmed the fat off the steak, gripping the knife so hard, her knuckles were white as the fat. When the steak was ready to be seasoned, she opened the door to the spice cupboard, and jumped at the sound of the squeak. The peculiar hand attached to her wrist numbly took salt, pepper, and garlic powder out of the cupboard and set them next to the steak.

Since the cupboard was open, and nobody was in the kitchen at that moment, Jordan whisked the bottle of burgundy out of its hiding place. Using her body to shield the wine from view, she turned the corkscrew for a seemingly endless ten seconds, and then babied the cork out of the bottle's neck to prevent it from popping. She threw the cork in the garbage, and took a large gulp of wine before returning the bottle to the cupboard.

In spite of the effort it took to make her hands do what she wanted them to do and a hyperactivity she could barely control, Jordan cooked a perfect dinner. She and her mother picked at their food, while Jude ate his own meal and finished what was left on the other two plates.

While Annie cleared the table, Jordan took Jude aside to tell him what was about to happen and swear him to secrecy.

"You're shittin' me! Does he know?"

"It was his idea. He wanted me to do it months ago, but I wasn't here, for one thing, plus I didn't have the nerve."

"So why now?"

"His pain is so bad he can't stand it without the pain killer I've been giving him. I'm about to run out, and when that happens he'll be back where he was, wishing he was dead and no doubt blaming me for his misery."

Jordan gave her brother an affectionate shake. "This is the best time for me to do this, Jude. You and Mom will have a chance to say some nice parting words, then his pain will be gone. Many people would choose to die this way, if they were given the opportunity."

Jude shook his head in disbelief, and looking older than his twenty-six years, dragged himself into the living room. Jordan helped her mother with the dishes, and then urged her to join him.

Annie searched her daughter's face. "Aren't you going to say anything to your father before you … are you leaving all the goodbyes up to me and Jude?"

Jordan shot her mother a withering look. "Give me a break, Mom. I can't be both his executioner and his shrink!"

Annie's mouth dropped open. "Well, excuse me," she said, her eyes smoldering. She turned on her heels and stomped into the living room.

Jordan set her medical bag on the kitchen table. In spite of their recent bath in warm dishwater, her hands shook when she repeated the process she had rehearsed in her mind at least twenty times that day. She methodically placed the tourniquet, syringes, ketamine and morphine in a neat row on the table. She counted and recounted the ampules.

You can do this, she told herself. *You've done this before, and every ticking minute you waste gives Kent more reason to fire you.*

Her frazzled nerves screamed for the soothing effects of the red nectar in the dark green bottle behind the cracker box, so she ever so slowly opened the cupboard door. When she didn't hear it squeak, she wondered why her father hadn't discovered that trick.

She took the wine out of the cupboard, and hovering over the bottle like a mother hen, lifted it to her lips. The wine made a warm path down her throat and gave her a momentary rush of pleasure. She took another gulp and was in the middle of her third when Annie walked back into the kitchen.

"What in the world are you doing!?"

Like a child hanging onto its favorite toy, Jordan hugged the bottle to her chest. "I need a little something to calm my nerves—that's all. Please go back with Daddy where you belong."

Annie rushed to her daughter and spun her around. "Give me that," she cried. Her hazel eyes were peppered with fury as she glowered at the bottle, and the expression didn't change when she turned her eyes on her daughter.

"Mom, don't look at me that way. You think this is easy?"

"Something is terribly wrong with this picture," Annie said, shaking her head. "You've hated your father all your life because of his drinking, but you can't put him out of his misery without having a drink?"

Jordan started to protest.

"How many drinks do you need, Jordan? One? Two? The whole bottle? I won't let you do this. If I have to rip that bottle right out of your hands, you're not drinking that wine!"

When Annie grabbed for the wine, Jordan spun away from her. Wrestling for control of the bottle, the two women banged against the refrigerator, then careened into the counter, spilling wine on the fronts of their clothes and splattering the kitchen floor. In less than fifteen seconds a mother's rage defeated a daughter's desperation, and with the determination of a she wolf protecting her young, Annie yanked the bottle out of Jordan's hands and poured what was left down the drain.

Jordan looked at the wine soaked shirt clinging to her breasts and started to cry. She sat down next to the supplies she had so carefully arranged on the table and sobbed into her hands.

Annie took a moment to catch her breath. "I'm afraid you have a problem, young lady—the same problem Dusty had; the same one I think Jude has. You were always my dependable one. It's too late to save Dusty, maybe even Jude, but by God, I won't let all three of you kids end up like your father."

Jordan cried so hard she nearly choked. As she let the tears pour out and her mother's words sink in, she couldn't escape the fact that two people close to her had accused her of drinking too much. Slumped in her chair and shivering with emotion, she mentally reconstructed the events of the last few days: sleeping through a ringing phone the night of the fire, being disappointed there wasn't a bottle of whiskey in the spice cupboard, buying wine at the grocery store, the disappearing glass of burgundy, the realization she had hidden her last precious bottle of wine in the same cupboard her father used to keep his whisky.

Jordan rested her forehead on the kitchen table. "I'll get a hold of myself, Mom, just give me a minute."

While her tears began to subside, she searched her memory for some clue as to when her relationship with alcohol changed. She remembered being in grade school when she first realized her father drank a lot of beer, and how her relatives and the rest of the world believed this was shameful. Even though this embarrassed her and convinced her that alcohol must be sinful, she once took a drink of beer when her father wasn't looking. That first mouthful tasted awful, and she wondered what it was about growing older that made it taste better. She drank whatever was around, and a lot of it, when she and Riley were dating, but couldn't afford liquor while she was in veterinary school. She bought her first bottle of scotch shortly after Kent hired her. Over time, this had become a bottle a week. She drank wine with dinner.

"Did Daddy always drink too much?" Jordan asked, raising her head.

Annie sighed. "Not at first. Not when we were too young to drink legally. It got worse over time. I don't remember exactly when I first realized he was addicted."

"He's got a brute heart, Mom, especially when he's been drinking. I've been afraid of him for years, but he's still my father. I can't believe what I almost did to him."

Tears began flowing again. "I don't feel it in here," she said, pointing to her heart, "but I know I love him somewhere—maybe in my corpuscles."

She sat up and wiped her eyes. "Thanks for stopping me, Mom." She took a ragged breath. "I'm not doing so well, as you can see, not nearly as well as people think. Why does life have to be so hard?"

"I don't know, sweetie, it just is," Annie said, putting an arm around her daughter's shoulders. "We would be better off if they taught us when we were little girls that life is tough, instead of filling our heads with stories like *Cinderella*. Cinderella should have bunions, and her prince should get drunk and fall off his horse."

Jordan smiled at her mother's fairy tale allusion, and thought about her own fantasy relationship with Kent. He was right to be angry with her the night of the fire, but why did he treat her like a stupid donkey the rest of the time? He didn't love her, maybe didn't even like her, probably still resented the fact she was a woman, so why was she so attracted to him? How could she have allowed the fear of losing him and the job attached to him, to hurry her into coming within minutes of committing a horrible crime?

Annie leaned forward and kissed her daughter on the forehead. Both women were silent as they contemplated the seriousness of what happened and didn't happen that night.

"Daddy's going to be furious," Jordan said, "but I'm *so* relieved I didn't go through with it."

She got out of her chair and stepped to the back door for a breath of air. When she poked her head outside, she was surprised to feel the cool kiss of snowflakes on her face. She raised her face and let the small white crystals soothe her burning eyes and cheeks and float down the front of her wine stained shirt.

"Look, Mom, it's starting to snow. Isn't this awfully early?" She turned around to see Jude standing in the doorway.

"What's going on in here?" he asked, staring at Jordan's wine-drenched shirt and the matching stains on his mother's clothes. "Are you two drinking wine in here?" He glowered at his strangely silent mother and sister. "I can't think of anything more to say, and he can't either. Besides, I gotta go—it's snowing, and my tires are bald."

Jordan closed the back door and walked over to her brother. "There's not even a quarter of an inch on the ground, but you can leave any time you want, because I've decided to let nature take its course."

Jude's jaw dropped. "Jeez, Jordan, he thinks it's gonna happen tonight!"

"Sh-h-h. Not so loud."

Jude grabbed his sister by the arm. "This is insane," he sputtered, lowering his voice. "I had to eat a mile of shit in there. I had to lie, if you want to know the truth, to say something nice to him. Now what am I supposed to do? Come on, Jordan. He's gonna die anyways."

"So you do it then, if you think it's so damned easy. Do you hate him enough to pump a gram of morphine into his veins? I have a feeling you aren't a complete stranger to needles."

Jude dropped his sister's arm and stepped back. His pale mouth quivered as his eyes darted back and forth between Jordan and his mother.

"I, I don't hate him," he stuttered, inching toward the front door. "Not anymore. He can't do nothin' to me anymore."

Their argument was suddenly interrupted by a choking sound, and when they trooped into the living room, they discovered what they heard was actually a gurgle of laughter—the kind of laughter that is the best a man can squeeze out when he can barely breathe.

"Why are you laughing?" Jordan asked, amazed her father could find anything to laugh about after what Jude evidently told him.

Cooper pointed a bony finger at the living room window. "Snow!" he said breathlessly.

With so much going on that evening, nobody had remembered to close the living room curtains when night fell. Framed by the front window, and illuminated by the streetlight, thousands of snowflakes were performing like fine-boned ballerinas, leaping and twirling for the small audience gathered inside.

After a string of breath-sucking coughs, Cooper managed a weak smile. Annie smiled, too, her eyes brimming with tears.

"The doctor said … I wouldn't last … till winter."

Jude poked his arms into the sleeves of his jacket. "It's not winter. It's not even Hallo …"

"Shut up, Jude," Jordan snapped.

She wiped her father's mouth with a tissue. The day's activities seemed to have exhausted him. His skin was the color of cement, and his eyes, more closed than open, quivered in between blinks. When she asked him how he felt, he moved his head to one side and smiled sadly.

"I'll fix you up with you one of my famous cocktails," Jordan said, trying to sound cheerful.

Cooper opened one eye. The one eye looked at her warily while his mouth opened and closed like a guppy.

"It's not what you think, Daddy, and it's not what you asked for, but it's all you're going to get."

CHAPTER THIRTY-SEVEN

A steel framed clock hung behind the reception counter in the spot previously occupied by the cuckoo. Two clients with cats in carriers and one with a Chihuahua in her knitting bag sat waiting to see Dr. Warner. Emily was busy with the billing process for another client whose excited black Lab had wrapped its leash around the man's legs. Emily's eyes widened when she looked up and saw Jordan standing there.

While Emily finished with the client, Jordan walked over to the aquarium against the back wall so she could watch the brightly colored fish lolling in their predator-free ocean. Watching fish was supposed to be relaxing. Instead, she felt like a sea mammal that was forced by its biological framework to rise to the surface every few minutes for a gulp of air.

After paying his bill, the man with the black Lab flew past her to the door. It was hard to tell if man or beast was on the leash, as a deliriously happy dog raced outside.

Arms outstretched, Emily hurried to the other side of the counter. "I knew you'd come back!"

Jordan felt a twinge of guilt when she gave Emily a hug, and though her decision to drive to Prineville the night before had been quick and decisive, now that she was back in her old stomping grounds with its familiar smells and the friendly small-town faces waiting with their pets, her resolve was beginning to weaken.

"Is he busy?"

"Yeah." Emily nodded at the woman with the Chihuahua. "He's neutering that woman's cat. He was supposed to get over to Keeney's Dairy yesterday but couldn't get away." She searched Jordan's face for some clue as to her intentions. "He sure could use your help."

"Hasn't he hired that Drew fellow?" Jordan felt herself flush.

"Not yet. He wants him to come back for a second interview before he decides." The phone rang, and Emily hurried behind to counter to answer it. "I'll tell him you're here," she said after she hung up.

Fifteen minutes later, Emily walked over to where Jordan and wished her good luck. Jordan nodded and squared her shoulders before walking past the examination rooms to Kent's office.

When she looked inside, he was sitting at his desk writing something in a manila folder. She rapped once and uttered a cheerful, "Knock knock."

"Come in," he said, without looking up from his work. Jordan tiptoed into the small office and sat in one of the chairs facing his desk.

"I didn't tell you to sit."

She jumped out of the chair as if it had emitted an electric shock.

"That was rude of me," he said, sounding almost apologetic. "Have a seat."

Jordan sat stick straight in the wooden chair, knees pressed together and mouth so dry her tongue was sticking to her teeth. Kent closed the file he was writing in and placed it with several others neatly stacked in a black metal tray.

She thought that for someone overworked, Kent looked coolly in control in his white, button-down collar shirt. His rolled up sleeves exposed smooth, suntanned forearms, and she wondered if the rest of his body was tan.

He pointed at the pile of files in his tray. "As you can see, I've got a lot of work to catch up on. Have you decided to agree with me and admit you have a drinking problem?"

Jordan opened her mouth to speak, but he waved her off.

"Never mind, we can talk about that later. How is your father?"

"My father? You've never asked about him before." Jordan lowered her eyes. "His funeral was yesterday."

"I'm sorry for your loss," he said, in the same impersonal manner as a policeman investigating a crime scene. "How long was he in the hospital?"

"He wasn't in the hospital. He died at home, where we'd all like to die, I suppose, if we had a choice in the matter." She brushed away a tear. "And free of pain, thanks to me."

Kent raised an eyebrow and began tapping his pinky fingers together pincer style the way he always did when he gathered his thoughts or calculated his next move.

"What do you mean, thanks to you?" His pinky fingers gathered speed.

Jordan focused on the finger motion, surprised she hadn't made the connection before. The way he tapped his pinky fingers together reminded her of the pincher on the butt of an earwig.

Momentarily distracted, she turned serious again. "I made sure he received an analgesic that was palliative," she replied. "That's not what I came here to talk about, though."

Kent leaned back in his swivel chair and folded his arms across his chest. A hint of a smile curled the edges of his mouth, but his eyes remained cold and condescending.

"I'm here to pick up my things," Jordan said, in a steady voice she hardly recognized. "I left rather quickly as you may recall."

The veterinarian's expression soured. "So you've decided to quit rather than face the fact you're a drunk."

Jordan stiffened at the sudden rebuke, and wiped her palms on the legs of her jeans.

"I owe you an apology for my actions the night of the fire. During my father's final days, I realized I was drinking for courage or escape, but for the wrong reasons whatever they were. I was definitely headed in the wrong direction, and I'm doing something about it."

"The fire wasn't that long ago. What makes you think you are all of a sudden a changed woman?"

Jordan scooted to the edge of her chair, so close her knees grazed the back of Kent's desk.

"I'm *not* a changed woman. I've always been smart and a hard worker. I'm good with animals and good with people, too. Except for that one night,

I've been your third and fourth hands. I deserve to be treated like a doctor of veterinary medicine should be—with respect."

She looked straight into his cold blue eyes. "I've decided to open my own practice."

Kent tipped his head back and laughed. "You don't have a pot to pee in. What makes you think you can open your own practice?" He leaned forward in his chair and narrowed his eyes. "Don't you dare try it here, young lady, or I'll crush you before you even find a landlord desperate enough to rent space to you!"

Jordan shook her head in disbelief. "Wow… that was brutal. My friends tried to warn me about you, but for some reason I didn't listen."

She stood up to leave. "Don't worry, Dr. Warner, I won't be competing with you. I've decided to stay in my home town and make my practice mobile. Instead of clients bringing their animals to my clinic, which, you're right, I can't afford, I will strictly make house calls for all animals, big or small. I think people will appreciate getting care for their animal companions in familiar, comfortable surroundings, and when it comes to final goodbyes, there will be no shivering little creatures getting their life-ending injections on a stainless steel table."

Bracing for some kind of explosion, Jordan was surprised when her ex-boss was silent.

"It will just take me a few minutes to gather up my things."

She took five giant steps down the hall, then turned around and took five giant steps back.

Still sitting at his desk, Kent was surprised to see her and wondered if she had changed her mind. He figured it would be just like a woman, especially this one, to torment him that way.

Jordan leaned against the door jam, relaxed and emboldened by the relief spreading across her shoulders.

"By the way," she said, smiling jubilantly, "tell Drew I said hello."

She didn't wait for a response. Dead was waiting for her in the Jeep, and she had packing to do.